# LAKEN

By Lawrence Gulley

LAKEN

Gulley, Lawrence
*Laken*

ISBN: 979-8-9881499-3-4

*Printed in USA*

This book is dedicated to Bleau Belle, with love.

# Table of Contents

# Chapter 1

This story takes place near a small town in south Alabama. The year was 1950.

*"Oh my,"* Laken thought to herself. It was as though her heart suddenly leaped into her throat, for she recognized the sound of the boisterous voice. It was Calvin! Luckily for her, she was in the back room. She did as her mother told her to do: she tiptoed over to the chifforobe, eased the door open and climbed in, making sure to hide behind the clothing that was hanging inside.

Laken was only five years old but had seen and witnessed enough things to last her a lifetime. Calvin was the worst of them.

Her mother called the ones that she took to bed, her clients. Some would just buy the homemade whiskey and never enter the door. Laken liked them the best, especially James. James brought her storybooks, clothes (especially in the wintertime), and candy. James never took Callie to bed, though. He did buy the liquor from her, but that was all— and most of the time, just a pint. Sometimes James would catch Laken on the outside. He'd run up to her, grab her under the arms, and swing her in the air, making her scream from excitement. Sometimes James would ride Laken on his shoulders or his back. Laken really liked it when James came. Besides the cold drinks, candy, and cookies, he always showed a general interest in the little girl. James always loved to sit on the front porch, while Laken sat in his lap and read the storybooks he'd bought for her.

James would always leave, though, when one of Callie's customers went inside. He'd tell Laken, after he'd hug her

1

neck, to stay outside if weather permitted, until the customer left. If not, he instructed her to go sit in her mother's truck until they left. Callie said she made double money when they crawled into the bed with her. If she was inside, Laken knew to go into the back room when that occurred.

She once told her mama she was scared of Calvin and wondered why Callie allowed him to come there.

"Little girl, you just don't know the ins and outs of my business. Calvin is the one who delivers the meal, or corn, along with the sugar. That's what I need to make the liquor, and that's what we live off of. Leastwise, that and the tricks I pull," she answered.

Callie continued, "What do you suppose would happen if we went into town and bought fifty pounds of sugar and meal or corn?"

"I don't know," answered Laken.

"I'll tell you: the law would be down on me like a duck on a June bug. They'd bust up my still and put me in jail, and then what would become of you? Where would you go?" her mama had asked.

Laken just shrugged her shoulders, gesturing that she didn't know.

Callie and Laken lived in an old, rust-covered, tin-topped log house. The house had four rooms and a wide front porch that extended the whole width of the front of the house. They cooked from an iron stove that used wood. The house was heated by a small fireplace. A clear water creek ran behind the house, and that's where they got all the water they used for the whiskey and for the house.

Laken thought one day as she squatted in the chifforobe. Her mama had several pictures on the mantle board that was nailed above the fireplace. One of the pictures was a picture of her mama, and Laken always thought how beautiful Callie was. Laken knew everyone had a mama and a daddy. She'd asked her mama who her daddy was. Callie just told her she would tell her when she was older. Laken doubted if her mama even knew who her real daddy was. Whoever he was must've had black hair, for Laken's hair was black, with just a hint of red in the sunlight. Callie's hair was dark red, and she wore it shoulder length.

# Chapter 2

So far, while Calvin was there that day, all she'd heard coming from the living room was the squeaking of the bed springs and a lot of curse words. Once, Calvin had hit her mama in the face and had broken her nose. Her nose was swollen for a couple of weeks, and when it finally healed, it had a twist to the right, and it disfigured her face.

Laken held her breath the whole time Calvin was there, waiting to hear her mama's screams, but fortunately it never occurred.

Finally, she heard Calvin as he told her mama that he'd tote the fifty pounds of corn meal and the "slip" of sugar to the front porch.

"You have my money ready when I get back," he told Callie.

Laken eased out of the cramped chifforobe, but still remained quiet in the bedroom, and she'd stay that way until Calvin left.

Callie's house was well situated for the business she was in. Her place, which consisted of twenty acres, had an old log barn and two or three small sheds. To get to the house, you turned off the highway onto a little "pig trail" road, then the road opened into a small, cleared area that was used as a parking area. Callie kept the grass cut with a hoe and a sling blade, which she kept on the end of the front porch. That's where Callie parked her truck, and also where her clients, or customers, parked. After you left the parking area, the route to Callie's house turned into a wooded trail, and you walked about seventy-five yards to the house. The vehicles were completely hidden from the highway. The customers felt safe with the situation, and so did Callie.

The still was situated inside the old log barn, out of sight from anyone. The old log barn had a dirt floor, so Callie could build a fire under the still and not worry about anything catching on fire.

The still held fifty gallons of mash. Laken had watched her mama many times. As she got older, she'd help Callie carry the water from Persimmon Creek to the fifty-gallon wooden barrel that held the mash. It took twenty-five pounds of sugar, twenty pounds of meal, and twenty-five pounds of regular corn. They finished filling the barrel with water, then put the mesh lid on it. It was according to the temperature, but usually in three to four days, they were dipping the mash out of the barrel, and putting it into the still. The fifty gallons of mash usually yielded seven to eight gallons of moonshine.

There were three copper pipes coming from the top of the still, and the copper tubing was curved to run into a wooden trough. Callie tended to the firing of the still, and when Laken saw steam coming out of the end of the pipes, she began dipping cold water from a tub and pouring it into the wooden trough. Soon, clear liquid would start coming from the end of the copper tubing into two five-gallon wooden barrels.

Hiram and Jimmie Beasley owned the land directly behind Callie's house, and on the south end also. Callie would always pour two gallons of whiskey into pints and half pint bottles. She'd hide the remainder on Mr. Beasley's land. They'd roll the whiskey in a wheelbarrow to where the creek was shallow, cross the creek and hide it across the fence in a densely wooded area. Callie would hide eight pints in the front yard in various places, then eight pints in the living room.

Usually in the fall of the year, Callie distilled twice a week, in order to have enough to last through the winter. Fermenting mash in the winter months was nigh impossible, for the mash only fermented at a warm temperature.

The land in front of Callie's house belonged to James' parents, the Jordans. In fact, they were the biggest landowners in the area. Callie was scared to hide her whiskey on the Jordans' property. James had told her that if his parents had a report of illegal whiskey on their land, they'd prosecute.

## Chapter 3

It was in the summer of 1950 when Laken met the Beasley family.

Laken couldn't remember when she couldn't swim. Sometimes, in the summer months she'd jump into Persimmon Creek behind their house. The water was at least ten feet deep. As the creek meandered southward, it became shallow until it ran into Flat Creek, then the water became dark and deep.

Callie didn't care if Laken swam in the creek, for she knew what a good swimmer the little girl was. Callie swam too, but usually she'd jump in with a bar of soap in her hand, which meant they were both in for a good bathing.

Callie was an accomplished fiddle player, and she was playing while sitting on the front porch the day she heard the Beasley family downstream. Laken decided to swim downstream and check them out.

It didn't take but a few minutes before Laken could see two children splashing in the water, and their grinning parents watching them as they played in the shallow stream. Laken saw that they were a young boy and a girl. The boy was wearing a pair of cutoff jeans, while the girl had on a bathing suit. Laken had seen pictures of bathing suits in the Sears and Roebuck catalogue that her mama kept in the toilet.

The Beasleys were startled, to say the least, when they first noticed Laken. The two children ran out of the cold water and stood close to their parents. The boy looked to be a year or two older than the little blonde girl.

"Don't be afraid. I live over yonder," Laken said, as she pointed upstream.

"Yes, we've heard that Callie has a daughter," the lady said, "but how in the name of Jesus did you get this far downstream?"

Laken looked puzzled, then said, "I swimmed."

"You mean you swam through that deep water?" the little blonde girl asked.

"I shore did," replied Laken. She then added, "I swim just about every day in the summertime."

The man grinned. "Well, you're a mighty pretty little girl," he said. then added "We're the Beasleys, and we live across the field," as he pointed toward their house. "That's Caleb, our son, and our daughter, Shelby."

"My name is Laken. My mama said that's the reason I can swim so good, 'cause she named me Laken."

Mr. Beasley grinned again, then said, "Alright kids, we've got to feed up, so you'd better get back into the water; you only have a few more minutes." Shelby and Caleb ran back into the water, and this time they had someone else to play with, and so did Laken.

Mrs. Beasley couldn't help but notice that the children went a little deeper into the water, and Caleb showed Laken how he could "dog paddle."

It wasn't long before Mr. Beasley walked toward their farm truck, and Mrs. Beasley called her children out of the water, then told Laken it was a pleasure meeting her.

"When will y'all be back?" Laken asked.

"I'll talk to Mr. Beasley, and if they're good in church Sunday, we'll bring them back Sunday afternoon," their mother said, as she handed them each a towel when they walked by her.

Laken could tell that Caleb wasn't ready to leave the water, for he was mumbling to himself as he dried off with the towel.

"It's nice meeting you, Laken," he said, then Caleb ran to the back of the truck and crawled in.

"Yes, it was nice meeting you; you're always welcome to come over and play with Shelby," Mrs. Beasley said.

"Yeah, that would be good. We can color, play hopscotch, or swing in the homemade swing," Shelby said enthusiastically. Then she added, "It's no fun playing by yourself."

Laken knew she couldn't invite them to her house, but she responded, "I'll ask my mama!"

"How old are you, sweetheart?" Mrs. Beasley asked.

"Mama said I was five years old on June 15th," Laken replied.

"My goodness, Shelby, you're only five days older!" Mrs. Beasley laughed, as they, too, headed toward the truck.

Shelby and Caleb waved at her as the truck pulled away.

Laken decided to walk back to the house. She was so excited about having some friends to play with, and she couldn't wait to tell her mama.

"Wonder who was playing the violin so beautifully?" Jimmie Beasley asked her husband as they bounced across the field.

"Probably Callie, the little girl's mama. Callie's paw, Mr. Pruitt, could play the steam out of that thing, and the banjo too. Along with making whiskey, he used to play at barn dances and such," replied Hiram.

"Strange, them living right here under our noses and I never gave them a second thought. Mr. Pruitt is deceased, isn't he?" asked Jimmie.

"Yeah, the train smashed his truck with him in it, while he was crossing the tracks in Frisco City," her husband said.

"So, no one is living there but Laken and her mama. What happened to Laken's father?" Jimmie asked.

"Far as I know, Callie has never been married. I know she's making and selling shinny over there. The way I look at it, she has to feed herself and that baby, so it's none of my business," Hiram answered.

"I don't ever remember seeing this Callie. I never even heard talk of her before now," Jimmie remarked.

"Well, by all accounts, she seldom leaves the place. Besides, we run in different circles, and we do stay plenty busy on the farm," Hiram told his wife.

"I know I'm getting nosey, but I wonder who the child's father is," said Jimmie.

"Well, I'm not being a gossip, but after all, you're my wife. I've heard tell that James Jordan hangs out there a lot, and he does drink a little," replied her husband.

"Lord, I'll bet you Victoria Jordan doesn't know about this child! She does favor James, though," Jimmie said thoughtfully, as they neared their narrow driveway.

"Well, the Pruitts are just uneducated; you can tell by the little girl's speech," Hiram said, as he parked the old truck beside the big barn.

"Bless her little heart," Jimmie replied, as she opened the door to the truck. They didn't say anything else, but Laken Pruitt was on the minds of every member of the Beasley family as they went about their day.

# Chapter 4

Laken's mama was still playing the fiddle when the little girl got to the house. Knowing better than to interrupt Callie, she went inside to change clothes.

After Laken had on dry clothes, she went outside to hang her wet panties and dress on the clothesline so they could dry.

"Boy, my fingers are getting sore," Callie said, as Laken stepped onto the porch. "Come here, girl and let me show you the chords to "Mary Had a Little Lamb.""

Laken thought she knew the chords already, but she gently took the fiddle from her mama's hands and began to saw away with the bow.

After Laken finished, Callie pulled her close and gave her a rare hug.

"Just wait, you'll toughen the end of those fingers. The more you play, the tougher they'll get, and you'll be a crackerjack," Callie smiled. "Now, let's do Turkey in the Straw."

Laken rubbed the tips of her fingers on her left hand, which were still shriveled from the cold water of the creek. Slowly, she began to saw away, then picked up speed as she went along.

When she finished, she looked at the tips of her fingers to see if they were bleeding, and they weren't.

"I want to learn some of the tunes you play," Laken said, then added, "They're beautiful, Mama," in an attempt to butter her mama up.

"I thought that was you, sawing away," James said, as he came from behind the house.

"Let's hear Old Rosin the Bow," James requested.

"Well, alright, but it'll cost ya," Callie said, as she puckered her lips and allowed James to give her a chaste kiss.

Laken was stunned, for it was the first time she'd seen them show the slightest bit of emotion.

Callie grabbed the fiddle and bow from her daughter and did something Laken had never seen. Callie did a jig on the porch as she played Rosin the Bow.

James reached over and pulled Laken into his arms, and they both smiled as Callie danced while playing the tune.

"Woop!" Callie exclaimed when she'd finished, then sat back down in the old straight-back chair.

Both James and Laken gave her rousing applause, while Callie caught her breath.

"I didn't know you still had it in you," James said.

"Oh, I pick it up now and then," Callie said, as she hung the fiddle and bow on a nail sticking out of one of the logs.

Laken knew it was time to strike, while Mr. James was there.

Still clutched in his arms, she began.

"Mama, while I was swimming awhile ago, I met the folks that live in the long white house that's across the field. They seem to be real nice people, and they invited me to come over and play with their daughter. Her name is Shelby, and she's the same age as I am," Laken told her.

"Haven't I told you to stay on our property?" Callie demanded sharply.

"It was just a few feet past the fence post. I heard them laughing and playing in the water, so I played with them for a little while. They seemed ever so nice," Laken added quickly.

"No, you don't have fitting clothes to wear over there. Laken, them folks are rich, and they'll be laughing at you." Callie started to say, "Like everyone does me," but she caught herself before saying it.

"Now hold on a minute," James interjected. "Hiram and Jimmie Beasley are good Christian people. I think it would be a good idea for our girl to be around them. She'll be going to school next year, and she needs to learn to be around other children."

*"There, he'd said it. He said, 'Our girl,'"* Laken thought. So now she knew.

"What do you mean, 'Our girl?' You weren't in that house when I thought I was going to die having her. You were off with Betty Jean Dale, having a good time," Callie snapped.

"You shouldn't talk bad about the dead, and if clothes are the problem, well, let's go get her some," James said, as he picked Laken up off the porch.

"That Mama of yours get word that you're driving Laken around, you're gonna catch it," Callie warned.

"Some things are worth it. Besides, we're not going to the Big Store in Excel where everyone knows me; we're going to Monroeville. Don't bother to cook supper. I'll bring you a hamburger back, because I know you're not going, you're afraid you'll miss a dollar," James said.

"Yeah, well most folks ain't rich like you are, and you'd better go on before I change my mind," Callie said, giving in.

Laken was excited, but she knew better than to let on. She just clung to James' back, as they made their way down the trail that led to his truck.

The little girl was thrilled about going to Monroeville, because it was a lot bigger than Excel and had more stores. The only time she and her mama would go to Monroeville was to pay taxes on their place once a year.

# Chapter 5

"You have a lot nicer truck than mama's," Laken said, as they stopped at the only traffic light in Excel.

"Thank you. It ought to be, for it cost enough," James answered.

Soon, they passed a long brick building on the left. "Look: that's where you'll be going to school next year. Have you been reading and coloring in your books I've been bringing you?" he asked.

"Every one of them. Shoot, I can even say my ABC's," Laken said proudly, as she recited them to him.

"My goodness, you'll be the smartest little girl in the first grade!" James exclaimed.

"I hope so. Mama said she hated school, but I'm going to try my best," Laken said.

"I was two grades ahead of your mama, and boy, was she a looker! She was the prettiest girl in her class," James told Laken.

"Yeah, I've seen pictures," Laken answered.

"Your mama didn't have the chance that I'm going to give you. I'm going to see that you have just as good as the rest of them. I'm going to teach you to drive, and after you get your driver's license I'm going to get you your own car. I'm going to see to it that you won't have to do the things your mama did to get money."

Laken had seen it all her life, and somehow, she knew what her mama did was wrong, but she didn't say anything.

"I only wish there was more I could do for you, but due to uncontrollable circumstances I can't at this time. If you ever need me, though, you know where I live," James told her.

"Mama pointed your house out to me; it's a pretty place," Laken said. She then added, "I can walk there."

Monroeville was the county seat for Monroe County. The downtown shopping area was situated around a square. The courthouse was located in the middle of the square. It was the tallest building Laken had ever seen. The brick building was three stories high, with a tall white dome extending from the top. The dome was rectangular, with huge  clocks on each side. The clocks struck each hour and half-hour.

The streets were buzzing with more people than Laken had ever seen.  Several of the men were wearing suits, and the ladies were all nicely dressed.

"Shore is a bunch of big shots in this here town," Laken said.

James laughed at the child's grammar but realized something had to be done before she started school.  He then thought he had a year to come up with a way to teach her to speak properly.

"Baby, they're just people like us. Most of the ones with suits on are lawyers or businessmen," James told her.

"Oh, I've heard Mama talk about lawyers. She said the best thing is to stay away from them."

James laughed as he steered his truck around the square.

"I guess your mama had me in mind when she told you that, for *I'm* a lawyer. I just don't practice at this time. I have farmland, trees, and a sawmill, then accounting work to do, and that keeps me busy," James told the small girl, as he parked his truck in front of Katz Department Store on the square.

Before he got out of the truck, he told the excited girl, "Always remember this: you're just as good as any of those men wearing those suits." He then ran his fingers through her long black hair in an attempt to get some of the tangles out. He did the best that he could do, before he kissed her on the cheek and said, "Come on, let's go inside."

An eager saleslady met them inside and asked if she could help them.

"Yes, fix her up with two Sunday dresses, with shoes to match. A pair of sandals, a pair of loafers, two pairs of jeans with elastic waist bands, five pairs of shorts..." James continued, "...five assorted blouses, and matching socks for each outfit, a hairbrush and mirror." Then he cleared his throat and said quietly, "See that she gets the appropriate undergarments for each suit of clothes."

The exuberant lady laughed about the hairbrush and mirror, but then said, "I'll fix her up. She's sure a cutie."

Laken couldn't believe all the items Mr. James was buying her, so she eagerly followed the lady around in the clothing store. James went over and began conversing with a man who was wearing a suit and tie.

There were a few other shoppers in the store, but other helpers tended to them, while the same saleslady continued sending Laken into the dressing room to try on clothes.

The kind saleslady noticed Laken kept looking at the bathing suits, so she walked over to James, while laying a pile of clothes on the counter. After she talked to James, she saw him nod his head, so the next thing Laken tried on was a blue bathing suit.

It took about an hour before the smiling lady began ringing the items up on the cash register.

Laken decided to wear her sandals and one of the summer outfits out of the store, so the lady put the dress she'd been wearing into one of the bags.

Laken didn't know how much the items cost, but she saw James pull out a roll of bills after looking at the sales receipt.

The man in the suit helped James carry the bags to the truck.

James made sure to put the things next to the door, so she'd be sitting beside him.

"Are you hungry?" he asked.

"Well, we had grits and butter for breakfast," Laken said shyly, not wanting to let on that she was starving.

"Oh, my goodness, and it's near four o'clock!" James replied.

Needless to say, the next stop was at the bus station, where they had a small diner.

"I've never eat away from home," Laken said, as they entered the eatery, and she saw pictures of food hanging on the wall.

"Well, you're about to," he told her, as he guided her to a table and pulled out the chair for her.

A young girl came to their table, and James ordered two hamburgers, fries, and two cokes. He then told the young lady to prepare another hamburger and an order of fries to go.

The whole day was just unreal to Laken. Meeting the neighbors at the creek, and Mr. James buying her all those pretty clothes…it was the best day of her life, and she told him so while they were waiting on their food.

"That's one reason I bought you the new clothes. You visit the Beasleys as much as you can. Pay attention to the way they act and talk, and learn from them," James told her.

"I talked to Mama about it, but she said no," Laken reminded him.

"Don't you worry, sweetheart, I'll talk to her too," Mr. James promised.

Laken then asked James something that melted his heart.

"I heard you and Mama talking about you being my daddy. Would it be alright if I called you Daddy?" Laken asked hesitantly.

"Well now, let me think. If you were an ugly ol' buck-toothed thing, I'd say no, but since you're the prettiest little girl I've ever laid eyes on, I'd be honored, so yes," James agreed, while holding back tears.

"Oh, that would be wonderful! Everyone else has a daddy, but me," Laken said.

"Well, I'm nothing to brag about, but if it pleases you," James said, as he reached across the table and held his only child's hand.

The young waitress soon returned with their food. Laken had eaten a hamburger before, but she had never tasted French fries. She watched her daddy as he ate his hamburger, so she tried to copy him. She had trouble stretching her mouth wide enough, so her daddy told her to mash the burger down, which she did.

James wound up eating everything on his oval-shaped plate, but try as she did, Laken couldn't finish all of hers. She drank all of her drink, though.

Before they left Laken told her daddy she needed to go to the toilet, so James led her to the door of the bathroom.

Laken had never sat on a commode before, but she soon figured it out.

After she finished, she washed and dried her hands, then met her daddy outside. He paid the waitress for everything, including Callie's to-go meal.

Excel was only about five miles from Monroeville, so it wasn't long before Laken began to recognize places.

"So, I'll be going to school there next year," Laken said, as they passed the school.

"Yep, and you'll be not only the prettiest girl in the first grade, but also the smartest," James told her. "When summer is over, we're going back to Monroeville and I'll buy you some winter clothes," he continued, as they passed the "Big Store" in Excel.

When they reached the parking area at Callie's, they noticed a long white car parked near the trail.

"That's Mr. White. He's just there to buy shinny," Laken said. She then added, "Mama has some new cotton sacks; I'll get one of them and bring it back. That way we can tote everything back at one lick."

James let her out of the truck, and she ran up the trail, wearing a suit of her new clothes and brown sandals.

*"My Lord, I need my rear end kicked for allowing my baby to be raised in such conditions,"* he thought.

He knew, though, that Callie would fight him in court if he tried to get custody, for she had told him so, and he'd have to prove that Laken was his child. He didn't know what Callie did with her money, for she certainly didn't spend much of it. Therefore, he knew she had the money to hire a lawyer. Plus, his mother would simply croak, and would never accept the child, so she'd probably have a miserable life living with him in the big house. It was nearly impossible for him to live somewhere else. He had his office behind the house, and the workers were constantly in and out, not counting his associates from different companies that he had business with.

James had really given a lot of thought to getting custody of his child, but with circumstances as they were, it was nearly impossible.

*"Such a mess,"* he thought, as he saw Don White come up the trail with a pint bottle sticking from his chest pocket.

The two nodded their heads at each other upon recognition.

About the time that Don fired up his car, Laken came up the trail with the folded cotton sack.

They put everything in the long sack but Laken's "Sunday" dresses, and of course, Callie's hamburger and fries.

Laken carried her mother's meal, while James handled the loaded sack. He was careful to make sure to not snag the bag with her dresses on the brambles and briars going up the overgrown lane.

Callie was sitting on the front porch, and she quickly stuck the money she'd received from Mr. White in her bosom.

"Oh, Mama, just wait until you see all my pretty clothes and things!" Laken burst out, as she handed her mama her supper in the bag.

"Yeah, I'm sure they're nice. Take 'em to your room and put 'em up. Make sure to hang those dresses in the chifforobe," Callie said, not bothering to look at any of them.

Callie remained on the porch, while James and Laken entered the house. When they reached Laken's room, James emptied the cotton sack on Laken's bed. He picked out the lacy socks and told Laken to wear them with her dress shoes and dresses.

"Yes, sir, I will," Laken promised, as she hugged each of her beautiful dresses before hanging them in the chifforobe.

James whispered to Laken, "I'm going outside and talk to your mama about allowing you to start spending time with the Beasley family."

"Okay," Laken whispered, then hugged her daddy and thanked him for everything.

"Looks like you spent a plenty," Callie said, when James returned to the front porch.

"I just got a few things she needed," James replied. He then added, "She told me she'd been invited to the Beasley place, so I figured she'd need clothes to go over there."

"Yeah, well, I'm not too sure about that. Then again, it would get her outta my hair some. I've been thinking about it. Since you've bought her some clothes, I suppose it would be alright, just long as none of them set foot on my property," Callie said.

"I'll speak with Mr. Beasley about it when I leave here, and I'm sure you won't have a problem with them. Besides, what business would they have coming here?"

"Well, I just figured if she went over there, they'd get to thinking their young'uns could come over here, and I'm not having it," Callie insisted.

"I've got plenty of work to do, but like I said, when I leave from here I'll go straight there and talk to Hiram," James replied.

Callie just took a deep breath and expelled the air in a long sigh. "Well, we'll see how it works out."

# Chapter 6

Laken had being going to the Beasleys' for two months, and both James and Callie could tell there was a change for the better in her grammar and the way she groomed herself.

"Shelby said she stroked her hair a hundred times each night, and she brushes her teeth each morning and night," Laken told Callie.

"Yeah, I reckon when she goes to the toilet she pees in a gold pot," Callie said sarcastically.

The sarcasm completely went over Laken's head. "No, Mr. Hiram and Caleb use an outdoor toilet, because they work in the fields. Miss Jimmie, Shelby, and I use the commode in the house," she said earnestly. "They have it made over there! Shoot, they have a bathtub inside, a sink in the kitchen and a small one in the bathroom. That's where Shelby brushes her teeth. They must all do that, for I see four brushes hanging on the wall. The house has electricity, and all you have to do is flip a switch and the room lights up!

"Miss Jimmie has a refrigerator that keeps things cold, and an electric stove. All she does is cook, wash clothes, hang 'em on the line, sweep and mop. Shelby and I help her when we're not playing. We have lots of fun over there; we color in books, play hopscotch, and swing in a swing that has long ropes. Miss Jimmie seems real pleased that I'm teaching Shelby how to read and write. They've even bought Shelby the same books that I have. When Caleb's not working, we play hide and seek. They have horses, cows, even a milk cow.

"Caleb has his own horse and he asked me to ask you if I could ride with him. Oh! Miss Jimmie wants to know if you wanted milk, she said she gets more than she needs," Laken said, finally pausing for breath.

"Shoot, yeah, I'll take some milk, and buttermilk too, but if you fall off that horse and break your neck, don't come whining to me," Callie said.

She wouldn't dare let Laken know, but she did miss her daughter being underfoot, and she probably wouldn't have allowed her to go over there if she didn't have her clients. Callie was saving every dime she could for them to move away. She'd get a job in a factory or something and wouldn't have to lead the kind of life that she was leading now. She still had Betty Jean Dale's purse that she'd found in James' truck.

Betty Jean had been killed in a car wreck. They were about the same age. The purse contained Betty Jean's driving license, social security card, and identification card—everything she needed to start a new life. She was hoping she could make it all come about before Laken started school.

Callie wasn't dumb by any means, just uneducated. Since Laken was born at home, she didn't even have a birth certificate. Callie knew she had to have one to enroll Laken in school. *"James is a lawyer, so he'd know about how to get her one,"* she thought.

If everything went as she had planned, she'd start their new lives the next year. Due to her name, she knew she couldn't get a job, and Laken wouldn't get a fair start with people knowing her background in this small town. *"Maybe Mobile or Pensacola,"* Callie thought. She could mail in the taxes on the house and twenty acres, for it had been in the family for over a hundred years. *"After all,"* she continued to think, *"land is land, and they don't make any more of it."*

Callie felt the hint of fall in the air late that afternoon, and she felt like playing her fiddle. She could see that Laken was coloring in one of her coloring books from the light of a kerosene lamp.

After a quick supper of pancakes and syrup, Callie got the old fiddle that had belonged to her grandpa. She returned to the front porch and started out playing The Arkansas Traveler.

She was interrupted a couple of times with people buying the shinny. As much moonshine as she had sold, she'd never drank it. Her daddy would get drunk and tell her to not do like him. "This stuff is meant to sell and not to drink," he'd say, so she stuck to his old saying.

Callie did a lot of thinking while she played. She knew that if she hadn't carried the Pruitt name, James would have married her. He was the only one that she'd ever loved, and still did, even though she wouldn't let him know it. She knew his mama, Victoria Jordan, was the meanest woman she'd ever encountered. Victoria had thrown a fit and threatened to have her arrested for prostitution if Callie didn't leave her son alone.

Callie wasn't prostituting at the time, but she was selling shine; she had to make a living somehow. She couldn't have the law coming around her place, so she had broken it off with James, but it was too late, for she was already pregnant. She started prostituting after Laken was born. She had such a hard time birthing Laken until she thought she must have done something to her insides, because she'd never gotten pregnant again. While lying in bed right after Laken was born is when she came up with the scheme of saving every dime she could, so her baby wouldn't have to lead the life she had.

She'd had a hard bitter life. She had been looked down upon as a child, and she still was. Callie shied away from public as much as possible, for she could see the old biddies turn their heads and whisper about her, what few times she and Laken were in public. Therefore, she limited her trips to the Big Store to the least amount possible. When she did go to the store, she only bought the bare essentials, but in large quantities.

There were other stores, a café, post office, and gas station in Excel, but Callie limited her visits to just the Big Store. It was called such because you could buy groceries, clothing, shoes, and household items there. Upstairs was where they kept the caskets for burial.

There were a few chickens on Callie's place, enough to furnish them with eggs, and to wring one of the slippery thing's necks to eat on special occasions.

Her land was so shaded, due to the large trees and bushes, that she couldn't grow much. She did hoe out enough soil to always have collards and other greens, such as onions, mustard and turnips.

The Beasleys grew acres and acres of corn, so when the season was right, she'd help herself to it, and they never said anything. Later, when the corn dried in the fields, she'd pull enough of it to feed her chickens. She stored the corn in one of the log cribs.

Callie wound up playing Tin Roof Blues that night about ten o'clock. She went inside and cleaned the dishes, checked on Laken and saw that she had gone to sleep, reading. The book was about a girl and her dog, and the pages had colorful pictures in it. James had bought Laken several books. Callie took the book and laid it on the stack with the others. *"What a smart little girl,"* she thought proudly.

After blowing out the kerosene lamp, she made her way to her bed, hoping she wouldn't get any more customers that night. She knew she needed the money for her goal, but she just wasn't in the mood, for she had the blues.

# Chapter 7

Everything was going real well with Laken spending time at the Beasleys, until one Sunday in October.

James had bought Laken her winter clothes, as he had promised. Laken's room was now full of nice clothes, so much so that Callie had to nail a wire in the corner of Laken's room to hang her clothes on, especially the "Sunday clothes."

Laken had gone with the Beasleys to church several times. Callie always made sure that the girl carried another suit of clothes with her. After church, Laken always stayed over a couple of hours to play, and Callie didn't want her to ruin her Sunday dress.

That particular Sunday, though, Laken came straight home after church. Callie could see that the child was upset about something, but she didn't say anything.

Laken always ate lunch with the Beasleys when she was over there, so Callie threw some wood in the stove, so she could scramble something for dinner.

Callie was laying the scrambled eggs, pancakes, and cane syrup on the table when Laken came out of her room.

"Come on and eat, baby. I know you haven't had time to eat with the Beasleys," Callie said.

She had a fire going in the fireplace and heat from the stove made it almost unbearably hot in the room, so she cracked a window to cool things off.

Laken put a small amount of food on her plate, then began talking.

"We went to a different church today. I didn't know it, but it's the church that daddy goes to. There were some special people singing, and Mr. Hiram wanted to hear them.

"Anyway, when I saw daddy come in, I ran over and grabbed his hand. An old lady slapped me on my arm and told me to turn her son loose. I didn't have to turn him loose, for she slapped my arm so hard until she almost knocked me down.

"I began to cry, so I went over to the Beasleys and took a seat beside Caleb.

"Daddy came over and tried to settle me down, but Mr. Beasley wouldn't have it. He told all of us that we were leaving, so we got up and left," Laken said.

"The old witch, she'll meet her come-uppance one day and it ain't gonna be good!" Callie snapped. "It's hard to believe she's Mr. Willie's wife and James' mother. You just always remember what I told you. You're just as good as the next one. You have nothing to be ashamed of," Callie told her daughter.

"Yes Ma'am, I'm just sorry that Shelby and Caleb witnessed it. Now they don't know what to think of me. They treated me as if I was a rattlesnake on the way home," Laken said, while stirring the eggs around on her plate.

"How did Mr. and Mrs. Beasley act toward you on the way home?" asked Callie.

"I could tell that Mr. Beasley was mad, but he didn't say a word on the way back.

"They were going to have a big eating when the folks got through singing. Miss Jimmie had taken some fried chicken and a big banana pudding for the eating. Before we left, we went into the back and we put her stuff that she had brought in the car. After we were in the car, Miss Jimmie said it was a good thing that she was a Christian, or she would have told Victoria Jordan what she thought of her," Laken said.

About that time someone knocked three times on the door. Not giving Callie time to answer the door, in rushed James Jordan.

"Oh, my baby, I went over to the Beasleys' and they're all upset about what my mother did, and they're terribly upset about you leaving," James said. He then picked Laken up and hugged her tightly.

Laken began to cry again, while James consoled her.

" Shh, shh," James said, while wiping tears from his daughter's face. "Everything is going to be alright. If it makes you feel better, mother was shunned so by the church people, until she left early," James said.

He then sat Laken back in her chair. "Now, you be a big girl and eat your lunch," he told her.

"The old witch! She thinks with all her money she can get by with anything. She don't want me to pay her a visit, I've about gone my limit with her. She's ruined my life, and now she's starting on my baby," Callie said, regretting saying the last of the sentence.

James looked at Callie with the same expression on his face that he'd had six years earlier.

"Don't get any ideas. Too much water has gone under the bridge for us," Callie told him.

James shrugged his shoulders, then pulled out the chair beside Laken and sat down.

"Well, my goodness, why don't you just make yourself at home?" Callie said, then returned to her meager meal. "There's a pot of coffee on the stove; you know where the cups are," she told James.

James got up to pour himself a cup of coffee, then sat back down beside his daughter, who had settled down and was eating her meal.

30

He looked around in the room and saw the fiddle and banjo hanging in their usual places.

"So, I hear tell that you're still playing your fiddle, late at night," James said.

"Yeah, I play it sometimes when business is slow," Callie said, as she finished eating. "I'm not the only one in the family who can play it either," she said, as she saw that Laken had eaten all she was going to eat.

"Laken, bring me the banjo here, then get the fiddle. Let's show the old man something."

Laken smiled, for James had never heard her play before.

After Laken handed her mama the banjo, Callie began to tune it while Laken returned for the fiddle and bow. Once she had tuned the old banjo, she told Laken to stand near the fireplace.

Laken did as she was told. As she put the fiddle in place against her neck, Callie said, "Now, play 'Old Joe Clark.'"

James was amazed at his daughter. After Laken played a verse, Callie accompanied her with the banjo.

"Woohoo!" James hollered, when the two got wound up.

Laken was smiling as she sawed away.

When they finished that tune, Callie told her to play, 'Bile Them Cabbage Down,' so they immediately went into the other tune.

About halfway through the song, James got up and did a jig, similar to buck dancing, which rattled things on the wall.

After they had played two tunes, Callie figured Laken's fingertips had all they could handle, so they didn't play another one.

When Laken had placed the two instruments back in place, she came and sat in James' lap.

"Boy, you two are ready for the road!" he exclaimed as he kissed his daughter on the cheek.

"Aw, pshaw," Callie answered, then got up to get herself a cup of coffee.

After she sat back down with her coffee, James went on about how well Laken could play the violin.

"It just come natural to her, and swimming, too. I'm telling you, she could swim before she could walk," Callie said.

"Oh, well, she took that after me," bragged James.

"Laken, get off his lap and go let that window down, then throw a piece of wood in the fire. It's beginning to get cold in here," Callie said.

While Laken headed toward the window, James got up and threw a piece of wood that was stacked beside the fireplace into the fire.

About that time, someone knocked on the front door.

James didn't recognize the voice, but Callie turned around and pulled a pint of shinny out of an old homemade cabinet. After the customer put the two dollars and fifty cents in her hand, Callie poked the pint through the opening of the door and thanked the person.

The person buying the whiskey had broken the exuberant atmosphere in the room, and after seeing that Laken was in a better mood, James said his goodbyes. First, though, he picked Laken up and swung her around in the room until she squealed from delight.

"Is there anything you need from the store?" James asked Laken. She cocked her head to the side, as though she was really thinking, then replied, "No, but thank you anyway."

"Ok, then, are you going to continue your visits to the Beasleys? They're really worried about you," James said.

"Yeah, I'm about over the mean old woman. It's hard to believe she's your mama and my grandma," Laken replied.

"Good, I've got work to do. You keep up with those violin lessons," James said.

"I will, I promise," Laken replied.

James then bent over and kissed her on top of the head, then making his daughter scream with delight, he walked around the table and kissed Callie on the top of her head.

Callie made a mock swing at James, then said, "Go on, get outta here."

Their actions only made Laken laugh louder, as James went out the door.

James smiled as he walked down the doorsteps, knowing he'd accomplished his mission, for the time being.

# Chapter 8

Mrs. Beasley had kept her promise; she was sending so much milk along with buttermilk until Callie told Laken to tell her just a gallon a week would be plenty. The only place Callie had to store it was in the cold water of Persimmon Creek. The milk's containers were glass gallon jugs, and the buttermilk was in quart glass containers. Callie would tie a string to the ring of the jug and ease it down into the cold water of the creek. As they used all of the milk, Callie would make sure to wash and rinse the containers before Laken took them back.

Callie didn't know it, but Caleb crossed the boundary fence and would carry the milk for Laken as far as the creek.

Callie and Laken's breakfast and supper diet changed after getting all the milk. As bad as Callie hated to spend money, they began to have cornflakes for breakfast. For supper, they ate a lot of cornbread and buttermilk. Usually the only time Laken had meat was when she ate at the Beasley house, and almost always, it was chicken.

Caleb was in school during the week. He was in the second grade. Mr. Hiram had bought Caleb a yellow pony, but he wouldn't let the girls ride the pony unless Caleb was there. Caleb had named the pony PeeWee. About the only time Caleb had to ride the pony was on Saturday and Sunday afternoons.

Mrs. Beasley had a small red radio that sat on top of the refrigerator. Hank Williams was a popular singer. 'Hey, Good Lookin',' and 'Cold Cold Heart' were two of his songs that got played on the radio a lot. Another good one was 'I Walk the Line,' by Johnny Cash.

From ten to eleven p.m., bluegrass music came on the radio. A group from Monroeville came on one morning, and some girl played the fiddle. She played 'Old Joe Clark.'

"Hey, I can play that," Laken said, as she sat down at the small kitchen table and finished listening to the tune.

"You can do what?" asked Miss Jimmie.

"Play that on mama's fiddle," Laken replied.

Jimmie stopped wrestling with the rutabaga she was trying to peel, and said, "Well, you'll just have to bring that fiddle over here and let us hear you," Miss Jimmie said.

"I sure will, if mama will allow me. She's mighty careful about her fiddle and banjo. You see, they belonged to her daddy, or either her grandpa. I'll ask her, though," Laken replied.

"Can you play the banjo, too?" Jimmie asked excitedly.

"No, but I believe I could, with a little practice," Laken answered.

Laken resumed her job of wiping the counter tops and table top with a damp rag, as though her talent was just a matter of fact.

Miss Jimmie continued, "Some nights, especially in the spring and summer, I open the window to our bedroom and can hear music coming from over there."

"That would be my mama; she's really good at it," Laken said.

"You know, baby, I feel for your mama. I don't guess I've seen her but a couple of times. I know she's bound to get lonesome over there. Please tell her she's welcome to visit anytime she likes," Jimmie said, as she hugged Laken's neck.

"I'll tell her, but I doubt if she'll do it; she stays pretty busy," Laken said, not daring to mention the whiskey.

"Lord, I know how that goes! It takes a lot to keep this place going. It seems that I never get caught up," Jimmie said.

"Well, our house isn't as big as this one, and mama doesn't cook as much as you. We usually just have one thing to eat, like grits and butter, or pancakes with syrup. Since you've started giving us the milk, we've been eating cornflakes for breakfast, then cornbread and buttermilk for supper. She keeps the butter in a syrup can. It stays in the creek along with the milk," Laken told her.

"I guess  you learn to do with what you have, and right now I have to get dinner going," Jimmie said, as she ran her fingers through Laken's shiny black hair.

Jimmie then leaned over and whispered in Laken's ear. "Don't tell Shelby I said this, but she is absolutely envious of your hair."

"I took it from my daddy," Laken replied.

"I know honey, I know," Miss Jimmie said, as she opened a quart jar of butter beans that she had canned.

"I try to cook enough so we can make two meals out of it. Today,  I think I'll surprise Hiram with some fried pork. He thinks he has to have meat and dessert with every meal. I'm sure you've heard the old saying, the way to a man's heart is through his stomach," she told Laken.

"Well, I'll help Shelby finish sweeping the floors," Laken said.

After Laken and Shelby finished sweeping, Miss Jimmie told them to go look under the pine tree in the front yard.

"Bring me four or five of those pine cones that are fully opened, and we'll make some turkeys for Thanksgiving. It'll have to be after dinner, though," she said. "Those things can be prickly, so be careful picking them up…or better yet, take a pair of Shelby's gloves," she added.

Laken had learned earlier that morning that Mr. Hiram had taken some calves to the stock yard in Frisco City to sell them.

"If he's not back by twelve-thirty, we'll go ahead and eat," Miss Jimmie told the girls.

It was a cold day, too cold for the girls to play outside, so Jimmie found them simple chores to do inside. She put them to work folding bath cloths and towels.

Laken loved the Beasleys' house. It had a living room, a den, three bedrooms, a kitchen with a combined dining room, a bathroom, and a big storage room. The house was heated with electric heaters that were built into the wall. The den was heated by a giant fireplace. The fireplace was built with yellow-colored bricks, not from stones like the one at Laken's house. The chimney was made from yellow bricks, too.

The girls finished their tasks, and Miss Jimmie had finished preparing the dinner and had it on the table. She then opened the door to the den and started a fire in the fireplace. When she came back into the kitchen, she closed the door that went into the den.

It was fifteen minutes before one o'clock, so Jimmie called the girls for dinner.

At Laken's house, they helped their plates straight from the boiler. At the Beasleys', Miss Jimmie dipped everything into separate floral colored bowls. The food was blessed before each meal, then the bowls or platters were passed around for everyone to help their plate or saucer.

Today, they had fried pork chops, butterbeans with whole pods of okra boiled with them, stewed Irish potatoes, and cornbread. For dessert they had chocolate pudding with meringue topping.

Of course, the girls ate more chocolate pudding than they did anything else.

After dinner, they all cleaned the kitchen and the girls spread a sheet  over the table to protect the food from unwanted pests.

The day was dark and cloudy, but after dinner, Miss Jimmie gave them a paper bag and a pair of gloves to collect the pine cones. They each put on their winter coats and ran outside.

Jimmie watched them through a windowpane on the front door.

Of course, they had to frolic some. She watched as they ran toward PeeWee's stable. Under the eaves of the barn, some green grass, which had been protected from the cold weather,  was still growing. Jimmie watched as the girls pulled up handfuls of grass and threw it across the fence, where PeeWee was waiting for it.

Jimmie continued to watch the giggling girls as they ran back toward the pine tree and started collecting the pine cones. Neither one of them used their gloves; instead they used their forefingers and thumbs to pick them up and drop them into the open bag.

*"Such a contrast,"* thought Jimmie. Shelby with her long blonde hair, with fair skin and blue eyes, while Laken was dark skinned, with black hair, and gentle brown eyes. Shelby was a little taller than Laken, but Laken was built more muscular and thicker.

Each had learned so  much from the other. Laken's grammar was much improved, and she was far better groomed. It was hard to believe that they were the first to take Laken to church and to cook her a decent meal. Shelby learned the joy of getting outside and having someone to play with.

Jimmie dropped the curtain, then turned to find paper for them to draw, then color the head and tail feathers of their turkeys.

The den was built off the end of the house, which had a long concrete porch from one end to the other.

When they returned, she heard them stomping their shoes on the cement doorsteps. The huge den was beginning to get warm from the roaring fire in the fireplace.

After hanging their coats on the coat hanger, Jimmie told them to get their color crayons, a pencil, and Shelby's scissors and bring them to the den, which they did.

Jimmie drew her turkey neck, head, and tail feathers, then colored them first, so the girls would know what to do. Next, she looked in the bag and picked a pine cone, and inserted the head, neck and tail feathers, making a turkey.

"Yay!" shouted the girls, as they got busy with their artwork.

Jimmie couldn't help but laugh at her own turkey, as she set it on the window sill, so the girls could see it.

It didn't take the girls long before they were attaching the parts of the turkey to the pine cones. Neither one of them were satisfied with their first creations; they got the necks too long, causing the heads to droop over, so they each started another one.

Their second ones were presentable, so they placed them beside Jimmie's.

"I'm going to color one for my room," Shelby said.

"Yeah, and I'm going to do one for Mama," Laken replied.

About the time the girls were placing their last turkeys on the window sill, Hiram's truck came past the house. Jimmie knew he was going to the barn to take the cattle trailer off, and he would be in shortly.

Jimmie was glad of one thing, and that was the fact that Hiram would just as soon to eat his food cold, so she didn't feel the need to re-warm his supper.

"It tastes the same, after you chew it a few times," he'd say.

The girls could hardly wait to show him their turkeys.

Hiram surprised them, though, for in a few minutes they heard the sound of his truck pass the house, heading back toward the highway.

Their house was about a hundred yards from the highway. Jimmie knew that due to the cold blustery weather, Hiram had gone back to the end of their lane to wait on the school bus.

"Well, baloney!" Shelby exclaimed, as she and Laken parted the curtains and looked, while Hiram's truck headed back toward the highway.

"No need to worry, girls, he's just gone to pick up Caleb from the school bus. You know school turned out for the Thanksgiving holidays today, and Caleb won't have to go back until Monday," Jimmie told them.

"Yay!" the girls said in unison, for they missed their part-time playmate, since Hiram kept him so busy on the farm.

Hiram had noticed the smoke coming from the den's fireplace. When he returned with Caleb, they came through the door that led into the den.

"Brrr!" Hiram exclaimed as he came through the door, with Caleb behind him. Caleb carried an arm load of schoolwork under his left arm, which he plopped down on the nearest table.

Caleb made fair marks in school, but by no means was he a scholar, as he had little interest in school. He would rather be helping his daddy on the farm.

"Dinner is still on the table," Jimmie told Hiram, as the two gave each other a smack.

"Look what we made," Shelby said proudly, as she and Laken picked up the prickly pine cone turkeys and showed him.

"Wow, they're nice! Now ol' Caleb and I won't have to waste time in the woods trying to kill a turkey for Thanksgiving dinner," Hiram said.

Both of the girls laughed, and exclaimed, "Nooo!"

After warming himself by the fire, Hiram headed toward the kitchen, closing the door behind him.

"Well, let's see what we have here," Jimmie said, as she picked up Caleb's schoolwork and examined it.

"Wow, you did a good job with your turkey drawing, but you didn't color him," she said.

"No Ma'am, someone must have swiped my crayons. Miss Sawyer said I'd need some when school opens back up Monday," Caleb explained.

The girls ran over to look at Caleb's turkey.

"Wow, I didn't know they had a big head like that," Shelby said, as she looked at the drawing.

Jimmie shushed Shelby, and said, "Well, I think he did a fine job, considering he didn't have crayons. Look, you can see Caleb standing beside that tree. He's about to lower the boom on that rascal," Jimmie said, as she pulled her son over to her, with her arm around his waist.

Jimmie began looking at some of his spelling words and saw where he had misspelled two or three of them.

She knew that Caleb didn't like her to hug or embrace him anymore. Sure enough, he pulled loose from her and headed toward the kitchen.

"Don't you be making a mess in my kitchen, and don't eat too much, for you won't eat your supper," Jimmie told him, as Caleb went through the door.

*"It seems like that boy is growing in leaps and bounds,"* thought Jimmie, as she saw her handsome son leave the room. She knew he was going into the kitchen to talk with Hiram about his trip to the stockyard.

Caleb's aloofness toward her recently worried her, so she talked to Hiram about it one night when they were in bed. Hiram assured her that he was just growing up, and she had nothing to worry about. "Boys are different from girls," he said.

The days were getting shorter, so Jimmie knew they'd have to eat an early supper, so Laken could get home before dark.

Jimmie put everything in the oven to reheat the food, while Hiram and Caleb bundled up to go to the pastures and feed the animals. They'd stack bales of hay into the back of the truck, and in various places, Hiram would stop, and they'd throw the hay out for the hungry cattle. The cows could drink water from Persimmon Creek, but he and Caleb had to feed and water the hogs and chickens by hand.

After the food was warmed, Jimmie put on her long coat, grabbed two pails and headed to the cow stall, where Belle would be waiting to be milked and fed the sweet feed. Jimmie brought the milk inside to the kitchen, then hurriedly went back outside to feed the chickens inside their pen and gather the eggs. Her last chore was to close the wire gate to keep the varmints out, when the chickens went to roost.

Hiram and Caleb finished their tasks at the same time as Jimmie finished hers. Caleb took the basket of eggs from his mama, and they all went into the house together.

After everyone washed their hands, they sat down at the table for supper. They took turns saying the blessing, and it was Laken's turn.

"God bless this food; God bless the Beasleys. Amen!" she said.

All that Hiram ate was some of the chocolate pudding, for it hadn't been long since he had eaten.

They ate a hurried supper, for the shadows were getting long outside.

Hiram told Laken that he'd be taking her home. "It's too late for you to be walking across that field," he said.

"Tell your mama I'll be sending over more milk and buttermilk tomorrow," Jimmie told Laken.

"Yes, Ma'am, and I'll ask her if I can bring over the fiddle," Laken replied.

"I'll tell you what, wait until the day after tomorrow; it'll be Thanksgiving. You can put on a performance for us after we eat," Jimmie said.

"Yes, Ma'am, I'll just bring the empty jugs tomorrow," Laken replied.

Caleb rode with them when they took Laken home.

Hiram wasn't sure how to get to the parking lot that Laken talked about, but she pointed out the directions and they soon pulled into the parking lot.

Laken had already hugged Mr. Hiram and Miss Jimmie's neck before she left their house, so she jumped out of the truck. Hiram stayed until she disappeared, going up the trail.

Hiram recognized Victor McMillian's and Leon Snyder's trucks parked in the lot and just shook his head. *"I guess they're getting ready for the holiday,"* he thought.

Chapter 9

It was Thanksgiving, 1950, and Jimmie had been cooking for two days. Of course, the girls helped her, especially with the cleaning.

Hiram and Caleb had bagged a big gobbler in the woods behind the cow pasture. They were so proud of themselves, they insisted that Miss Jimmie take time off from her cooking to get the Kodak out and take their picture holding the turkey by the neck.

Laken and Shelby helped pluck the big turkey. Shelby grimaced at each feather she pulled from the turkey, but it hadn't seemed to bother Laken.

Callie had allowed Laken to carry the fiddle over to the Beasleys', telling her, if she tore it up to just stay over there and don't bother to come back home.

Even though Laken loved staying over at the Beasleys' in the daytime, when it started to get dark, she like spending the night in her own bed. Even though she had to spend a lot of time in the chifforobe at night, she didn't have to do it in the daytime.

Laken had never eaten most of the things that she had at the Beasleys'. Jimmie just couldn't understand it; no matter how much Laken ate, she didn't seem to gain an ounce (not that she was skinny).

Laken didn't know several of the dishes on the table that day, but everything looked delicious. The table was so full of food that the girls had trouble finding room for their plates and glasses of iced tea. The aroma in the room smelled delicious. Miss Jimmie had the desserts on the counters. They consisted of a coconut cake, egg custard pies, and apple pies. In the center of the table set a big platter with the golden-brown turkey in it.

Everyone gathered around the table, and Hiram blessed the food. He also thanked the Lord for his family, Laken, and their many blessings, including their farm.

When he said "Amen," he began to carve the turkey, and everyone sat down to eat.

Laken didn't know what some of the food was, so she put a small amount of each dish on her plate. She discovered that she liked all of it, but she found that she liked the cornbread dressing and fruit salad the best.

"Everything is so good! I wish Mama had a dish," Laken said, while she was eating.

"Well, we'll just have to send her a plate back," Jimmie said.

"Oh boy! Thanks ever so much," Laken remarked.

Jimmie continued, "We'll send her a plate of food back at Christmas, too."

"I'll tell her tonight when I get home," Laken said.

Neither Laken nor Jimmie knew that Callie wouldn't be around on Christmas.

Jimmie was so tired she didn't feel like eating much. She just picked at her food, while she thoroughly enjoyed watching everyone else around the table eating.

Her mind flashed back to the time that she had met her husband. She had traipsed along with her father to the stockyard in Evergreen, Alabama. Jimmie and her family lived on a farm near the town, which was about eighteen miles from Excel. Hiram and his father had ridden over to check out the prices of the cows. Hiram and Jimmie struck up a conversation, and the rest was history. Jimmie looked at her husband as he ate his dinner. *"What a lucky woman I am to have a Christian man for my husband!"* she thought.

Even though she didn't leave home and work like a lot of the local wives, she made up for it by working in the house and keeping things running on an even keel. She made a little money selling milk, eggs, and butter, even though she didn't charge Callie or any of the needy for their milk. Jimmie kept the money she made in a cookie jar and spent it only occasionally.

They weren't rich, by any means, but they didn't owe anyone for anything, as far as she knew. They had a family car, farm truck, and two tractors with the equipment. Of course, Hiram had inherited the land and house from his father. They'd built onto the house and Hiram saw to it that things were kept up.

Jimmie didn't worry about money; she left that up to Hiram. He saw to it that they got what they needed, but they weren't extravagant, as were some in the area, like the Jordans.

Hiram didn't tell her so, but she knew that he'd taken the young cows to the sale, so they'd have money for Christmas.

They centered their lives around the church, their family, and the farm. Once in a blue moon, they'd take their children to the theater in Monroeville. Jimmie thought that Hiram liked the Western movies as much as Caleb did. They'd always eat supper at "Home Café," which was located on the square in Monroeville. It would give Jimmie a break from cooking.

"Whoo! I'm full as a tick, but I've got to have a small slice of that coconut cake," Hiram said, as he took his empty plate to the counter.

Jimmie jumped up to get a saucer and slice the cake.

Hiram sat back down at the table with the slice of cake. "Mm-mmm, Miss Jimmie, you've really outdone yourself with this cake," Hiram said.

"Ah, pshaw, that's what you say every time I cook a coconut cake," Jimmie remarked, adding, "You and Caleb just like coconut."

Everyone soon finished, and after things were stacked on the counter, they headed for the den.

Once everyone was seated, Hiram reached over to turn on the radio, but Jimmie announced that Laken had a Thanksgiving treat for them.

Laken began to unwrap her coat from around the fiddle. She figured her old coat would protect the fiddle, since she didn't have a case for it.

Everyone was amazed as they watched Laken put the instrument up to her neck and pick up the bow.

"I can't play but three or four tunes; my fingers are too tender to chord the strings for long," she said.

Everyone was still amazed and continued to stare at Laken as she stood by the fireplace and begun to saw away with, 'Cripple Creek.'

"My Lord, would you just listen to that!" said the stunned Hiram.

Laken played flawlessly. Her next tune was, 'Old Joe Clark,' followed by 'Ode to Joy.'

Laken patted her left foot as she played.

"The last one, I'm dedicating to Shelby," she said, as she put the burning tips of her left hand to the strings and started playing, 'Jingle Bells.'

After Laken finished, everyone yelled and applauded.

"*How* old did you say you are?" Hiram asked.

"Ah, honey, I've already told you, there's only a few days difference in the girls' birthdays," Jimmie said.

Laken carefully rewrapped the fiddle and laid it behind the curtain on the windowsill, where she had hidden it.

"Honey, you belong on the radio. You have them beat that play every Sunday morning; you're gifted!" Hiram said exuberantly.

"I only know a few tunes, but if my fingertips get tougher, I could learn more," Laken told Mr. Hiram. "Mama can play for hours," she added.

"Yeah, we've heard her over the years, and she's good, but she's not five years old, either," replied Hiram. "My goodness. We're going to have to find a way to toughen those fingers. Maybe if you help ol' Caleb chop some wood?"

"Hiram Beasley!" Miss Jimmie exclaimed.

"Honey, I was just kidding," Hiram said, then he reached over and turned the radio on.

Hank Williams was singing, 'Move it on Over.'

"Did I ever tell you kids that I saw Hank Williams?" Hiram asked.

Laken didn't know who Hank Williams was, for they didn't have a radio at their house.

"Is he the one singing now?" she asked.

"Sure is," Hiram said. "Jimmie and I saw him in Monroeville. He was just a gangly kid then. He has relatives in Fountain, Alabama, and he was visiting them."

"Did he have on a cowboy suit?" asked Caleb.

"No, he was just like me; he was wearing a pair of overalls," reported Hiram. "I'll bet he never dreamed at the time that he'd be famous today. Shoot, he couldn't be much over twenty-five years old now."

49

"He's the pride of Alabama. He was raised not far from my hometown, about eight or ten miles," Jimmie remarked. "From what I've heard, he had a rough time of it coming up."

"Sure did, leaving me to believe if he can make it, anyone can," Hiram said, aiming his voice toward Laken.

The children soon tired of listening to the adults talk about Hank Williams, so Hiram turned the radio down and, in just a few minutes, he was nodding off.

The girls and Miss Jimmie went into the kitchen to clean the dishes, while Caleb went to his room to look at a catalogue. His daddy had told him when he turned nine years old, he'd buy him a .410 shotgun and he'd found pictures of them in the catalogue.

After raking all the food scraps out of the dishes, Jimmie told the girls, "Boy, the hogs are gonna have a feast tonight."

"I know. I wish daddy would let us have another dog," Shelby commented.

"Yeah, I know, but I think he's still grieving over Bully; he had that dog when we married. I imagine when Caleb really puts the pressure on him, he'll relent and let him get one. He'll soon be the age to go hunting by himself," Jimmie told the girls. "Ol' Bully would sure enjoy these scraps," Jimmie added.

Several times, Laken had to really think what some of the words Miss Jimmie and Mr. Hiram meant. It took her a few seconds to realize what "Relent" meant, but like all the other times, she soon figured it out.

"If Caleb goes hunting, Laken and I are going with him!" Shelby exclaimed.

"Little girls are supposed to learn to be in the house learning how to be a good housewife," Jimmie said, as she kissed Shelby on the cheek.

"Baloney! Times have changed, Mama. A lot of wives at church, work," Shelby said.

"I know, but their husbands aren't farmers, and they don't milk cows, slop hogs, and feed chickens," Jimmie replied. "Besides, your daddy doesn't want me to work publicly. Could you imagine me behind a sewing machine sewing for a company, driving a taxi, churning milk, or mopping someone else's floors?" she asked.

Both of the girls laughed.

"No, Mama, you wouldn't have the time," Shelby said, then added, "Especially the churning the milk part; that takes hours."

After they'd cleaned the kitchen and put the bedspread back over the table to protect the leftovers, they walked back into the den.

Hiram, who had awakened from his nap, said, "Guess what, girls? They just announced over the radio that 'Rio Grande' will be playing at the movies Saturday night. Let's make plans to go. Caleb and I can feed the cattle earlier, while you get the chickens into the pen and gather the eggs."

"Oh my, it must be a John Wayne movie," Jimmie said, as she sat down on the couch.

Hiram laughed. "How well you know me! It's John Wayne and Maureen O'Hara," he said.

The girls squealed from excitement.

"I just hope Mama lets me go. How long does it last? I've never been to the movies," Laken said.

"Sure, she will. Why I'll send James over there to talk to her," Hiram said.

He then thought he might have opened his mouth when he shouldn't have, for so far as he knew, James having any connection to Laken had never been mentioned around the girl.

"I'll ask her tonight, and if she says no, then you can talk to him about it," Laken said, failing to mention that she called James, "Daddy."

"Hey, maybe you can spend the night. Just don't forget to bring your church clothes for the next day, though," Shelby said. Then she added, "I've never had anyone to spend the night with me."

"I'll see, but I've never spent the night away from home," Laken said.

"Well, then, it'll be an adventure for the both of you," Jimmie said, smiling.

For the remainder of the evening, the girls spent their time in Shelby's bedroom. They'd draw colorful characters or creatures, then color them with Shelby's crayons.

It wasn't long before they were eating again, then chores were done. Shelby and Laken fed the chickens and collected the eggs, making sure to lock the gate behind them. When Miss Jimmie milked the cow and brought the milk inside, she immediately prepared Callie a platter of food, then wrapped it with wax paper, and taped it on the bottom.

Jimmie then strained the milk, as she always did, making sure it didn't have a speck of trash in it.

When Hiram took Laken home, he saw Barney Jones' vehicle in the parking lot. He went around and got the platter from Laken while she got out of his truck.

"Hold the platter on the ends, and be careful," he instructed, then he patted her on the back, before she began her trek down the trail.

"Uh-uh-uh, no telling what the child is liable to walk in on," thought Hiram, for Barney was known to be a womanizer.

Laken recognized Barney's vehicle, too, so she came in through the back door, which led to her room. She stayed there until she heard Barney leave. She was glad, too, for it was freezing in her room with the door closed. There were only two rooms in the old log house and both were heated from the fireplace in the living room.

Callie was getting out of the bed when Laken came into the room and rushed to the fireplace. She laid the platter of food on the hearth.

"The Beasleys sent you a Thanksgiving meal," Laken told her mama.

Callie sat up in the bed, and Laken could see that she was naked.

"Well, bring it here, before the platter gets hot," Callie said, while pulling a quilt over her lap.

She tore the waxed paper from around the platter, then set it in her lap. Seeing the bounty of food, she said, "My Lord, no wonder you like to go over there!" She then told Laken to bring her a fork.

The kitchen was located at the other side of the room, so it didn't take Laken but a minute to return with the fork and a kitchen towel for her mama to use as a napkin.

Callie was already chewing on a piece of turkey when Laken handed her the fork, then laid the towel beside her.

"Mm-Mmm, best turkey I ever 'et,'" Cassie said, then she grabbed the fork and began to shovel in the variety of food.

Laken was constantly correcting her mama's grammar, but it didn't do any good. She certainly didn't want to get Callie in a tizzy before she asked her if she could go to the movie show and spend the night with Shelby on Saturday night.

Laken tossed a piece of wood into the fireplace and watched as her mama wolfed down the food.

"I don't know what this is called, but it's good," Callie said.

"That's fruit salad. Shelby and I helped Miss Jimmie with some of the things," Laken told her. Choosing her moment, she said, "Mama? The Beasleys have asked me if I could go to the movie with them Saturday night, then spend the night with Shelby."

"That means you'll need to take two suits of clothes with you when you leave from here Saturday morning. One to wear to the movies, and another for church," Callie said.

"Yes, Ma'am," Laken quickly agreed, a little surprised at how quickly her mama had made up her mind.

"Well, word is I'm having over several clients Saturday night. A bunch of squirts from high school are coming over. Heaven knows, I need all the money I can get, so it's probably a good thing that you won't be here. You'd be in that chifforobe for a long time," Callie responded, while still finishing up her supper.

For once in her life, Laken was okay with her mama's occupation. *'It's a good thing she'll be busy anyway. She just worried about the spending the night part,"* Laken thought.

# Chapter 10

Laken wore her western shirt, that snapped instead of being buttoned, along with jeans and her brown penny loafers, to the theater that night. The weather had been cold and windy all day, so the girls had stayed in Shelby's bedroom most of the day. Laken taught Shelby the alphabet, and when Shelby learned it flawlessly, she ran into the kitchen to repeat it to her mama.

Jimmie sat down at the table and listened to her baby.

'Oh my! I was in the first grade before I learned to say mine," she said, after Shelby had finished.

"Laken taught me," Shelby informed her.

While they were in the car on the way to Monroeville, Shelby kept saying the alphabet.

"Shut up!" Caleb said, after the third or fourth repetition.

"Caleb, don't you talk to your sister like that," his father corrected.

"Well, she keeps saying the stupid alphabet over and over," Caleb complained.

"She's just proud of herself, and she has a right to be. As I recall, you didn't learn them until you started to school," Hiram told his son.

After that, Shelby settled down and so did Caleb.

The sun was going down when Hiram parked the car on the square in front of the courthouse.

"Boy, we have a long walk. Either the café is busy, or folks are waiting on the theater to open," Hiram said, as they got out of the car.

On the way to the café, Jimmie held one of Hiram's hands, while he held Laken's hand with his other one and

Jimmie held on to Shelby's. Caleb trudged along behind them.

The Home Café had a buffet, or you could order from the menu.

Of course, the three children ordered hamburgers and fries, with Coca-Cola, while Hiram and Jimmie ate from the buffet.

After eating, they walked along the sidewalk until they were in front of the theater, then rushed across the street. They had to wait in line for about fifteen minutes before Hiram was finally paying for the tickets.

There was a popcorn machine in the lobby, which was popping corn right before their eyes. It smelled heavenly.

The auditorium was well lit, so they didn't have trouble finding a place to sit.

Hiram and Jimmie had already planned the seating arrangements. They sat on the ends, and the children sat between them, with Caleb sitting next to his daddy.

In a few minutes, the lights were dimmed, and the red curtains trimmed in gold opened to reveal a large movie screen.

Laken was in awe. She'd never seen so many people, not even in church.

First the news came on. President Truman was talking about the Korean war, and it showed actual battle scenes of the conflict.

Later, a cartoon came on, and it was about Popeye the Sailor Man and Olive Oyl.

"Olive Oyl looks like Miss Davis, at church," Shelby whispered to Laken. They both giggled.

After the cartoon was over, the movie came on, and Laken was just enthralled. She'd never seen anything like it, or even heard of such a wonder.

Just as the Indians were attacking, the intermission came on. Hiram took the three children to the lobby and bought them all a Coke and a bag of the delicious popcorn.

They were still enjoying their snack when the lights were dimmed, and the movie came back on where it left off.

While watching the movie, Laken, Shelby, and Caleb never dreamed they'd be performing on that very stage one day.

When the movie was finally over, they all went to their respective bathrooms, then waited in front of the theater until the traffic cleared. They then made their way back to the car.

The town had street lights everywhere, and even the insides of some of the stores were well lit. Laken thought that she had never seen such a beautiful sight.

A full moon shone on them all the way home.

"I do believe that I could drive with my headlights off," Hiram said.

"Sure is a bright and beautiful night," Jimmie agreed.

As they started up the lane to their house, Hiram said, "You know, Pap Gulley has some mighty pretty pups. He brought two of them to the sale the other day, and I think I'll get us one. We need some kind of watchdog here when we leave."

"You'd make Caleb a happy young man," Jimmie said.

Caleb was thinking about his bed, but with the mention of a puppy, he snapped to.

"What kind of pup is he?" the boy asked eagerly.

"Heaven knows, but he said they make big dogs, and they're solid black. He's saving a boy pup for you; we just haven't had time to go get him," Hiram told his son.

"Let's go after church. I'll make him a warn place in the barn when we get back with him," Caleb said excitedly.

"We'll see," Hiram answered.

Laken had thought to bring her toothbrush and hairbrush, but she didn't own a pair of pajamas, so Jimmie loaned her an old pair of Shelby's.

After brushing their teeth and giving their hair a hundred strokes apiece, the girls said their prayers and jumped into bed, squealing a little as they recounted the night's excitement. There was a dim nightlight shining in the room, along with the moonlight, which made everything cozy for Laken. She had feared she would be lonesome for her own room, but it wasn't like that at all.

After whispering to each other and giggling some more, the two were about to go to sleep. All at once, Shelby turned to Laken and said, "I always wanted a sister, and I love you like you were my very own sister!"

Laken was stunned, and she didn't know what to say, so she murmured, "I love y'all too."

They were both smiling when they fell asleep.

The next morning was like all the other Sunday mornings, except Laken didn't have to tramp across the fields in order to reach the Beasley house. Once everyone was at the table, they ate a good breakfast of grits, eggs, bacon, and homemade biscuits.

All Caleb could talk about at the table was the black puppy, and how much he hoped they were going after it that afternoon.

Miss Mary Surmon and Annie Kimbro had ordered two dozen eggs each. Since Shelby and Laken had gotten ready before everyone else, Miss Jimmie asked them if they could get the eggs ready, which they did. The crates were made from cardboard, so they had to be careful. After putting them into the paper crates, they carefully set them in double bags.

They always went to Sunday School, then regular church services on Sundays.

There were several homemade swings outside the church, and the day was sunny. The Sunday School teacher allowed Shelby and Laken's group to go outside for a few minutes.

In the few minutes they were outside, they made a new friend. Her name was Ann Cobb, and she could swing higher than anyone. In the short time they had, they discovered that Ann lived near them. They didn't get to talk long, though, before it was time to go inside for church.

The church had two choirs, one composed of adults, and the other with children, who aged from six to twelve.

Brother Kenneth Johnson, the preacher, had talked to Caleb about joining the choir, but so far the boy had held off. Caleb told his mama that he'd feel silly wearing the long robe.

The choir loft was exactly that; it was in the loft of the church. It was beautiful up there, though, and Laken and Shelby had been up the stairs to look at it. There were nice, smooth mahogany benches, and on each end were beautiful stained-glass windows with Jesus holding a lamb.

Unlike Caleb, Laken was eager to be in the choir, and had talked Shelby into joining it when they turned six.

The service was short that day, so by twelve o'clock, Brother Kenneth was standing at the front door shaking everyone's hand. The preacher's wife was Miss Julia, and she made it a point to always stand by her husband and shake the ladies' hands or tell them how lovely they looked.

After changing out of their church clothes, the girls stayed home with Miss Jimmie while Hiram and Caleb made the trip to Pap Gulley's to see about the puppy. Miss Jimmie had told them that dinner would be on the table when they got back.

Jimmie deposited her egg money, which was two dollars and forty cents, into the old cookie jar. She'd cooked most of the Sunday dinner that morning, so she didn't have much to do to finish preparing the meal.

Laken donned the long-sleeved western shirt and jeans that she had worn to the movies. Shelby loved the plaid shirt and pleaded with her mama to buy her one.

Jimmie asked the girls to set the table, then told Shelby she'd talk to her daddy about it. She then added, "That shirt looks expensive; I'd be willing to bet it was bought at Katz Department Store."

"Yes, Ma'am, I picked it out. My daddy took me up there," Laken said.

"Who is your daddy?" asked Shelby.

"Shelby!" Jimmie said in a harsh voice.

Shelby didn't know why what she had said was wrong, but Laken spoke up and said, "James Jordan."

"Gollee, that's one of daddy's friends. Boy, your grandma is a doozie," Shelby added.

"Shelby, what's come over you? Why are you so curious today?" Jimmie demanded. "And don't you say another bad word about Victoria Jordan," she warncd her daughter. "Mrs. Jordan is our neighbor, and you shouldn't say bad things about your neighbor."

"Yes, Ma'am," Shelby said, and she remained silent as she and Laken finished setting the table.

After the girls were done with the table, they went into the den and turned the radio on. Then they waited until the puppy arrived.

When Hiram's truck stopped in front of the house, the girls dashed outside to see the new puppy.

"His name is Jim," Caleb said, as he stepped out of the truck.

The girls made a mad rush toward the black puppy.

Caleb felt he had to turn his puppy loose, or the girls would have torn him in half.

"Don't pet and love on him so! I'm going to make a hunting dog out of him," Caleb told them, as Laken hugged the puppy.

"Hey, let the girls take care of him while you get a cardboard box out of the barn," Hiram told his son. "Put a little hay in it and put it on the front porch. It'll be a good place for him to sleep until he learns the place."

Hiram headed toward the house with a smile on his face, knowing Caleb would have a battle on his hands with the girls.

Caleb ran toward the barn and returned in a jiffy, for he didn't want the girls to spoil his dog by petting and loving on him. The boy grabbed Jim and told the girls to go inside and bring him a pan of water, then he placed the puppy in the bed of hay at the end of the porch. Caleb waited outside and stroked the puppy on the head several times.

The girls soon returned with a pan of water and the morning's leftover breakfast of bacon and a biscuit.

One whiff of the food, and Jim wolfed the bacon down, then started on the biscuit. Barely giving the food time to hit his stomach, he began to lap the water.

"That dog was starving for food and water," Caleb said, smiling at his new puppy's appetite. "Look at him go!"

Hiram came to the door and told them to come inside for dinner. "He's eaten and drank water, so he's not going anywhere," he assured the children.

Reluctantly, they followed Hiram into the house, with Hiram staying at the door to push the puppy back out onto the porch.

The three played with the puppy that afternoon until it was time for the chores.

The inquisitive Jim learned his boundaries that afternoon, especially after he got too close to the rooster and the rooster flew into him. After being pecked and spurred, Jim ran back to his box.

The girls collected the eggs and fed the chickens that afternoon, while Jimmie milked the cow.

She warned them that the next day, they'd be churning. "We need some buttermilk and butter," she said.

After a quick supper, it was time to take Laken home.

Hiram felt better as he left Laken that afternoon, for he didn't see another vehicle in the parking area for a change.

Jimmie had put Laken's Sunday clothes and two pairs of pajamas inside a pillow case. Hiram got out of his truck to help the child get out.

"You take care, and we'll see you in the morning," Hiram said, then he gave Laken the usual pat on the back, before she headed up the trail.

"Did you bring in more food?" Callie asked, as Laken came into the house.

"No, it's my clothes," Laken said, as she headed toward the back room to put on a pair of the pajamas and hang her Sunday clothes up.

Callie had been hoping that Laken would bring in more food, but when she saw that she didn't, she got up from her chair and began to scramble some eggs.

Laken soon returned to the front room.

"Well, what did you think of the movie?" Callie asked.

"Oh, it was heavenly! We ate out and everything, and we had the best popcorn at the movies," Laken said. She then added, "Caleb got him a black puppy today after church."

"Well, as long as he don't come snooping over here when he gets older," Callie said, as she sat down at the table with the scrambled eggs. She didn't bother to take them out of the pan.

"He won't mess with anything over here," Laken promised. "He's a good dog."

"What have you got on?" Callie asked.

"It's pajamas. I think everyone wears them," Laken answered.

"Well, I guess it's better than sleeping with just your panties on," Callie said, as she wolfed down the eggs.

After Laken was warmed from the fireplace, she told her mama that she was going to bed.

"I'm heading in, too. I thought I could sleep today, after such a busy night last night, but no such thing. Everybody and his brother was thirsty today," Callie said.

Laken left the door open so her room would stay warm. Before she blew out the lamp, for the first time Laken took a good look at her room.

*"Such a difference,"* she thought, and she wished she was back at the Beasleys'.

She never knew when one of her mama's clients might come in, and she realized that she slept with fear each night—a fear that someone would come through her door.

# Chapter 11

It was getting near Christmastime. Callie even had a Christmas tree decorated with cotton balls up in the corner of the front room. The tree was a small cedar tree that Callie had hacked down near the trail that led to the parking area.

*"It's so much different from the tree at the Beasleys' house,"* Laken thought, but she didn't say anything. The tree at the Beasleys' was about eight feet tall, Mr. Beasley said, for it went to the ceiling of the den. The Beasley tree was decorated with electric lights and silvery icicles as well as pretty ornaments.

Caleb had found the tree while he and Jim were traipsing through the woods. He told Mr. Beasley what they'd found. Hiram had taken an axe along with them, and sure enough, they dragged the tree home. Caleb was so proud of himself!

Jim had only been at the Beasleys' a couple of weeks, but he had learned his way around the farm. Boy, did his tail go to wagging when he saw the school bus stop at the highway for Caleb to walk home! Jim always met Caleb about halfway up the lane, and it was a joyful reunion.

James Jordan made it a habit of visiting Hiram two or three times each week. Once, he'd even brought his father along. Laken liked the older fellow; he told the girls a bunch of tongue twisters and bent over laughing when they couldn't repeat them.

By now, the Beasleys thought it was a common occurrence for everyone to know that James was Laken's father, so nothing was thought about it.

One day, Laken saw her grandfather slip Mr. Hiram some money. She didn't know what it was for, so she didn't think anything about it.

Laken began spending more nights at the Beasley house. Of course, she'd always ask her mama first.

Callie did tell her, though, that after the holidays, she was going to put a stop to it. "I'm mighty busy, it being the holidays and all, so I'm having a lot of clients and selling a lot of liquor. I just hope I have enough made to last until it warms up, enough so we can make some more," Callie told Laken.

Even though as far as she could remember, her mama made and sold whiskey, Laken had even begun to help her. Somehow, Laken knew it was wrong, and even though she knew how to make it, she didn't intend on doing it when she was grown.

What little time they had together, Callie taught Laken more and more about the fiddle, and even a few chords on the banjo. She also taught her daughter that if she rubbed the ends of her fingers with pine needles, it would toughen them.

One day, on a Monday evening the worst of the worst occurred; Calvin showed up. He nearly knocked the door down as he knocked and kicked.

Laken hadn't intended on spending the night with the Beasleys, but Callie told her to get her coat and run to their house. "You can come home tomorrow," Callie told her, adding, "Hurry, before he knocks the door down!"

Laken quickly did as her mama said. She grabbed her coat and ran out the back door, straight into her daddy's arms.

"What's your rush?" James asked.

"Calvin is in there! He's mean. Mama told me to run over to the Beasleys,'" Laken said.

"Go on then, and know that I love you," James said, as he hugged her and put her down. "Run, before it gets dark!"

Laken ran to where the creek was shallow and looked back to see James going in the back door, holding a pistol.

About halfway across the field she heard two gunshots, but she sped up and continued on. She could see the Christmas tree lights shining through the den's window, and she felt better.

Back at Laken's house, Callie finally made her way to the door.

"When I knock, you answer," Calvin told Callie gruffly, as he slapped her across the room.

James opened the door, and Calvin made a lunge toward him, opening his long, wicked pocketknife as he did.

Callie knew her nose was broken again, for blood was gushing from it. She was still on the floor when James fired the two bullets into Calvin's enormous stomach.

The bullets didn't seem to slow Calvin, for he continued toward James, swinging his knife and cursing.

James kept backing up until he backed out of the door and was on the ground. His pistol must have ran out of bullets, for he kept pulling the trigger and it didn't fire. Calvin kept coming after him, still swinging the shiny knife blade at James' stomach.

Callie wiped the blood from her nose and ran toward the front porch.

With her nose pounding, Callie thought, *"I've had enough of this."* She then grabbed the sharp, deadly sling blade from the front porch and ran toward the back of the house.

James had backed up as far as the creek, when Calvin sliced James' stomach open with the knife. James held his intestines with one hand while taking a swing at Calvin with the other. Calvin blocked the blow with the knife, and Callie saw more blood fly as Calvin kicked James into the swift current of the creek.

"What's it going to take for you?" Callie screamed as she struck Calvin with all her might across the top of his head.

The sharp sling blade cut through his skull into the brain, and Calvin toppled into the creek.

It was beginning to get dusk, but Callie ran to the shallow part of the creek, where Laken had crossed.

She saw James' body, and it was under the water, so she knew he was dead. In a few seconds, Calvin's lifeless body rushed down the stream, with the sling blade sticking from his head.

Callie grabbed James by his familiar hands and pulled him to the rocks in the middle of shallow stream.

Callie began to cry, but she knew she had to think, so she wiped her eyes.

"James, I always loved you," she whispered, and then she headed back toward the cabin.

The first thing she did was to lock both doors, then she grabbed the two battered old suitcases she owned. She loosened the familiar stone on the hearth and brought out the two cloth sacks of hoarded money. She knew she had to be fast in case Laken showed back up with the Beasleys.

After packing as much as she could in the suitcases, including the money, Callie threw some shoes into a pillowcase, along with her hairbrush, mirror, and rouge. She couldn't carry everything in one trip, so she grabbed the two suitcases. She prayed that at least one of the men had left the keys in their truck.

Before leaving the only home she'd ever known, Callie ran to the creek, carrying one of her winter dresses. Bending down, where the two men had bled, she rubbed her dress into the congealed blood and threw it into the cold stream.

As it turned out, Calvin's old truck had the keys in the ignition. Not wanting to take a chance with her money, Callie locked the suitcases in the truck. She then ran back up the trail for the remainder of her necessities.

Callie knew she was only taking the bare minimum, but she also knew if she didn't get away fast, she'd be going to jail for murder.

She didn't know what she was going to do about Laken, but she thought she'd figure it out later.

Callie fired up the ignition on Calvin's truck, and after she made it to the highway, she headed south. Her nose had stopped bleeding, but it was hard for her to see, her vision was so blurred.

# Chapter 12

Callie had never been in such a predicament. She wanted to keep driving until she reached Texas, but between Excel and Mobile, she decided to stay in Alabama. She didn't know how she was going to do it, but she planned on getting Laken back. She knew one thing, she wouldn't be selling her body anymore, and she wouldn't be making and selling whiskey.

She planned on keeping a low-keyed life, one that would make it hard for the law to track her down. She still had Betty Jean Dale's identification and social security card, so from this night on, she was Betty Jean Dale.

Callie reached the outskirts of Mobile about eight o'clock. She went through the Bankhead Tunnel and was driving through downtown Mobile by nine o'clock.

She saw a well-lit motel on the west side of Mobile and pulled in. After presenting Betty Jean's ID, she rented a room for three nights. After paying thirty dollars and carrying her things into the room, Callie realized how alien things were for her. She'd never had electricity or running water before.

It took her a few minutes to figure out the shower, but she soon did. Once she had taken a good hot shower, she felt better. The happenings of the night had worn her out, but she had to think. She put on her robe and slipped on a pair of loafers. She knew the tag on Calvin's truck could lead the law straight to her. She went outside and pulled the top of the tag down, making it hard to read.

After making her way back to the room, she emptied the two grungy sacks of money onto the top of the bed. She heard the sound of a vehicle outside the door, and she happened to think the door wasn't locked. With her heart in her throat, she ran to the door and locked it.

Cracking the curtain, she saw that it was just a young couple, and they were walking toward the office.

She soon figured out how to turn the lamp on that sat on a table next to the head of her bed. After doing so, she turned off the bright overhead light, and sat in the middle of the bed. She made sure that her back blocked the view from the outside.

With shaking hands, she separated the bills and began to count the money. When she had finished, she found that she had four thousand, two hundred dollars. Putting the smaller bills in her purse, she rolled the larger bills around each other and packed them into some thick socks.

Callie thought of the ways she had earned the money. She hated the taste of whiskey, and the only good sex she'd had was with James.

*"What a fool I've been! If only Victoria Jordan hadn't hated me so, things would have turned out differently,"* she thought.

She thought of James and the love she'd had for him over the years. Strangely, though, she'd never let him touch her sexually after she'd started fooling with other men. She guessed that she loved him enough that she didn't want to defile him; she could never figure it out. *"Poor thing, he died defending my life,"* she thought.

She also thought of the hated Calvin and wondered why no one had killed him before James and she did. She knew he liked rough sex, and if she hadn't been getting the liquor ingredients from him she wouldn't have had anything to do with him.

Callie's lips cracked a smile, however, when she thought of Laken. *"How smart and talented she is to just be five years old. I just pray she got away safely,"* she thought. She had it in the back of her mind to get Laken back. *"First, I've got to get a real job and get myself established. I'll start on it tomorrow."*

She got up from the bed to check on her nose. After looking in the mirror, she discovered that her nose was still swollen and red, but it looked like Calvin had knocked it straight again.

It was painful, but her next move was to brush her teeth. She was starved, but she managed to brush her teeth, then her hair before she crawled into bed.

She had a lot on her mind, but she was so exhausted she fell asleep right away.

## Chapter 13

The next morning, Callie didn't take any chances. She dressed warmly, for it proved to be a cold morning.

Adjoining the hotel, she saw a flashing orange light. "Get a good country breakfast here," the flashing light read.

Callie couldn't believe her good luck. She walked the few feet to the diner and went inside.

There was a woman with stacked red hair behind the counter.

"Can I help you?" the woman asked, as she handed Callie a greasy plastic menu.

Callie looked over the menu, and ordered grits, two fried eggs, ham, biscuit, and coffee.

"How would you like your eggs?" the woman asked.

"Fried," replied Callie.

The lady nodded, turned around, cracked two eggs and dropped them onto a greased flat metal cooker. She then took a smoked ham out of the refrigerator, sliced a thin piece and also threw it onto the hot metal.

After handing Callie a big mug of coffee, she said, "You can eat here or at one of the tables. You'll find the condiments on the tables."

Callie didn't know what condiments was until she chose a table, and soon figured it out after seeing the cream and sugar, along with little shakers of salt and pepper.

She guessed the grits and biscuits were already cooked, for in just a few minutes the lady slid her tray of food on the table. The eggs were raw on the tops, but Callie didn't say anything. She just dropped them over into the hot grits, while she buttered her biscuit.

Needless to say, it didn't take her long to polish off the meal. Callie enjoyed finishing her coffee, then took the tray of empty containers back to the counter.

"Oh, how sweet," the woman said, as she headed toward the cash register. "That'll be a dollar nineteen," she continued, after mashing some buttons on the register.

Callie was wearing a pair of jeans, so she reached into her pocket and handed the lady a dollar and twenty cents. The lady opened the register again and gave Callie a penny back.

Callie pulled her old thick coat from the back of the chair where she had been sitting and put it on. She was ready to face the cold and her immediate problem at hand.

She found some empty gallon jugs in the trash barrel outside. She picked out one that had a lid on it and put it in the floorboard of the truck.

When she pulled out of the parking lot, she had no idea where she was going, for she'd never been to Mobile. She really surprised herself at how well she could drive in the morning traffic.

According to the gauge in the dashboard the truck was low on gas. She found a gas station on the outskirts of town and pulled in. Surprisingly, gas was only twenty-four cents a gallon. Gas was twenty-seven to thirty cents a gallon in Excel.

Callie told the attendant to fill the gallon jug and put the remainder in the truck. She handed him two dollars.

She had no idea where she was going; all she knew was she needed to find a secluded place.

It took close to an hour before she found a gravel road. After turning onto a dirt road, she found that several more dirt lanes led from that, so she turned down one of them. She found that the lane led to a wide stream of water.

She stopped on the bank of the stream.

In the back of her mind, something told her to look under and behind the seat of the truck. She pulled out a pile of papers and an old, tattered coat. The coat was heavy, so she began to go through the pockets.

"Aha!" she said aloud, as she retrieved two bundles of twenty-dollar bills. The money still had the wrappers on it. "First National Bank," the wrappers read.

*"Undoubtedly, that snake Calvin must have robbed a bank,"* thought Callie, as she stuffed the money deep in her coat pockets.

After giving the truck a thorough going over, she didn't find anything else of value.

Callie took the penny she'd gotten back after paying for her breakfast and unscrewed the screws holding the tag on the truck. She threw the tag into the black water.

Next, she soaked the interior of the truck and under the hood with the gasoline that was in the jug. She stood back and threw a lighted match inside the truck and ran. The truck went up in flames. Callie then walked away from the scene and didn't look back.

She had to walk back to the highway before she could hitch a ride. The man that picked her up said his name was Lonnie and he worked at International Paper. Callie just told him her name was Betty.

The first car dealership they came to, Callie told him, "This is where I get off," so he pulled into the dealership and left in a hurry.

The day was Wednesday, December the 20th, when Callie made the deal to buy the two-door coupe 1948 Plymouth.

They haggled about the price until the man settled for eight hundred dollars, tax and all. The salesman said he'd fill it up with gas.

Callie asked to use the bathroom. While inside, she peeled off forty of the twenty-dollar bills of Calvin's money.

The salesman never asked for identification; he just took her word, so Callie gave her name and address as Betty Jean Dale, 654 Parker street, Mobile, Alabama.

By noon, Callie left the dealership in her shiny green Plymouth coupe.

She didn't have a problem finding the motel, for she'd made a point of staying on the main road. After getting to her room, she counted the money and discovered she had three thousand and two hundred dollars to add to her stash. Plus, she had the bill of sale to the car, which would come in handy in the future.

She was hungry from the morning's events, and she was planning on going back to the little diner, but Callie discovered from the motel clerk that the diner was only open for breakfast.

"Hmph!" Callie exclaimed, then walked back to her room.

Once there, she stuffed two hundred dollars into her pockets, then hid her stash back where she'd had it. She thought she'd found the perfect place. She'd discovered the dresser was bolted to the cement floor, as was most of the furniture in the room. She guessed it was bolted so no one could steal it. Callie stuffed the rolled socks back into the tight opening behind the dresser, making sure her hoard wasn't visible to the naked eye.

She wasn't only going after something to eat; she was going clothes shopping. She knew she needed a job and she had to look presentable.

As she had done that morning, Callie stayed on Highway 90, so she wouldn't have trouble finding her way back to the motel. She loved her Plymouth; she'd never had anything as nice.

Luckily, she found a diner open. Next to it were several department stores. After eating, she began shopping.

The places were packed with Christmas shoppers, but by the middle of the afternoon, she'd bought five skirts, three blouses, two dresses, two slips, two brassieres, six new pairs of panties, a new beige coat that came to her knees and three pairs of shoes.

She didn't see a single woman with pants on, for they were taboo for a woman to wear in public. She'd noticed other women staring at her, because of the ragged clothes she had on, and she sure didn't want to be noticed. She would change into something new to wear as soon as she got back to her room.

Callie had noticed a newspaper rack in the lobby of the motel. After changing into one of her new outfits, she thought she'd walk over to the lobby, and buy a local paper. She was hoping she could find a job, so after purchasing the paper she told the clerk her ambitions.

She couldn't believe it when the clerk told her that the owner of the motel was looking for someone to cook at the diner. "You see, Miss Ruby is moving to Mississippi in about a week. You'll need to talk to the owner if you want the job. There's a little room in back that has a refrigerator, stove, and bed, everything you'd need to make it a cozy little place. The place is only open from six to ten o'clock.

Shoot, you have the looks, too," the young man said nervously, as he looked down at the floor.

"When can I talk to the owner?" asked Callie, ignoring the clerk's awkward remark.

"He'll be here at nine o'clock in the morning to take his money to the bank," replied the young man.

Callie looked at the name tag pinned to the clerk's shirt.

"Gee, thank you Jesse, I'll be sure to be here," Callie said.

She was whistling as she made the walk back to her motel room.

Even with the prospect of a job, Callie had trouble going to sleep that night. She thought of Laken and James. *"Boy, James would be proud of me now, especially if I land the job,"* she thought. Any other night when she was anxious or worried, she'd play her fiddle. *"But I don't even have that, now."*

Callie's nose had a bruise across the bridge of it, she noticed as she looked into the mirror the next morning. She really dusted it with facial powder, and it helped the looks of it. She'd taken a hot shower, and felt good about herself, as she smiled, showing her perfect white teeth. *"Shoot, I am pretty,"* she thought, as she looked into the mirror.

It had been a long time since she felt good about herself. She knew the reason she'd felt like she had, was the way she had been living.

Laken had taught her to give her red hair a hundred strokes each night, and she had to admit it looked better.

Callie was twenty-four years old, and had never worked in public before. She had intended on working somewhere, but after her Paw had been killed in the wreck, she'd had Laken. She had no one to leave her with, and no money to pay them. Her Paw made whiskey and sold it, and he'd taught her how, so she did what she thought she had to in order to survive.

Callie put on her prettiest dress over her new slip, then put on her new coat. She walked across the parking lot to the diner. It was six o'clock; she wanted to be the first customer and talk to Ruby.

She ordered the same thing as the morning before.

When Ruby delivered her meal to the table, Callie asked her about the job, and what she'd been told.

Since there weren't any more customers, Ruby pulled up a chair.

"Yeah, I'm leaving on the last day of this year. It's on a Sunday, so not many people come in anyway. You work seven days a week. You're only off on Christmas Day, the first day of the new year, Fourth of July, and Thanksgiving. He'll start you off at thirty dollars a week. I'm making thirty-five, because I've been here three years. There's a nice little room that goes with it. No water bill or electric bill either. It comes with the job," Ruby said. She continued, "If you get the job, I'll show you the room, and the ins and outs of the job."

Callie was moving into her new address on January 1st, 1951, for she had gotten the job. She thought she had learned enough from Ruby to run the place. She had to work free to learn, though, and also continue to pay for her motel room until she moved out.

She really liked Mr. Hill, the owner of the motel and the diner.

In two weeks' time, she could zip around in the small diner and wait on customers like she'd been there for years.

She bought a small radio for her room and listened to the local channels at night. She'd also called the local

79

newspaper in Monroeville and subscribed to the weekly paper for a year. Of course, she'd used the name B. J. Dale, and given the name of the hotel, which was 'The Blue Moon.'

Callie had the dishes, floor, and tables cleaned by eleven o'clock every morning, and she had the rest of the day to explore Mobile. She tried to keep her mind busy, but no matter what, there was a painful, relentless ache in her heart for her little girl, Laken.

# Chapter 14

Sheriff Nichols found the two bodies the morning after the killings. He also found Callie's dress, which had gotten hung up on the root of a tree that protruded into the stream.

Hiram had gone to the site with the sheriff.

They looked around the stream behind the house, but it had come a downpour the night before and they couldn't find a single track.

"Poor boy, looks like he'd tried to drag himself from the water, even in the shape he's in," said the sheriff.

"Yeah, I hate it for Willie and Victoria. He was a good boy, too. I don't know who'll run the operation now," Hiram said, as he watched the sheriff go through James' pockets.

Neither the sheriff nor Hiram recognized the body of Calvin, but the sheriff would soon know who he was.

After Sheriff Nichols had put all of James' belongings in a pull-string bag, he then began going through Calvin's pockets.

"Uh oh, look what we have here," the sheriff said, as he pulled three stacks of twenty-dollar bills from the inside coat pocket that the dead man was wearing. "Good thing he had his coat buttoned, or money would be floating into Escambia Creek by now. Who knows, there might have been more," the sheriff told Hiram.

Sheriff Nichols finally got to Calvin's wallet.

"Calvin Neely, Rural Route One, Gosport, Alabama," the sheriff said aloud. Then thinking for a few seconds, he said, "Five will get you ten, this money has been stolen somewhere."

"Do you know of anybody from Gosport by the name of Neely?" asked the sheriff.

Hiram shook his head side to side, indicating he didn't.

"The identification is probably stolen, too. Look, here's a ring of burglary tools hooked to his belt. He was a doozy for sure, but I've never heard of that name," Nichols remarked.

"Laken said that the man's name was Calvin," Hiram told the sheriff.

Sheriff Nichols walked back to his car and brought back two blankets. Hiram helped him cover the bodies, after the sheriff worked the sling blade out of Calvin's skull.

"You know what puzzles me is, how did this Calvin get here? There's only two trucks out there, Callie's old clunker, and James' truck," Nichols said.

"Beats me," Hiram answered.

"It leads me to believe that Callie left in this Calvin's vehicle. But then, someone could have been with him, discovered what happened, and simply drove away. If that's the case, then Callie's body is tangled up in those roots in that creek," the sheriff mused.

"I haven't the slightest, but the little girl needs to get into that cabin to get her things. If we see or hear anything from her mama, we'll sure contact you," Hiram said.

"If she wasn't so young, I'll bet she could tell me some things. Just ask her if she sees anything of her mama's missing. Meanwhile, I'll contact the sheriff in Clark county about this Calvin Neely and put some No Trespassing signs up at the entrance," Sheriff Nichols told Hiram.

"Just out of curiosity, did you know she was selling shine?" Hiram asked.

"Sure I did, and selling herself, too. I've never heard of any trouble going on here, though, and the Jordans didn't help her with that baby. So, I guess she did the only thing she knew how to do," Nichols replied.

"Well, Laken and the others are waiting at the house. For all she knows, everyone is still alive. She said she heard two gunshots as she was going across the field, and that's it," Hiram said.

"Poor child! Well, when the ambulance picks up the bodies, I'll tell Willie and Victoria. You can handle the little girl. And another thing: don't allow the children to come down here for a couple of days. I'm going to have this creek thoroughly checked," Sheriff Nichols instructed.

"All right, we'll just come get her things this afternoon, then I'll nail the doors closed," Hiram agreed.

"No, don't nail the doors and windows shut yet. I need to go through the house first. Just get whatever she needs out of there today. I'll get some padlocks and put them on the doors this afternoon," the sheriff said.

He then told Hiram, "The ambulance will more than likely bog up going across that field. Is there any way you can get the bodies to the highway?"

"Sure, I can take the tractor and wagon down there, but I'll need someone to help me," Hiram replied.

Sheriff Nichols laughed. "No, let the two men in the ambulance handle them. Make sure you take them across the terraces in that cotton wagon," he said, and laughed again.

# Chapter 15

Hiram had thought of a way to tell Laken about the whole ordeal. He decided to just tell her the truth yet be gentle as possible.

"What about Mama…you didn't find her?" asked Laken.

Hiram told her about the dress. "That's all we found," he answered.

"And my Daddy? What about him?" asked Laken.

"I'm afraid, honey, both he and this man Calvin are gone. They're on the way after the bodies now," Hiram said, as he continually stroked Laken's black hair.

Both Laken and Shelby had backed up until they were against Jimmie's legs.

"Well, can I live here,?" the trembling Laken blurted out.

Jimmie didn't give her husband time to answer, before she said, "Honey, we wouldn't have had it any other way."

"Poor Daddy! He was a good man. Calvin, he was a mean one, though. I'm sure going to miss Daddy," Laken said, but she never once mentioned her mama's name.

Hiram had to call his wife into the kitchen and talk to her.

"I've got to hitch up the cotton trailer, in order to get the bodies from down there. Please try to be strong and don't cry in front of the girls. Poor child, she's lost both parents; she'll need strength to get through this," he said. It was a tribute to the strength of their marriage that he didn't question his wife's decision to take Laken into their home.

Jimmie wiped her eyes with the hem of her apron, then walked back into the den.

Caleb wanted to go with his father, even though he had no idea where he was going.

"No, you stay here with the girls," Hiram said, as he walked out of the door.

Hiram only had to wait a few minutes before the ambulance arrived. The two bodies were secured in the ambulance and gone in thirty minutes.

Hiram returned to the house, and just Laken, Caleb, and himself went to the Pruitt place, for Laken's things.

After seeing how Laken lived, Caleb was shocked, but he didn't say anything. Laken had gotten some cotton sacks out of the barn, and the three packed her things into two of them.

All Laken carried to the truck was the banjo and fiddle, and she made sure to wrap them good with clothes she'd found on the floor.

Laken knew it was her mama's blood that she saw on the floor, from where Calvin had hit her.

Somehow, she felt her mama's presence in the room, and it gave her the willies.

The next few days were hard for Laken. Even though they were told to stay away from the Pruitt place, Laken would tell Hiram and Jimmie that she had forgotten something or the other, so over there they'd go. They brought back trivial things, but Hiram thought that Laken was just looking for signs of her mama. She stopped asking to go there, however, when she saw that Sheriff Nichols had secured the house and barn.

Hiram figured that she had given up on finding her mama.

The most pitiful day was the day of James' funeral. It was a closed casket ordeal, due to the fish tearing away some of the flesh of James' face. It was also just a graveside service.

The funeral was held on Saturday, December 23rd, at 11:00 am.

Sheriff Nichols must have been looking for trouble, for he and one of his two deputies attended.

Hiram had done his best to keep himself and his family in the background, for the graveyard was crowded with mourners.

Reverend Johnson gave a nice funeral, and even sang, 'In the Sweet By and By' near the end of the service. At the end of the service, Brother Johnson quoted Revelation 21:4, then shook the immediate family's hands.

Laken pulled herself from Hiram's grasp and ran to the grave site. Standing at the end of the line of the family, Reverend Johnson shook Laken's hand, then hugged her.

Hiram walked over to  Laken and picked her up. He saw that Willie Jordan had his hand on Victoria's shoulder, preventing her from walking.

Hiram walked by Willie and smiled, then nodded his head.

On the sly, Hiram and Jimmie had done most of the Christmas shopping. Willie Jordan had slipped Hiram a hundred dollars to go toward Laken's gifts.

They had heard that Willie and Victoria's church were serving a meal for the family. Hiram, not wanting to push their luck with Victoria, told Jimmie they would go to Monroeville instead. "We'll get a burger, and I know you have Christmas to buy, especially Christmas groceries," Hiram told her.

They announced their intentions to the children, and of course, they wcrc all eager to go.

They stopped by the house for a short while, allowing everyone to go to the bathroom, then change clothes.

Caleb emptied his piggy bank to buy Jim a dog collar.

"We can't tarry, because as usual we've got to get back to our chores," Hiram announced, as they crawled into the car.

Not being as extravagant as the Jordan family, Hiram parked in front of Bedsole's Dry Goods. They bought each child two sets of clothes. Hiram, who was a big, tall man, had a little trouble finding himself a new work shirt and khaki pants. With Hiram's urging, Jimmie bought herself a new loose-fitting dress and a pair of everyday shoes.

Their next stop was at the Jitney Jungle grocery store.

The girls went inside, while Hiram and Caleb ran to V. J. Elmore's five and dime to look for Jim a dog collar.

Hiram knew how Jimmie was inside the grocery store, so they weren't in a hurry shopping for a dog collar. Caleb soon found one he liked. It was brown leather with plenty of holes, so it would still fit as Jim grew bigger.

Hiram and Caleb sat outside in the car until Jimmie came to the door. Jimmie had already paid for the groceries, so Hiram and Caleb began to put the bags in the trunk of the car.

On the way out of town, they stopped at a hamburger place and ordered burgers, fries, and drinks.

Hiram thought they had time to eat inside the car, but he made sure they didn't spill anything on the seats.

When they reached home, after carrying everything into the house, they hopped to their chores.

Jim didn't care too much about the collar, but he soon grew accustomed to it. The dog also thought it was his job to ride on the back of the truck and bark at the cows, as Caleb threw off the bales of hay. Jim didn't seem to like the hogs, though, for he just watched, as Caleb threw the ears of corn into the pen.

By the time the eggs were gathered and the chickens were fed and locked up, Jimmie was usually through with the milking.

Ol' Belle was always eager to be milked. It not only relieved her bag, but she got to eat the sweet feed that Jimmie poured into her trough.

After straining the milk, Jimmie came back into the den to  spend time with her family.

Hiram and the children were gathered around the radio. They were listening to a local channel, and it was playing nothing but Christmas music.

Someone had plugged in the Christmas tree lights, and it was truly a heavenly sight to see.

The girls were playing tic-tac-toe, Caleb was looking at the gun catalogue, and Hiram patted the cushion next to him, indicating for his wife to sit next to him.

Jimmie wasn't a big woman, but she was what they called "full figured." She sat down lightly next to her husband.

Every once in a blue moon, a memorable occasion would take place, and Jimmie would tell herself, *"Make yourself remember this."* This was one of those occasions, she thought. In spite of the things they'd  gone through the last few days, the girls had smiles on their faces. Caleb was dreaming of hunting with the gun promised him, and everything was at peace in her world.

In a little while, she'd get up and roll out a pan of biscuits, then make a pan of tomato gravy to go with the biscuits. A simple meal, for she'd start cooking for Christmas the next day. In that moment, she realized, as she often did, that she had everything she needed—and she felt truly grateful.

## Chapter 16

It was Christmastime, 1950.

Hiram had gone to the barn where the bicycles were hidden and brought them into the house. The girls had training wheels on theirs, but not Caleb's, because he could already ride one. He just got one a size bigger than the girls'. All three of the bicycles were red in color, for Hiram didn't want them picking and choosing.

Christmas Eve fell on Sunday, so they just had communion, and Brother Johnson just said a short passage from the Bible.

The church had a big Christmas tree, and Delores, the treasurer, made sure that each child got a wrapped gift. The girls got jump ropes, and Caleb got a baseball. He and Jim sure had a good time with the baseball that afternoon, while the girls enjoyed playing with their jump ropes.

The next morning was total bedlam. Christmas wrapping paper covered the den floor. Of course, the big presents for the girls were their bicycles. It was the big one for Caleb, too, until he opened the long box that contained his BB gun. He figured the remainder of his gifts were clothes, so he ran to his room to pull off his pajamas and put on some warm clothes.

Jimmie just had a platter of ham and biscuits on the kitchen table, so Caleb grabbed some of each as he went by.

Besides their bikes, the girls opened packages that contained clothes, coloring books, and books to read with colorful pictures. They really liked their charm bracelets, too. Each bracelet only had three charms. Jimmie told them for each good deed they did, they'd get another charm. "That doesn't mean doing chores around the farm, but something extraordinary, like doing good for someone at church or something like that," Jimmie said.

"I'm going to ride my bicycle over to my grandparents and get to know my grandma Victoria better. That should get me another charm," Laken said.

"No, I wouldn't do that just yet," Jimmie was quick to respond.

"Another thing, I'd better not catch you girls crossing that highway. Now, you can ride your bikes around the yard, and halfway up the lane, and that's it," Hiram said.

"But Caleb rides his bike to the mailbox," Shelby argued.

"Caleb is older and can ride his without the training wheels," Hiram told the girls.

Shelby knew she was wasting her time, so she changed subjects, while Hiram and Jimmie opened their gifts.

Hiram discovered he had a new pair of thick cotton gloves, just what he'd been wanting. He also got a denim coat, lined with a woolen fabric. The coat had a corduroy collar, and a big pocket on each side.

"Now, I really need this," Hiram said, as he slipped on the coat and modeled it for Jimmie.

"Believe it or not, the only place I could find one in your size was at the Big Store in Excel," Jimmie said.

"Well, open your gifts," Hiram told her.

"You shouldn't have," Jimmie said, as she drew a deep breath, looking at the mahogany jewelry box he had given her.

"It plays a tune, too. Of course, you have to wind it on the bottom," Hiram said.

Jimmie held the top of the jewelry box and wound it three or four times, but nothing happened.

"I think you have to open the top," Hiram said.

"I know; I'm just being gentle with it. It's so beautiful and delicate looking," Jimmie said, as she turned it over and opened the lid.

"Once I Had a Secret Love," began playing.

"You romantic rascal," Jimmie said, as she leaned over and kissed her husband, making the girls giggle.

"Well, open your other one," Hiram said, so she did. After unwrapping the small box, she found that it held a beautiful silver cameo stick pin.

"Oh, honey! This is too expensive for a farmer's wife," Jimmie said, but then added, "Just wait until Sunday."

"Now I won't have to put my jewelry in a cigar box," Jimmie said, admiring her jewelry box again, before she began her day.

The girls were wanting to go outside, but Jimmie told them, "Not before breakfast."

Caleb came back into the den with his BB gun.

"I've got this baby loaded," he told his dad.

"Hold on there, cowboy, first you have to get breakfast. No shooting at animals, anything that's glass, or your sisters," Hiram told him.

"I've already had breakfast, and yes sir on all the other," Caleb said, as he rushed out of the door, calling Jim as soon as his feet hit the porch.

The others ate their breakfast, and after two cups of coffee, Hiram remarked that he had to round up Caleb and feed the animals.

"I thought you were going to help us with the bicycles?" Shelby pleaded.

"Just as soon as I get back. You girls dress warmly. It'll be warmer by then, too," Hiram said.

Hiram knew that Jim would be hopping in the back of the truck, so he took the morning's food scraps with him. Caleb usually fed the dog, but Hiram knew he was too excited to think about it.

After he'd reached his truck, Hiram heard Caleb scolding Jim. From the looks of it, Caleb had shot a jaybird and Jim retrieved it, only Jim wouldn't turn it loose.

"Come on, boys," Hiram shouted. Jim must have seen the food, and he knew he would get to bark at the cows, so he came running. Caleb was right behind him. Before Jim reached the truck he turned the bird loose, and Caleb picked the nearly featherless thing up.

Jim had recently learned to jump into the back of the truck without assistance. He'd take a long running start, then hop with his back legs, always skidding halfway down the back of the truck. Jim was a greedy dog, so he didn't waste time gobbling down the few scraps.

It took twenty bales of hay twice a day in the wintertime to feed the cows. Hiram planted two fields of rye grass each fall. The cows had eaten one field down to the nubs, and the other field wasn't high enough to turn the cows loose in.

Bahia grass grew well on Hiram's land, so that's what he baled for hay in the winter months, and the cows loved it. It took half of Hiram's land to supply grass for the cows year-round, and the other half he farmed peanuts and corn.

Three acres behind the house was used for a garden. Beans, peas, sweet corn, snapbeans, squash, and tomatoes, along with onions, and watermelons were planted for consumption in the house. Everyone stayed busy in the hot summer months gathering the garden crops. Miss Jimmie had the hot job of canning the vegetables for the cold winter months.

When Hiram and Caleb's job was over and they returned home, the girls already had their bicycles in the yard and were actually riding them.

"That's the way to do it," Hiram said, pleased with what he saw. "Shoot, by summer, I'll be taking the training wheels off," he told them.

Laken had a little more trouble getting on her bike than Shelby, for her legs were shorter than the other girl's.

Jimmie had already milked the cow and was busy with the Christmas dinner.

Hiram fed and watered the hogs, then found a sunny place to watch the children play. After about thirty minutes, Hiram saw Caleb run into the house, holding another jaybird to show his mama. He came out faster than he went in, though, and Hiram laughed about it.

Caleb soon tired of chasing Jim for the birds, so he went inside with his BB gun, and came out with his new bike.

Hiram went inside to see if he could help Jimmie.

"Yes, you can pick up all that Christmas paper off the floor and burn it, then watch the girls. I've got this under control in here," she said.

Jimmie was stirring something, but he put his arms around her, then squeezed her tight.

"Alright, that's night time stuff," Jimmie said, but when he turned her loose, she kissed him, then said, "Now get going."

By twelve o'clock, Hiram could tell the girls were beginning to tire, so he sent them inside to help Jimmie.

Willie Jordan came driving up the lane about the time the girls went inside.

After the two men talked a while, Willie asked if he could see his granddaughter.

"Sure, any time," Hiram said, and the two walked into the house.

Jimmie had the girls in the kitchen, so Hiram opened the door and told them that Mr. Jordan had come to see Laken.

Not quite knowing what to do, Hiram sat down in his chair, after he'd pointed to a chair for Willie to sit in.

When the two girls entered the room, Willie motioned for Laken to have a seat in his lap.

Laken remembered what Callie had told her, "Don't ever sit in no man's lap, but yo' daddy's," so instead of sitting in her granddaddy's lap, she just stood beside him.

Willie slid his arm around her, and after pulling her near him, he asked how she liked her bike.

"I like it," Laken replied.

"So ol' Santa was good to you?" Mr. Willie asked, as he patted Laken on her arm.

"Yes, sir," replied Laken.

"Honey, you're mighty young to be telling you this, but don't pay your Grandma Victoria any mind. James could have married the King of England's daughter, Elizabeth, and she wouldn't have been satisfied. I want you to know that I love you, and if you ever need anything, get word to me through Mr. Beasley, you hear?"

"Yes, sir," Laken answered, then added, "Thank you for coming to see me."

Hiram could see the tears in Mr. Jordan's eyes, when he patted Laken on the arm again, and said, "Well, run along and go about what you were doing."

After the girls went back into the kitchen, Mr. Willie pulled out a handkerchief, wiped his eyes, then blew his nose.

Hiram, who felt uncomfortable about the situation, got up and threw a piece of wood into the fireplace.

"Nice place you have here, real cozy," Mr. Willie said.

"Yes, sir, we've done a lot of work to it," Hiram told him.

"I remember," replied the old man.

The two continued to talk for a few more minutes, and during the course of their conversation, Hiram discovered a few things. Mr. Willie told him that he was going to close the sawmill and rent out his farm land.

He then remarked that he had enough forest land to live quite well off the trees. "I hate it about the sawmill though, it'll put a lot of men out of work," he replied.

"It'll sure hurt the economy around Excel," Hiram agreed.

"So, what are y'all planning on doing with my granddaughter?" Mr. Willie asked.

"Well, I talked to Sheriff Nichols about it. He said to wait until after the holidays to apply for custody, then we'd have to wait six years to adopt her," Hiram replied.

"I am so glad. That way, I can watch her grow up, and if you need help financially, get word to me," Mr. Jordan said, as he got up to leave.

"Yes, sir, but maybe we can make it," Hiram said, as he slipped on his new coat and followed Mr. Jordan to his truck.

Laken didn't know it at the time she had thought about her mama's words, but one day she would sit in another person's lap in the future, and he was in that very house.

# Chapter 17

It was March of 1951, and Callie was very proud of herself.

The Blue Moon diner was near the newspaper, 'The Mobile Press.' Several of the workers rushed in each morning for a quick breakfast, or just a cup of coffee. Almost everyone left tips, and Callie made it a standing rule to save every one of them, plus half her pay.

Her goal was to save enough money to buy a place of her own, so that she could sneak into Excel and get Laken.

Surprisingly, Callie's nose had settled to its original position, leaving only a small bump at the very top.

Callie wore her own clothes to work each day. She wore an apron over her clothes and a net over her red hair. The apron tied around her neck and her waist, which really complimented her shapely figure.

She ate breakfast at the diner, and seldom cooked anything in her room. If she did, it was usually just a stir fry meal.

She was constantly getting hit on by the customers. She thanked them for their compliments but paid them little attention. She had one goal and stuck to it.

A young editor that worked at the Mobile Press told her by chance that they needed someone to deliver the afternoon papers.

"You just deliver them to about seventy-five stands; most of them are on Highway 90 at different businesses," he said.

Callie applied for the job when she got off work and got it. She was given a map, showing each place she had to stop. One of them was The Blue Moon Motel.

It took very little gas for the job. The hardest job was loading all the papers, but she handled it. The paper gave her twenty-five dollars a week, more money that she stashed with the other.

Callie knew very little about banks, but she also knew it was dangerous to have so much money on hand. By July, she had money hidden all over the little room.

She had only gone to school long enough to keep the truant officer from coming to their cabin. What little she went, she made good grades, though. The reason she didn't like school was some of the other girls picked at or made fun of the clothes she wore. The boys liked her, however, for she could play baseball with the best of them. Both the girls and boys really took notice of her when she reached maturity and filled out in the right places.

One thing Callie could say about her Paw, she didn't have to sell the whisky. She did help him make it, and it was a good thing she did.

She saw very little of the money, though, for he drank most of the profit.

Callie didn't want that kind of life for her daughter, so just for the fun of it, she began to look for a house to buy.

On July 4th, while she was off work from the diner, she counted her money, and it totaled nine thousand one hundred and fifty-five dollars.

In two stacks, she put four thousand and five hundred dollars. She thought the bank might suspect something if she put all her money in one bank. She wasn't sure about the money that came from Calvin's coat pocket. *"Knowing him, it's probably stolen from somewhere and the money is marked,"* she thought.

She thought about just putting the nine thousand in a safety deposit box, but they charged rent. She wanted to make money by putting it into saving accounts. The next day while delivering the papers, she found two banks that were relatively close and set up two savings accounts. One of the banks even gave her a red piggy bank, with "Farmer's Bank" stenciled on the sides.

The very next day she had to have Betty Jean's driver's license renewed. She'd practiced Betty Jean's signature, so she came out of the courthouse without a problem, with a new license.

After about a week, Callie hadn't heard anything from the banks, so she deposited fifty more dollars in each of them.

She turned twenty-five years old on July the ninth, which fell on a Sunday. She celebrated by going to the theater. "Rio Grande," starring John Wayne and Maureen O'Hara, was playing. Callie had never been to a movie before, but she waited in line until it was time to pay for her ticket.

She picked out a seat near the back. About an hour into the film, she thought, *If only I didn't have to hack Calvin over the head. Oh, how I miss my baby!*

## Chapter 18

Things were going full steam back at the Beasley place. It was July, and all three children had celebrated another birthday. Caleb turned nine on May 28<sup>th</sup>, and the girls celebrated together on June 12<sup>th</sup>. The girls were now six.

They'd all stayed busy picking and shelling beans and peas, plus other chores.

Hiram had two tractors: a big one, which he operated, and a small Ford, that he had taught Caleb to operate. They stayed busy cutting and baling hay and plowing around the corn and peanuts. Caleb also had the job of cutting the grass with a push mower. This task included not only the yard and around the barns; he also had to cut down the grass on each side of the lane that led to the mailbox, next to the highway.

Hiram saw to it that the three children had time to ride PeeWee, and refresh themselves at the creek two or three times a week, especially on Sunday evenings.

One Sunday, the three walked to Laken's old cabin. They found everything secure, but the weeds had about taken the place over.

Jim made every move they did, and he always ran ahead of them, looking for snakes.

Hiram knew that Laken had to have a birth certificate to get into school. The Beasleys already had custody of her. Laken told Hiram and Jimmie that she wanted her last name to be Jordan.

"I'm not trying to be mean, but I look like my daddy. You all have blonde hair and mine is black like my daddy's," Laken said.

Both Hiram and Jimmie laughed and didn't take offense to what the child said.

For legal work, Hiram always used lawyer Robert Barry. He told them that Callie had to be missing for seven years before they could adopt Laken.

"Well, we'll just have to wait a few years. We'll be back, though, Mr. Barry," Hiram told him.

During that first summer, Laken had taught Shelby how to strum, 'Down Yonder' on the banjo. Laken wasn't sure about it herself, but to the Beasleys, Laken was a child prodigy when it came to music. By the time school started, Shelby could strum three different tunes on the banjo, accompanied by Laken on the fiddle.

One day in August while Hiram was in Monroeville, he stopped at a pawn shop and bought a ten-dollar guitar. He also bought the chord books for the banjo, fiddle, and the guitar. The owner of the pawn shop tuned the guitar for him.

Once he got home with the guitar and books, Laken played around with the guitar for only a few minutes before she sang and picked 'Jesus Loves Me.' Of course, Shelby learned to pick the song on the banjo.

"Just listen to these girls! How lucky we are to have two musicians in the family," Jimmie remarked.

That Sunday, for the first time in public, the girls picked and sang, 'Jesus Loves Me,' in church.

After church, Jimmie asked the girls if they were scared while they performed in front of so many people.

Both of them replied, "No, I enjoyed it, it was fun."

"Lord have mercy, I'd been scared to death," Jimmie muttered.

With their fingers toughened, some nights after supper, the girls would take the banjo and fiddle to the front porch and play several songs for everyone else in the household.

One night, Mr. Willie heard them and came over. He never got out of the truck; he just listened.

"Amazing," was all the old fellow said, then slipped a hundred dollars into Hiram's shirt pocket.

"For school clothes," he said.

Hiram tried to give the money back to Willie, but he wouldn't take it. Hiram had to get out of the way, as Willie began to turn around in the driveway.

Jimmie had caught up with the canning and reserving of the fruits and vegetables by the first week in August, so it was time to shop for school.

It was a good thing, too, for the children were growing so fast that the clothes they were wearing were getting too small for them.

Laken wasn't growing in height like Caleb and Shelby; Jimmie figured they would be tall like their daddy.

They all gathered into the car one Saturday and made a day of shopping in Monroeville. Again, they bought their clothes from Bedsole's Dry Goods, and their school supplies at V. J. Elmore's.

Bradley's Drugstore not only sold medicines, but they also had a small diner. They didn't serve hot meals, just sandwiches and drinks.

They heard the "Dong, dong, dong," of the clocks from the old courthouse, as they walked to Bradley's.

They were seated, and each ordered a burger and milkshakes. The children had never had a milkshake, but after sucking a few sips from the straw, they loved them. Everyone just got vanilla.

Each item was twenty-five cents, meaning Hiram paid two dollars and fifty cents for everything.

Hiram and Caleb had sold the peanut and corn crop, so Hiram wasn't hurting for money. He figured that if nothing major broke down, he could make it until he sold the butcher calves before Christmas. He and Caleb already had them shut up in a stall of their own, making sure they were fed until they were stuffed.

They didn't stick around to go to the theater. Jimmie said she was tired, and the girls wanted to get home so they could ride their bikes and go swimming. Caleb didn't say so, but he wanted to go too, and he knew Jim did. Even though Jim wasn't much for swimming, he loved to just wade in the water, and lap at it with his tongue.

Jim was turning out to be the very dog that Hiram had wanted. He was already a big dog, and still growing. Jim was very alert, running ahead of the children as they went to the creek, searching for snakes or other varmints.

Hiram and Jimmie seldom went to the creek with the children. Of course, they lectured Caleb each time they left, though, about the rambunctious girls, telling him to make sure they didn't get too deep into the stream.

Callie had told Laken if she stayed in the deep water she wouldn't have to worry about the snakes. "It's too cold for them," she had said.

When they made it back to the house, everyone carried their clothes to their rooms and slipped on their swimsuits.

Jimmie noticed as the girls ran by her that their swimsuits were getting too small for them, and they'd need new suits the next year.

"Caleb, you keep an eye on the girls," Jimmie said, as Caleb ran by her.

"Yes, Ma'am, I will," Caleb promised, as he went out of the door.

Jimmie went into the girls' room first, to get their new clothes straightened out. She and Hiram had taken out Shelby's double bed and replaced it with two single beds. There was only one drawback, though; there was just one closet. Things on the right were Shelby's, and Laken's items were on the left. The closet was already stuffed full, so everything below the size of 5, Jimmie began to take out. The church had a clothes closet for the needy, and she thought she'd give the things to the church the next day.

After hanging and folding, then putting away the girls' things, she started with Caleb's. It took only a few minutes with Caleb's, as most of his things were pull-over T-shirts and jeans.

The girls, along with Caleb, had gotten to where they'd go further into the stream, where it was deeper and they could swim farther.

Caleb had dared them to tell anyone. "After all, I'm in charge of you," he boasted.

The girls responded to his last statement by giving him a good dunking.

While Caleb was under the water he saw something wrapped around the root of a tree, so he grabbed it. With one big yank, he snatched it loose, and walked to the shallow part which was on their land.

"Look," he said, as he showed the girls a pistol.

"Let's go show Daddy," Caleb said, so without drying themselves, Shelby grabbed the one towel they brought and headed across the field. As usual, Jim led the way.

Hiram was feeding the "feeder calves" when Caleb showed him what he had found.

After looking at it, Hiram said that he needed to notify the sheriff. "That's probably the pistol that James shot that fellow with," Hiram said.

"Yes, sir. Reckon the sheriff will give it to me, since I found it and all?" Caleb asked.

"Now, what do you want with a pistol?" Hiram asked, as he looked at his son.

Caleb couldn't think of an answer on short notice, so he said nothing.

The girls didn't pay the pistol much attention, as they had learned to ride their bikes without the training wheels. They jumped on their bikes and headed up the lane, still wearing their bathing suits.

"Caleb, go catch those girls and tell them I said to get in the house and put them on some clothes!" Hiram said.

# Chapter 19

School had started in all its glory. Both girls were in Mrs. Sawyer's room, while Caleb was in the fourth grade. Miss Grant was his teacher, who was known for not liking boys.

School wasn't a problem for the girls, for they could already read simple words, and knew their alphabet.

Caleb had to work hard to make decent grades, which took him away from Hiram and his chores. Jimmie's word was the law when it came to school work, though. While Laken and Shelby were outside playing, Caleb was inside doing his homework.

Hiram missed his son's company, so one day he went into Caleb's bedroom, and saw that he didn't understand his multiplications. Hiram got a sheet of paper, and after doing a few examples, Caleb caught right on.

"There now, you see, there's nothing to it. Work a few examples, then come outside and ride ol' PeeWee around. I think maybe you're just scared of your teacher. Son, always remember, she might be mean, but she can't eat you," Hiram told him.

Caleb laughed, then said, "Boy, just wait until tomorrow. We have a test and I'm going to ace that sucker."

Sure enough, the next day, Caleb brought in a B on his arithmetic test. From then on, he often thought of his daddy's words, and he wasn't scared anymore.

When the autumn winds began to turn cool, the girls would play their musical instruments on the front porch. Hiram and Jimmie really enjoyed their little performances. Laken and Shelby also continued to play and sing once a month in church. The girls were now old enough to sing in the children's choir, but Caleb still held off.

Hiram and Jimmie were very proud of their children's school grades. Each six weeks, the Monroe Journal would print the honor roll students' names in the paper. Shelby and Laken always brought home straight A's, while Caleb would bring in a B now and then. Hiram and Jimmie didn't understand it, but Caleb would bring the B in on different subjects.

His name was still in the paper, though, and they were just as proud of him as they were of the girls.

"After all, he is a boy," Hiram told Jimmie.

Truth be known, Caleb had rather be on a tractor farming, than studying in a book.

Hiram and Jimmie didn't know it, but Callie was reading the Monroe Journal too, and would smile when she read her baby's name.

One day, a few days before Christmas, Sheriff Nichols pulled his police vehicle into the yard.

Hiram was loading some hogs to take to the sale, so he closed the chute that led to the back of his truck, in order to talk to the sheriff.

Nichols walked over to Hiram's truck, and the squealing of the hogs was deafening.

Hiram stepped away from all the noise, and the sheriff motioned for him to have a seat in the patrol car.

Nichols was a short man, so he had to roll the seat back to fit Hiram's long legs.

As soon as Hiram was seated, the sheriff said, "I have news for you. That Neeley fellow was wanted by the Sheriff's Department in George County, Mississippi. Seems that Neeley robbed a bank in Lucedale and killed two people getting away. Whoever killed him deserves a medal! Of course, Judge Kilpatrick won't look at it that way. By the way, the slugs taken from his belly were fired from that pistol your boy found."

"Well, sir, no telling what went on over there that led to the killing," Hiram said.

"I think I have it figured out. Jordan showed up while Neeley was there. They got into a fracas, and Jordan shot him, probably after Neeley cut his guts out. I believe Callie whacked Neeley over the head with that sling blade, then skipped out in Neeley's vehicle," the Sheriff said.

"About what I figured, but I wouldn't want the girl to know that her mama was a murderer," Hiram told Sheriff Nichols.

"No, she's a sweet thing, and smart too. She wouldn't have stood a chance with Callie." Nichols continued, "The tax collector told me you paid the taxes on the Pruitt place."

"Yes, sir. It'll go to Laken when she turns eighteen," Hiram said.

"You're a good man, Hiram, no matter what Miss Jimmie says."

The sheriff cranked the vehicle as Hiram laughed, then drove away after Hiram got out of the vehicle.

Once Hiram had sold the hogs and collected the money, he stopped by Ace Hardware and bought Caleb a basketball goal and a basketball. He had the goal mounted to the wall of the barn by the time the school bus ran.

Needless to say, Caleb immediately noticed the goal and ball on his walk from the bus.

The wood for the fireplace was getting slim, so Hiram was hauling wood with the tractor and trailer when he first saw Caleb dribbling the ball. Hiram smiled, for he knew Caleb had been working at his school work, and he was also a good help around the farm. *The girls have their musical instruments and their voices, and maybe Caleb could make it as an athlete,"* thought Hiram. *"Of course, Caleb will always have the farm, but I don't want my son to be like I was."* The farm was all he had. He, like Caleb, was the only son, and Hiram had to work on the farm, or the family would have gone hungry. He believed Caleb was going to grow to be a tall young man, and he thought he could make it in basketball.

The Christmas holidays came and went. It was hard for everyone to believe another Christmas had gone by.

Caleb got his .410 shotgun, as promised. He had to agree, though, that it was forbidden for him to load it until he was ready to fire it. From that day on, the family never lacked for squirrels, rabbits and other small game, and Jimmie could make the best squirrel stew. She was glad for the meat but was as nervous as a cat from the time Caleb left with the gun until he came safely back in. Caleb would find that not only was Jim a snake dog, but a good squirrel and rabbit dog.

The girls got mostly clothes for Christmas that year.

Hiram surprised the whole family that Christmas by having a telephone installed.

The theater in Monroeville was hosting a two-hour program for all the local talent. Jimmie read about it in the paper and after talking it over with Shelby and Laken, she entered the girls in the contest. The program was being held from 1-3:00 p.m. on a Saturday, December 30th. The first-place prize was fifty dollars.

They all thought they'd get haircuts before the competition. Caleb and Hiram liked Miss Emily, who had her shop in Frisco City, to cut their hair, so they went there.

Jimmie, who could drive the car, took the girls to Janice Gulley's shoppe in Monroeville. Janice was Pap Gulley's wife, the man who had given Jim to Caleb.

Neither of the girls liked bangs, so all Janice had to do was trim their hair, along with Jimmie's graying blonde hair.

The girls were eager to perform the next day. They could only sing two songs, so they chose 'Uncle Pen,' and 'Dear Old Dixie,' two fast ones.

Of course, the names of the contestants were printed in the Journal. Callie always got the paper on Friday. As she read her daughter's name, she smiled as usual, then cut the clipping out and pasted it in her "Laken" journal. Callie began to wonder.

*"Could I pull it off?"* she wondered. She knew if she was discovered she'd be going to jail, to say the least.

"It would be worth it to see my baby," she said aloud.

She knew that by the time she got back to Mobile, she'd be late delivering the Mobile Press, but she didn't care. At this point, only one thing mattered: to see Laken.

The next day, after closing the diner, she put on a plain green skirt and a brown sweater, with a long black coat that came to her ankles. She arranged all of her red hair so it would fit under a black scarf. *"After all, it is freezing cold weather out there,"* she thought. Her last thing was to paint her lips ruby red.

Callie left Mobile at 10:30, knowing it would take at least two hours to make the trip.

She arrived at the theater five minutes before the show was to begin, paid the dollar fee, and went inside.

Surprisingly, the place was packed. She was wanting to sit in the back row, but she had to go about middle way before she found a seat at the end. *"Good,"* she thought, *"quick and easy for me to get away."*

Laken and Shelby didn't perform until after two o'clock. When they performed 'Uncle Pen,' over half the audience stood up and applauded. The girls, now having confidence, immediately started on 'Dear old Dixie.'

Again, the audience stood up and applauded, not wanting the girls to go back behind the curtains. They did, but it was only because the theater manager said there were more performers waiting in the wings.

Tears ran down Jimmie's face as she witnessed the reception the girls received. *"And to be so young,"* she thought.

Jimmie wasn't the only one crying, but Callie managed to wait until she got inside her car.

Callie didn't take time for the others to perform; she left immediately. She felt a ping of melancholy as she passed the old courthouse as it was dinging three o'clock.

She was pretty sure the girls had won the contest, and she was surprised at how much Laken had improved. She also recognized the banjo and fiddle as being hers.

As bad as she hated to admit it, she could tell that Laken was being well taken care of. She also saw Mr. and Mrs. Beasley and their son in the audience, therefore she knew Laken was still with them. She was glad about that. *"At least she's still close to home,"* Callie thought.

She couldn't help but break down when she passed the road that led to her old place. She pulled the handkerchief out of her coat pocket and wiped her face. She then wiped the ridiculous lipstick from her lips. As she had a year ago, she took a deep breath and headed toward Mobile. Again, she felt as though she had the world on her shoulders and in her heart.

# Chapter 20

By August of 1955, the girls were now ten years old, and Caleb was thirteen.

It seemed that Caleb was growing in leaps and bounds. He was outgrowing his clothes and shoes before he could get full use out of them. Jimmie and Hiram could also tell that his voice was deepening. Caleb began to have friends coming over. They'd either go swimming in the creek or take turns shooting the basketball.

Sometimes, if Caleb had chores to do on the farm, they'd all pitch in and help him.

The girls thought the boys were silly and paid them little attention.

They all had bigger bicycles, and Caleb was even allowed to ride his to Excel, or to visit his schoolmates that lived nearby.

Excel High school had started a new program, the junior football program. It was for boys in grades seven through nine, and Caleb was in the seventh. He was already six feet tall and weighed a hundred and seventy pounds. Due to the farm work, there wasn't an ounce of fat on him.

Caleb, who lived about two miles from the school, rode his bicycle to practice each afternoon. The coach, after watching him throw the ball during practice, chose Caleb to be the quarterback.

Usually, boys in the eighth or ninth grades were the quarterback, and at first, the older boys made it hard on Caleb. After they saw they weren't going to run him off, and how well he could throw the ball and run with it, they eased up on him.

By the time school had started, Hiram had sold all his peanuts and corn that he had intended on selling. Of course, he'd kept the foliage of the peanuts to use as fodder for the animals to eat.

One day, Mr. Willie paid them a visit. While he was there, he brought up the subject that if Hiram had a couple of silos, with driers, he could get much more for his products.

"I know, Mr. Willie, but that costs money, and running the place and raising three children are expensive. Especially with them being involved with every activity that comes along," Hiram said.

Mr. Willie thought for a short while, then said, "As you know, I'm renting out all my farmland, and I haven't the slightest intentions of using my silos again. You come over to my barn and measure the cement foundations, then have two new foundations poured here. I'll have my men take the things apart and put them up over here on your place."

"Why, Mr. Willie, I couldn't ask you to do that," Hiram replied.

"Aw, pshaw, look what you're doing for me. If only Victoria wasn't such a prude," Willie added.

"Well, if you're sure, I'll start measuring tomorrow," Hiram said. "And I appreciate it."

Willie smiled, and said, "It's long overdue for me to do my part."

The next day, Hiram was building frames and having cement poured. By the middle of October, the two huge purple silos were sitting on Beasley property, and Hiram was waiting for the next harvest.

You could see the tall silos a mile before you reached the house. Jimmie said they looked like something from outer space.

Hiram laughed and told her that they'd get a lot more for the peanuts and corn.

"You see, dear, when I sell the peanuts and corn, the co-op is forced to dry them before they can sell them. I'll have them dried already, so I'll be getting top-notch price. Those silos are big enough to hold other farmers' grain and nuts too, and I'll charge them for drying, plus money for storage," Hiram told her.

"Lord, we've hit the big time now. Maybe I can get me a deep freeze and won't have to stand over that hot stove canning in jars anymore," Jimmie said.

"Yes, you can, my dear," Hiram told her, and snuck a rare daytime kiss from his wife.

Due to Caleb's ball playing, they spent Friday or Saturday nights at football games. Sometimes they were required to drive to different schools.

Hiram couldn't believe their son had such athletic abilities, *"And at just thirteen years old!"* he thought proudly.

Caleb was making such a good name for himself that several places where Hiram would go, people would say something good about his son.

Jimmie kept her eyes closed most of the time her son was on the field, and she was just glad that on ball game night, she didn't have to cook supper. They always ate hamburgers or hot dogs at school from the concession stand.

Laken and Shelby socialized with their friends while they were at the games. They, like Jimmie, had no interest in the sport. It also made them sick to their stomachs when they saw the older girls swoon over Caleb. Another thing that they laughed about behind Caleb's back was all the

"Vitalis" hair oil he started to put on his hair. He'd began to comb his hair in what was known as a "duck tail."

The bathroom at the Beasley place stank profusely of the greasy hair oil. The girls had complained about it to Jimmie, but she just laughed it off, saying that Caleb was just growing up. "He'll find himself eventually," Jimmie told them.

"Lord, I hope we don't start to put that stuff on our hair when we get his age," Shelby told her mama, with Laken agreeing.

"No, you probably won't be putting oil in your hair, but no telling what thirteen-year-old girls' styles will be by then. Shoot, I've been reading that young ladies up north are shaving their legs and wearing pants!" Jimmie told them.

Jimmie was in the kitchen, as usual, when Shelby asked, "That 'Mum' that he smears under his arms, what's that about?"

"You're too young to know such things, but in time, I'll tell you. What you girls need to know is how to do household things; now get busy sweeping the floor. You two can take turns, and it'll keep your mind off Caleb," Jimmie told them.

The girls knew that Christmas was right around the corner, so they hopped to it.

Football season was over by the first of December, and Caleb could help more around the farm. Hiram had sure missed his help, too, especially when he baled the hay, then put it in the loft of the barn. Hiram always tried to put his children's wants first, as long as he felt it might be good for their future.

After the football season, Caleb resumed his farm duties. Sometimes he'd get his friends to help him, particularly when it was cutting firewood.

That year for Christmas, Hiram bought something for the household that would change their lives forever. He bought a television. It was a thirty-two-inch Bendix. Like all televisions in the area, it would only pick up three channels, 3, 10, and 12. Channel 3 was in Pensacola, 10 was in Mobile, and 12 was coming in from Montgomery. The television had to be hooked to an antenna. Channel 12 was fuzzy. It was in the opposite direction to the other two channels. If you wanted to watch something from Montgomery, someone had to go outside and turn the antenna, which was usually Caleb.

At midnight, all the channels signed off with the playing of the national anthem and came back on at five o'clock the next morning. All three channels started the day with the local news.

Everyone learned from the television, especially the girls. They found out right away what Mum was used for. They learned that all grown-ups stank, unless they smeared Mum under their armpits.

Even though they might be worn out from farm chores, Hiram and Caleb soon discovered that wrestling came on at ten p.m. on channel 3. There was always aa good guy and a mean one. It was a good thing the television was in the den, behind closed doorways, for the two could really get absorbed in a match.

Their two favorites were two brothers, Bobby and Lee Fields. The meanest one was Mario Gilento.

Of course, for Christmas, they all made a day of it, shopping in Monroeville.

A new restaurant had opened in Monroeville, 'Bowen's Ice Cream Parlor and Restaurant.' Of course, they tried it out, and liked it.

Jimmie could tell that Hiram didn't seem to be in a hurry, and she figured something was up.

When they did make it home, she found that a new fourteen-foot chest freezer was setting on the front porch.

Jimmie never concerned herself with money, she left that up to Hiram. If they had it, he'd buy the necessities, and if they didn't have it, they'd do without until he did get it.

"Hiram!" she exclaimed, "How in the world, and the television too?" she asked, for she knew he wasn't going to charge anything on credit.

"The hogs; we had twice the amount we needed, so I sold twice as many," he said.

"Now we can buy ice cream," Shelby said.

"We sure can, baby," Jimmie said, as she hugged Hiram.

It didn't take but a few minutes before Hiram and Caleb had the freezer in the kitchen, and it was humming away.

For Christmas, the girls had more clothes under the tree than anything else, plus some board games. Of course, their charm bracelets  were already loaded with charms. They expected a charm for each occasion.

Caleb got clothes, boots, and three boxes of .12-gauge shotgun shells.

Caleb looked at Hiram quizzically, as all he owned was the .410. Hiram reached behind his recliner and brought out his grandpa Beasley's old rabbit-eared double-barreled shotgun.

"You already know who this gun belonged to. It was made by Mossberg in 1912. My grandpa brought it home from World War I. I don't know if he used it in the war or not. He left it to my daddy, and now I'm leaving it to you," Hiram told his son. He then added, "I've cleaned it good for you, and it's ready to shoot."

Caleb grabbed the gun and looked at it with keen eyes.

"It has 'C. B. 1912' whittled into the stock. What does that stand for?" Caleb asked.

"His name was Charles Beasley, and I imagine 1912 was the year he got it," Hiram answered.

"I know what I'll be doing this afternoon, and I'll be wearing my brand-new boots, too," Caleb said.

"This gun is more powerful than the .410. It'll teach you to shoot small game in the head," Hiram told Caleb.

"Yes, sir, I know," Caleb replied, as he went to his room to put the shotgun in his closet.

The girls were busy rolling the dice that went with their Monopoly game.

Everyone received new winter coats that Christmas, including Hiram and Jimmie.

Christmas fell on Wednesday that year, and of course, Jimmie had cooked another big meal. Neither of the girls liked anything to do with the kitchen, but Jimmie was teaching them to make simple things.

Both Shelby and Laken were interested in music, though, and had learned to play almost everything in the chord books that Hiram had bought them.

That Christmas night, the television was turned off, and they played for over thirty minutes. On some of the tunes, they sang along with the music.

The girls' favorite tunes were 'Blue Moon of Kentucky' and 'Pretty Polly.' They had performed the two songs at the talent contest at school before Christmas and won the first place.

They didn't win a prize, or money, but they earned the respect of the entire school, from that day until they graduated.

Little did they know that Callie was standing in the middle of the field listening to them. She'd run over brambles and briars in her old Plymouth, then beat her way with a stick to get through the old path. After she'd made her way to the house and sat on the porch for a few minutes, it was beginning to turn dark.

She had hopes of seeing Laken, if only through the window. As she neared the house in the early darkness of the night a black dog began barking at her, so she stopped in her tracks. Not wanting the dog to chase her, she stopped in the middle of the field, and that's when she heard the music. The dog stopped barking, so she stood in the freezing cold weather and listened to its entirety.

*"If only I could just see her,"* Callie thought, as she turned and followed her tracks back to her car.

As on the other time, Callie made her way back to Mobile with tears in her eyes.

She gave herself hope, though. *"Maybe when she's a little older she can understand,"* Callie thought.

## Chapter 21

By 1957, Callie had found a place of her own, and it was just what she had been looking for.

The place was on the outskirts of Mobile. In the rear of the long building was the cooking area, a small bedroom, bathroom, and storage room. The place was still equipped with a huge walk-in freezer, a fryer, grill, cooking utensils, dishes, silverware, and a buffet bar, everything she needed to go into business.

A man and his wife had owned the former restaurant. The lady's husband had died, and she wanted to move to Ocean Springs, Mississippi to be near her family.

Callie met the lady delivering newspapers to the place and learned that the owner was asking twenty thousand dollars.

Callie offered sixteen thousand five hundred dollars for the building and all the equipment. After thinking on it for a week, the owner accepted it.

Callie had twenty-one thousand dollars in the two banks, plus a few hundred dollars in her room at 'The Blue Moon.'

The former owner said they only served dinner and supper. "Most people eat from the buffet; a few order from the menu. We opened at twelve and closed at seven. Make sure you have plenty of rib-eyes and oysters on Fridays and Saturdays," she said. She then added, "The delivery men will help you a lot, by knowing what, and how much to deliver. We were closed on Sundays.

She also told Callie that she'd need a woman to help in the kitchen, and a young, pretty girl to take orders and deliver food. "I'm sure the help I have now will be glad to stay on."

Callie began to think that she'd bit off more than she could chew, but she was determined to go ahead. *"If all else fails, I'll have a roof over my head,"* she thought.

The name of the place was 'Margie's.' Callie changed the name to 'Laken's' and painted the name with scrolling red letters on the big plate glass window herself.

The place had twenty tables, with red and white checkerboard tablecloths. A stack of paper napkins was placed in the middle of each table. Each table had four chairs.

The place never closed during the change of ownership; when Margie moved out, Callie moved in and took control of Laken's.

To begin with, she and Raymona, the cook, were constantly bumping into each other. Half the food in the buffet was either to be thrown out, or Raymona and Cathy Jo, the waitress, took it home with them.

Callie tried cutting back on the food in the buffet, and still the customers wouldn't eat all of it. Finally, after a month of barely clearing enough to pay for the help, utilities, and food, Callie knew she had to make a decision.

To start with, she took all the menus off the tables.

"From now on, the buffet will be closed. We're only selling rib-eyes or T-bone steaks. For seafood, we'll have oysters, shrimp, or crab claws. Of course, we'll have burgers and fries for the kids. The only vegetables we'll be having are cole slaw and green salad. The only drink we'll serve is sweet tea or water. For dessert, it'll be doughnuts from Krispy Kreme," Callie told Raymona and Cathy Jo.

Right off, Callie could see a change in her clientele. More affluent looking people became regular customers. Cathy

Jo, who preferred to be called C.J., liked the new setup, since the customers left bigger tips.

Without running around in the small kitchen, cooking all the buffet foods, Raymona and Callie soon worked out a system. Raymona washed the dishes and Callie did most of the cooking.

Some of the men asked for beer with their meal, but Callie's simple answer was, "Sorry, we don't have a license to sell alcohol."

Sometimes, the ladies would thank her in private.

Callie dressed nicer at 'Laken's' than she did at 'The Blue Moon,' and the customers took notice, especially the men. Since she didn't have to stay in the kitchen all of the time, Callie had a little time to mingle with the customers. That's how she met Paul.

Paul Lindsey was a young lawyer. He didn't work with a firm, and he was always hustling for cases. He had asked Callie for a date one night, but she'd turned him down, saying she had to work too much.

She had taken noticed how the other ladies dressed and wore their make-up, so she began to dress more like a lady.

*"After all,"* she thought one morning, as she looked into the mirror applying her make-up, *"I'm just thirty-one years old. Shoot, I should go out now and then and kick my heels up. Just let Mr. Paul Lindsey ask me out again,"* and she laughed.

Callie opened Laken's in January, and by July, the place was really paying off. She traded her old '48 Plymouth in on a 1955 black and white Crown Victoria Ford. She'd even managed to put over a thousand dollars back into her savings account. The other bank, she used for a checking account to pay the delivery men, her help, and utilities.

123

As more and more time went by, Callie thought less and less about killing Calvin. She thought as long as she stayed away from Monroe County, and east Mobile, she might just squeak by. She knew that now and then people from Monroe County had to see doctors in Mobile and go shopping at the malls. That's why if she needed anything personally, she avoided the malls, and as usual she did her best to keep a low profile. She did her best to stay in west Mobile, where she felt safer.

Paul Lindsey kept asking Callie for a date, and she kept refusing, until one night he told her he was going to a class reunion. She knew he'd graduated in Pascagoula, Mississippi, so she accepted the date.

Paul reminded her so much of James. He had the same coal black hair, pearly white teeth, was about the same height and weight, and even spoke in an educated manner, like James did.

Callie had never been on a date in her life. James and she had gone parking, but never on a date in front of people, fearing Victoria would get wind of it.

People just didn't know how hard it was for Callie to even learn to speak halfway properly.

*"If he thinks when we go out, we're going to have sex, he had better think twice,"* she thought.

C.J. went with Callie to help her find a nice outfit for the date.

"They'll probably have a small meal, then dancing after they introduce themselves and their dates," C.J. said.

"Oh Lord! I've never danced in my entire life," Callie said.

"Ain't nothing to it; I'll show you how when we get back," C.J. told her.

They wound up choosing a short-sleeved taffeta dress. The dress was white, trimmed in gold colored lace material around the bodice, sleeves, and the bottom of the dress. A small matching zip-up purse went with the dress. No spike shoes for Callie; instead, she chose a pair of white low quarters.

Callie caught right on to the slow dance. It was hard for C.J. though, for she danced the man's part.

They practiced inside the diner, with the curtains pulled. They danced to music on the radio.

Callie had caught on until Elvis' record, 'I Just Wanna Be Your Teddy Bear' came on.

"Just sit down if a fast one comes on," C.J. told her.

The reunion was on a Saturday night. Callie worked until five o'clock. C.J. had one of her friends come in and help her and Raymona.

Callie didn't have a piece of jewelry to put on. *"Darn, I didn't even think of jewelry,"* the nervous Callie thought, as she looked at herself in the mirror. She was satisfied with what she saw, thinking if she brushed her hair one more stroke, the red would come out.

Paul picked her up at fifteen minutes before six o'clock.

Callie was waiting for him at the door of the diner. She'd never been to Pascagoula, so the entire thing was alien to her.

She went outside when she saw Paul park his car. *"My goodness, he's even washed his car,"* she thought.

She was so nervous that the thought ran through her mind to run back inside.

Paul came up to her and said, "Aww, you're so beautiful you take my breath away." He then embraced her, and then they kissed. Suddenly, all of Callie's nervousness disappeared.

# Chapter 22

The girls had turned twelve the week before—and yes, they were both now using Mum deodorant under their arms. They were also shaving their legs and under their arms. Miss Jimmie had already given them the "woman to woman" talk, but to her surprise they already knew about it. To Jimmie's disbelief, they'd learned about babies and such at school. They were also helping Jimmie with more of the domestic chores around the house.

The girls were beginning to fill out in places where young ladies do. They'd each gotten a new bathing suit and a beach towel for their birthday.

Attorney Barry had pushed the papers through, and they finally had the adoption papers on Laken. Again, they could have changed Laken's surname to Beasley, but as before, Laken said she wanted to leave it Jordan.

Caleb was now fifteen years old, and had his driver's permit, meaning he could drive on the public roads, but a licensed driver had to be in the vehicle with him.

Hiram was still paying the taxes on the Pruitt place each year, so he asked Laken if he could fence the end next to the road. "That way, my cows could get in there and keep most of the briars and brambles eaten," he said.

Laken hugged Hiram's neck, not knowing he'd been paying the taxes on the place for years. "So, it's still in the family?" she asked.

"Well, you could say that, for it's yours, or it will be the day you turn eighteen," Hiram told her.

Hiram fenced in the land, then increased his herd to twenty more cows.

The family car was always known as "Miss Jimmie's" car and the farm truck was referred to as simply the farm truck.

Hiram was making money drying and storing some of the local farmers' corn and peanuts. He made enough that he bought the farm another truck, then Jimmie a newer vehicle.

The older truck was kept on the farm, along with Miss Jimmie's older car. Caleb didn't know it, but they were planning to give it to him when he turned sixteen, so it was kept in the barn until then. Miss Jimmie's newer vehicle was a 1955 ford, with an automatic transmission, and Jimmie loved it.

The girls had also learned to drive the old farm truck, so now they didn't have to walk across the field to go swimming.

Hiram was right about the cows eating the briars and brambles around the old log cabin, and Laken and Shelby had gotten to where they spent more and more time there. Using the old porch sure came in handy after a cold dip in the stream! They'd spread their beach towels on the porch and talk about their future. Surprisingly, it would never be about marriage and family, for they sure didn't see any fun that Miss Jimmie had. All she did was work and watch a little television at night. They talked about music, creating their own band and writing their own music.

Being at the old cabin really brought back memories for Laken. Strangely, they were never any of the bad things. The girls wanted to go inside the cabin and the big barn, but both of these were still locked tight.

One day they were talking about things in the past, and Laken laughed.

When asked what she was laughing about, Laken told Shelby that her mama always told her that "y'all were big shots and to stay away from y'all."

Shelby laughed, too, then said, "Boy, we were big shots alright. From daddy's account, we lived from season to season."

"There's no telling where I'd be today if I hadn't swum down the creek that day," Laken said.

"Let me correct you: you said you had *swimmed* down the creek," Shelby teased.

"Alright, don't rub it in," Laken said, and they both slapped each other on the shoulders, laughing. Laken then got serious, and said, "You know, being with you guys was the best thing that could have happened to me."

"I feel the same way, and always have. Strange though, I never knew y'all existed until you showed up that day," Shelby confessed.

"Aw, it was because mama sold that old whiskey," Laken said, while leaving out the part about prostitution.

Laken continued to talk, while they laid on the porch.

"You know, somehow, I never believed my mama drowned in the creek that night. Calvin's truck wasn't found in the parking area, so I believe she left from here in it. I've really been giving it thought, especially as I've gotten older. I think she's out there somewhere, and scared to come back because she's afraid they'll get her for killing Calvin.

"Wherever she is, I hope she's safe, because she had a terrible existence living here. I just pray she will never come back to get me, because if she does, I'm not going," Laken ended.

"Brr, hard to believe your birth mama killed someone," Shelby said, shivering.

"Well, those two shots I heard, I believe Calvin shot my daddy, and mama had to kill him, or he would have killed her too. Calvin was a mean one. When he'd come, I was told to hide in the chifforobe, and I did," Laken told her.

"Wow! Have you ever told mama and daddy this?" asked Shelby.

"No, they've never asked me anything about it, but I think they already know," Laken replied.

Laken felt bad about it sometimes, but she'd always harbored a secret from the Sheriff, and Mr. Hiram. She knew where her mama had kept her stash of money. She had been too young at the time to realize the significance of it, and by the time she did, the cabin was locked tight. In a way, she was scared to look under the loose rock in the hearth, for if the money was still there, it meant Callie was long dead. *"Maybe when I turn eighteen,"* she thought.

"Let's change the subject. It's hard to believe that such a thing happened at this peaceful place," Shelby said.

"One other thing, do you know what I'm going to do when I get this house?" Laken asked.

"No, what?" replied Shelby.

"I'm going to roll that chifforobe out here into the yard and burn it. Every minute I spent in there, I was terrified that someone was going to open the door," Laken revealed.

The girls ended their time together at the creek that day talking about the next season of school.

"Hard to believe we'll be in the seventh grade," Shelby said.

"Yep, and Caleb will be going into the tenth. I wonder if he'll be going to college?" Laken asked.

"Shoot, I doubt it, he'll probably stay right here on this farm. I can't see him doing anything else," Shelby said.

Jim would always go with them on their treks. He'd always ride in the back of the truck. For some reason, he'd balk if someone tried to put him in the cab. He'd rather stay in the back of the truck and bark at the cows across the fence.

While the girls were at the cabin, Jim would sniff around in the dirt, or tree squirrels.

Caleb seldom came with them; he preferred to swim with his friends. That is, when he found the time, for Hiram kept him busy on the farm from the day school was turned out, until football practice began.

# Chapter 23

No one but Jimmie realized the hours it took for Hiram to keep the farm running smoothly. He left out of the door at daybreak. The first thing he tended to were the hogs, feeding and watering them. Next were the feeder calves, which had to be fed and watered year round. The cows in the pasture pretty well took care of themselves, except in the winter months. That was when bales of peanut hay, mixed with an assortment of grasses, were thrown into the pastures. The pasture cows drank from Persimmon Creek, but the feeder calves (the ones going to the sale) had to be watered.

Caleb did his share and more, but Hiram always put his schoolwork first.

Hiram knew he needed more help, especially after the silos were in full swing. Farmers were constantly coming in with products or to pick up the finished goods.

Luckily, Hiram's farm was in about the same season as the others, so it wasn't like he'd have to get off his tractor from the middle of the fields to tend to the silos.

He usually started to break his land the first of March, which took two weeks, if the weather was agreeable. The last two weeks of March, he planted corn. At the beginning of April, he started planting peanuts. Until harvest time, everything had to be plowed around to keep the weeds out.

Hiram had tried planting cotton, but the government had so many regulations on it that he didn't find it feasible.

Every minute of Jimmie's time was accounted for, too. She, like Hiram, began at daylight, milking the cow, and tending to the chickens. Next, it was cooking breakfast, then getting the children up and ready for school. Next was washing the clothes and hanging them on the clothesline to dry. Luckily, Jimmie had a wringer type washing machine that was set on the back porch. She could well remember when she had to boil the clothes in a big black pot and wring them out by hand.

Jimmie always chose Thursday morning for her churning. She'd fallen in love with the 'I love Lucy' and the 'Danny Thomas' shows, so she'd churn while watching television.

During the school months, she'd usually stir up a small meal for Hiram and herself. Supper was their main meal. So, she'd start it about two thirty.

Being a farmer or his wife, there was always something to do. It was the only life Jimmie and Hiram knew, though, and they wouldn't have it any other way.

They thanked the good Lord at suppertime for their many blessings that were bestowed upon them, whether the meal was slim, or a feast.

Laken and Shelby still sang in the church choir, only now, they sang in the young adult group. They still did their solos once a month in church, however.

The church was of the Methodist faith, and Hiram had been going there all of his life. The name was 'Woodlawn United Methodist Church.'

Miss Julia always had a big meal on every holiday, and people sure enjoyed the get-togethers.

School started in the fall of 1957, and Caleb played his first varsity football game. He found out that he'd be playing 2nd string quarterback, so he spent a good bit of time sitting on the bench. He didn't grumble to the coach about it, though, for the quarterback was a senior, and had played longer than Caleb.

Hiram and his family still attended every game, and Jimmie was satisfied with the situation.

The first day of school, Laken and Shelby came in and complained to Miss Jimmie. Laken said that every girl in their class was painting their fingernails.

"Yeah, and some are even wearing lipstick," Shelby chimed in.

"Well, they can paint all they want to, because they're not my girls. Wouldn't y'all be some pretty things singing in the choir with lipstick and painted fingernails?" Miss Jimmie asked. "The deal is the same as always; you can start painting your fingernails when you're in the ninth grade," she added.

"What about a light shade of lipstick?" pleaded Shelby.

"That, too, comes with the ninth grade, but I'll pick out the shades of lipstick and rouge," Jimmie told them.

They knew it was useless, so Shelby finally stomped the floor, folded her arms and said, "Hmph!"

"Alright, one more word out of you and I'm going to talk to your Daddy," Jimmie said, then added, "I'll find y'all something to do!"

The girls quickly decided to go to their room and start on their homework, before it was time to tend to the chickens.

After the girls got into their room, Shelby said, "You know, I think we got Mama so worked up that in a little bit, she would've sent us out there to milk ol' Belle!"

# Chapter 24

Callie was really surprised at what a wonderful time she had at Paul's reunion. She had been worried that she wouldn't fit in. After looking at some of the wives, who were overweight and talked with worse grammar than she did, she began to relax.

Everything was sort of informal. The event was held in the school auditorium. It was like C.J. had predicted; the food was mostly finger food, and no alcohol was present. As much of it that Callie had been around, she smelled it on some of their breaths, though, including the ladies. Of course, some of the ladies and men were well dressed and looked prosperous.

Callie knew that Paul was proud of her, for he sure seemed to enjoy introducing her to everyone.

She wasn't sure what a valedictorian was, but she intended to find out. Paul was introduced as the class valedictorian and was asked to give a speech, which he did. He grabbed Callie by the hand and led her with him to the podium, and, with his arm around her waist, he introduced her. He made the speech short, but everyone applauded him, as they returned to their table.

Someone had rigged very large speakers to a record player, so after everyone ate, the dancing began.

Callie found that she had natural rhythm, and dancing with Paul was easier than dancing with C.J. Callie didn't know who had picked the music out, but most of it she could dance to.

Not everyone danced, and with the fast ones, Paul must not have known how to dance fast either, for they didn't get out on the floor.

Callie noticed some of the men gave her the eye, but she didn't pay them any attention. She noticed that Paul saw them too, and she giggled to herself.

The whole affair was over by eight thirty, and Paul surprised her by stopping by his parents' house. To Callie's surprise, the house was just a moderate home and was set in a subdivision.

When they got out of the car, she smelled a different air than she did in Mobile. She mentioned it to Paul as they walked up the brick lane that led to his parents' home.

"That's the salt air; the bay is across the street," he said.

His parents were watching 'Gunsmoke' on the television when they entered the house.

Mrs. Lindsey, whose given name was Charlotte, almost ran to Callie and hugged her.

"It's so nice to finally meet you," she said.

"Nice meeting you too," Callie replied.

Paul's dad had his hand stuck out to shake Callie's hand, when his wife turned her loose.

When Callie called him Mr. Lindsey, he said, "Please, call me John," as Paul's mother directed them to have a seat on the couch.

"It's plain to see where Paul gets his looks," Callie said, as soon as she had a seat on the sofa.

"You don't have to tell me, honey; he's the spitting image of his daddy," Charlotte agreed.

She then offered them a drink or snack of some sort, but they both waved her away, saying they were stuffed.

They talked of trivia and current affairs, and Callie had to admit, she was lost on a lot of the subjects. She just smiled and nodded her head.

"Paul tells us that you own and operate a diner," John said.

"Yes, sir. It's a lot of responsibility and hard work, but it beats working for someone else," Callie answered.

"Well, don't you let ol' Paul freeload on you," John told Callie.

"No, sir, he pays like everyone else—when he has the money, that is," Callie teased, then she laughed and leaned against Paul's shoulder.

Everyone else laughed at Callie's last words.

"Well, he has a mighty slick tongue; that's why I believe he'll make a good lawyer, so keep a close eye on him, young lady," John advised.

"Oh, I keep an eye on him," Callie said, then nudged Paul on the shoulder again with hers, making  Paul's face turn red, and his parents laughed.

"She sells seafood, burgers, and steaks, along with the stuff that goes with them. No alcohol, though," Paul said.

"Some ask for beer or wine, but I look at it this way: it's a family diner. Children are there with most families, so I don't sell it," Callie remarked.

"So, you don't drink?" Mrs. Lindsey asked.

"No, Ma'am, nary a drop, and never have," Callie replied, then added, "Its iced tea or soda at 'Laken's.'"

"Laken…such an unusual name. How in the world did you come up with such a pretty name?" asked Charlotte.

"Exactly that, I knew a little girl once and her name was Laken, the prettiest little thing you'd want to look at, so I needed a name. I think it beats 'Margie's,' the name of it when I bought it," Callie answered.

"Then, you're from Mobile?" Charlotte asked.

"Yes, Ma'am, I came from Mobile," Callie said, as she crossed her fingers.

She kept talking, before Charlotte had time to ask. "My Mama died when I was thirteen, and my daddy was killed in a vehicle wreck when I was sixteen. We were renting, and I had no income, so I started running a small diner in Mobile. We only served breakfast. It had a small bedroom in the back, and the rest is history," Callie said.

"Bless your heart, so you've accomplished what you have on your own?" Charlotte inquired.

"Yes, Ma'am, every penny, because I've never been married. Shoot, I've been so busy, until I've never even dated. Then, this handsome devil of yours came along," Callie answered, as Paul pecked her on the cheek.

"Well, since Charlotte has run you through the grinder, I must say, I'm pleased with my son's choice," John said.

"Thank you, sir, and I'm pleased with my choice too," Callie replied with a smile.

"Well, before you break out the photo album, I've got to get this pretty thing back to Mobile," Paul said, nodding toward his mother. He then arose and pulled Callie by her hand.

After hugging necks and shaking hands again, Paul and Callie went out the door.

"Well, you've passed the test," Paul said, as Callie slid in beside him on the car seat.

"You think so? Well, I was just being myself." Callie said, as she patted Paul on his right knee. "Thank you for inviting me to your class reunion. It was the first one I've ever been to, and I learned a lot."

"Oh, yeah, and just what did you learn?" Paul asked.

138

"You're gonna think I'm silly, but I learned that I'm no different than anyone else. I've been so busy just trying to make it, until I had no time for socializing. I have the responsibility of my two workers too. Shoot, we're so busy on Friday and Saturday nights until it's pitiful. I've either got to build on or buy a bigger place. I need more help, too. C.J. is satisfied due to all the tips she's getting.

"Poor Raymona and I catch it. One time a man came in and wanted to rent the place for a club he belonged to. He told me to give him a price. It was tempting, but I had my regular customers to think about," Callie said.

"Hmm. Sounds to me like you have growing pains. You may want to advertise in the Mobile Press that you need a cook for just Friday and Saturday nights. If anyone wants to rent it, rent it on Sunday nights, the night that you're closed to the public. Up Raymona and C.J.'s pay. You'll be able to afford it," Paul told her.

"Will you run the advertisement for me? I'll give you a free steak supper," Cassie offered. She then added, "Say I'll interview them at the diner, and it's just for a cook. That'll give me time to help C.J. with the orders and serving."

"I'll do it if you go to church with me tomorrow," Paul answered.

Callie laughed, and said, "But you're already getting a free steak."

"Baloney. Come on, I want to show you off, and I'm getting tired of going by myself," Paul pleaded.

Callie thought for a small while, then asked, "It's not one of those snake-handling churches, is it?"

Paul grinned, and said, "No, it's a Baptist church. It's between here and Dauphin Island."

"Sure, it will be good for me," Callie finally agreed.

"Good, I'll pick you up at ten o'clock," replied Paul.

Callie thought, *"Paul sure is different from any of my old customers and clients. He's easy to talk to, and so kind-hearted!"* Then she thought of James being the same way.

She just prayed that Paul didn't find out about her past, which was always a continuous dread for her.

The radio was turned down low, and Paul had his arm around her, and they talked the entire way until they reached the diner.

Expecting to have to push him out of the front door when they arrived, surprisingly, they held hands until Callie unlocked the door. They embraced and kissed. Paul let out a deep breath, and said, "I'll see you at ten."

That night, Callie was still smiling as she drifted off to sleep, and for once, all her dreams were sweet.

## Chapter 25

In that same year of 1959, the girls were promoted to the ninth grade, and Jimmie broke down and allowed them to paint their fingernails.

Laken and Shelby had a thirty-minute slot, picking and singing at the local radio station. They had to wear their church clothes, though, for they didn't have time to come home to change. They left the station and went straight to church.

Caleb didn't like the idea, since he was the one who had to drive them there and back.

The girls were now fourteen and had really rounded and filled out their clothing. Things were like Jimmie had predicted; it was now acceptable for girls to wear pants, anywhere but school and church.

Caleb was going into the twelfth grade. He was shaving, but his beard, like his hair, was so blond that it was almost invisible. The only way the girls could tell he was shaving was the long sideburns that he grew.

The girls at school swooned over him, and it made Shelby and Laken sick.

Caleb, like the girls, had rules. He was given Jimmie's old '49 Chevrolet when he got his driver's license, but he wasn't allowed to date until he started the twelfth grade. There weren't many places to go, but Caleb found what few there were.

Surprisingly, he liked to dance, and Bowen's Ice Cream Parlor had a good Rockola juke box and a smooth dance floor. Caleb made a point of going there on Saturday nights, unless he was having a ball game, and that would be in the fall. He didn't have anyone special, so he danced with all the girls that didn't have a partner.

The girls found out about Caleb's shenanigans through the grapevine.

A momentous occasion happened at the Beasley's house that summer: Hiram had a telephone installed. Now, instead of going to the creek so much, the girls stayed on the phone.

Jimmie didn't know how the girls knew so many numbers. In fact, she never answered the phone unless it rang twenty or more times. Scared of the expense of a long-distance call, Jimmie wrote to her sister that lived in Evergreen and told her what her telephone number was. The children had strict warnings about calling long distance too.

Since the young people had outgrown PeeWee, Hiram sold the Shetland pony to a friend at church, who had a young son. Of course, the girls brooded for a small while, when they found out PeeWee was sold, but they soon got over it.

Both Shelby and Laken really practiced their picking and singing that summer, after the telephone got old. They had their dream and were sticking to it. As usual, if the old farm truck was available, they drove across the field to the old log cabin.

After landing the play time at the radio station, they thought they'd increase the size of their duo.

Miss Anne Brown, from Frisco City, could play the steam out of a mandolin, so they called her, and she agreed to join them. She also told them she listened to their program on Sunday mornings, and that what they needed was a bass fiddler. "Buddy Cater, why, he lives right there in Excel.

Why don't you call him? He can make a bass fiddle get up and walk," she said.

So, Laken called him, and he, too, agreed to join their group.

"I'll see Miss Earnestine and ask whether she'll let us practice on the porch at the Big Store this Saturday afternoon," Shelby told Laken.

"Yeah, we'll liven up Excel this coming Saturday," Laken said. Then they both hollered "Woo-Hoo!"

The next day, they phoned Miss Anne and Buddy, and they were all for it. Buddy had only one exception; he said his wife, Angel, had some chores for him that morning.

"But I'll be free that afternoon," he told them.

"Good; see you at two o'clock," Laken said.

"Now all we need to do is talk to Miss Earnestine, but I don't see why she wouldn't agree to it. Truth be known, she should be paying us," Shelby remarked.

They talked with Mr. Hiram about their plan that night at supper. He listened patiently, then told them they had left out one person.

"Who's that?" inquired Shelby.

"That would be Miss Jenny, the mayor of Excel. She has the say-so of everything in the city limits," Hiram told them.

"Oh, Dad, please call her," Shelby pleaded.

"I will, if you girls clean the kitchen after supper. Miss Jimmie wants to watch The 'Ed Sullivan Show.' I think ol' Elvis is gonna be on tonight, and I believe she likes the way he twists and carries on when he's singing," Hiram said, grinning.

Caleb, who had just shoveled a big spoon of creamed corn into his mouth, had to put his hand over his mouth to prevent spitting on the table.

"Lord have mercy, you have discovered my secret!" Miss Jimmie exclaimed, making everyone laugh, but Hiram, and he soon joined in.

After supper, both the girls and Hiram kept their promise.

Miss Jimmie didn't watch The Ed Sullivan show, though; instead she watched 'Rawhide,' for she knew Hiram enjoyed the program.

When Hiram called the mayor, her response was a resounding 'yes.' "Under one condition: they must sing 'Pretty Polly,' and dedicate it to me," she responded.

Hiram laughed, and said, "I'll be sure to tell them."

The new foursome not having played together before, they decided to get together and practice on the Friday afternoon before the event. Knowing the girls weren't old enough to drive, they chose the big barn at the Beasley place. None of the musical instruments required electricity, so it wasn't a problem to practice in the barn.

They didn't have to go over but about three songs, and Miss Anne realized they were meant to be together. They learned that Buddy could not only play the bass fiddle, but also had a beautiful baritone voice.

The foursome also realized that very day that Miss Anne was the boss. It was just her nature.

Miss Anne was about sixty years old. No one knew why she was referred to as, 'Miss Anne,' for she had been married and had two grown children. She also had grandchildren.

Hiram jokingly replied when asked by the girls that night why she was referred to as Miss Anne, "Because of her charity work for the town of Frisco City. It doesn't hurt any that she has most of the money in United Bank, and she's on the board of directors. Her husband died years ago, and she's turned his retirement into a small fortune, due to shrewd investments." he told the girls. He then added that she'd argue just as hard over fifteen cents as she would fifteen hundred dollars. "In her mind, right is right and wrong is wrong, and there's no other way."

"Well, I like her, and she can make that mandolin talk," Laken replied.

"I liked the idea that she's going to try to get money out of the radio station. She said it wasn't right for us to be performing on Sunday mornings for nothing," Shelby said.

"If anybody can do it, Miss Anne can," Miss Jimmie replied.

Needless to say, the girls were so excited that night, they found it hard to fall asleep. They stayed anxious until it was time for them to perform the next afternoon.

Surprisingly, Miss Jenny, the mayor, had a farmer pull a flatbed trailer in the middle of the parking lot of the Big Store. Some wooden homemade steps were next to the trailer, making it easy for them to step onto it.

Miss Anne and Buddy were already there when the Beasleys arrived.

Miss Anne looked stunning. She was tall and slender built, with natural white hair. She was wearing black pants, a white blouse and a short black jacket that came to her waist.

The girls were just wearing one of their Sunday dresses.

Buddy, who was well over six feet tall, muscular built and weighing about two hundred pounds, was just dressed in jeans and a T-shirt.

Before they began to perform, Miss Anne situated them on the flatbed trailer. "I'll talk to you later about your clothes," Miss Anne told each of them, as she told them where to stand.

Word must have gotten around via telephone and by word of mouth, because the parking lot was almost full of people. Some were even across the street and had set up chairs under the awning.

Miss Anne couldn't resist the opportunity; she ran down the steps into the Big Store. She returned with a big cardboard box, and with a black magic marker printed, "All donations are appreciated" on the outside of the box.

All of the girls' jitters dissipated as soon as they stepped onto the trailer.

Laken and Shelby recognized almost everyone there. Some of them were their classmates. They saw Bobbie Wright, Sara Lee, Sonny Hinson, James Watford, and Sonny Dawson. Sonny wasn't in their class, but he was in Caleb's.

"Okay, on the count of three," Miss Anne said, then they started with 'Pretty Polly' with Buddy joining in with his baritone voice.

Miss Anne never sang, but it was as though lightning was flying from those mandolin strings. Sometimes, Buddy would dance and go around and around with the bass fiddle, never missing a beat. Angel, his wife, was standing in the front row and would just howl as Buddy danced around.

Several people came up and threw money into the box.

They did about twenty songs and even took some requests. At the closing of their performance they sang, 'Amazing Grace.'

Laken looked over at Mr. Hiram and Miss Jimmie several times and saw they were smiling from ear to ear throughout the entire act.

People meandered around the trailer for a short while, telling them how much they enjoyed the show. Just as many bragged to Hiram and Jimmie about the girls' talent.

As the people left, Miss Anne took the box containing the money to her car and counted it. She found the amount was exactly thirty-six dollars, so she gave each of them nine dollars. She also told them how pleased she was with their performances, and she'd see them the next morning at the radio station.

After the girls were in the car with Hiram and Jimmie, they told them that Miss Anne had told them she had cases for our instruments.

"Oh boy, I've looked high and low for that very same thing. I guess she beat me to them," Hiram said.

"Another thing, Mama won't have to cook supper. Shoot, we have eighteen dollars; let's go out for supper," Laken said.

"I was just thinking about that. Here it is going on four o'clock and I haven't even laid anything out of the freezer," Jimmie replied.

"Suits me," Hiram agreed. "I'm so proud of you girls, I'll pay for it myself. I thought for a minute there y'all had Miss Jenny so worked up she was going to start buck dancing!"

Everyone laughed, "Yeah, she was really getting into it when we opened with 'Pretty Polly,' and with Mr. Cater joining in, it really enhanced the song," Laken added.

After everyone changed clothes, and the girls hung their instruments on the wall, they did their outside chores. Caleb came in to help his daddy, then left before Hiram had a chance to tell him they were going out for supper.

Once everyone had changed back into decent clothes, Hiram took the family to a different place. It was called 'The Hi-Ho,' and it was a step up from just a burger place. They went in, and a waitress directed them to a table. She then asked them what they would like to drink. They all chose sweet tea, and she gave each of them a menu.

After they had time to go over the menu, the girls ordered their regular, hamburger and fries. Hiram and Miss Jimmie ordered fried Alabama catfish, cole slaw, and snap beans.

For dessert, there was pound cake, lemon pie or coconut pie. Everyone ordered coconut pie.

The place was packed with other customers, and several people walked over to tell the girls how much they enjoyed their program every Sunday morning.

"Boy, they don't do this at the hamburger places," Laken whispered to her family.

Hiram knew several of the other customers, and would nod his head at them, when they would acknowledge him. Two of the couples were Delano Raines, Larry Booker, and their wives.

After they finished their meal, Hiram called the waitress over to get the bill.

"Oh, there's no charge, it's added to those gentlemen's ticket over there," the waitress said, then nodded toward Larry and Delano.

Hiram left a two-dollar tip on the table, then all four of them walked over to thank the two couples.

The ladies said they just had to hug the two girls, and they did.

One of the ladies even requested a song, for the next morning, which was, 'House of Gold.'

"We'll sure do it, and thank you, Ma'am," Laken answered.

"I hope you girls know how proud we are of you two. Y'all have come a long way, and I believe with Miss Anne being y'all's manager, there's no telling how much further you'll go," Hiram told them.

As usual, the girls were proud that he said it, but they felt somehow, they *were* going places…and it would be further than Monroeville. They had no way of knowing just how far from home their music would take them, but they were ready to go.

# Chapter 26

Callie had never gone to church. It wasn't that she didn't believe in the Lord, either, for she did.

With her being shunned and made fun of, due to her upbringing, she'd never been invited to church. All she knew was making and selling whiskey, then after Laken was born, prostitution.

At times, especially when she was alone and in her bed, she wondered how she could have led such a life. She asked the Lord every night to forgive her sins.

She knew she had enough clothes to wear to church a few times, but if she continued to go with Paul, she would need more.

When Paul arrived, they embraced and kissed, then he told her how pretty she was. "And dressed for church, too, you'll be turning heads," he said.

Callie loved his strong embraces, and kisses too, but of course, she wouldn't tell him.

She was ashamed to admit to him that she'd never been inside a church, but somehow, she was eager to go.

Paul wasn't wearing his usual blue suit, but a brown one.

"Boy, don't you look mighty handsome this morning," she told him, as they were still holding on to each other.

"Thank you, Ma'am," he said, then added, "Well, we'd better get going."

The appearance of the church wasn't what Callie had expected. It was small, with a tall, sharp roof. The roof had a steeple, and the bell was clanging and clanging.

A few men stood on the outside in their Sunday best, talking.

One of the men recognized her, from Laken's. After introducing himself, he said, "I sure wish you were open for supper on Sundays. Our wives don't want to cook on Sundays."

The other men laughed and nodded their heads at the couple when they walked by.

Callie looked back and said, "I'm considering that very idea, and thanks."

"Boy, ol' Paul is lucky; she's a pretty little thing," Callie heard one of them say, as they headed toward the wide cement steps, hand in hand.

The front door opened to a vestibule, and after going through it, Callie saw rows of comfortable looking long benches. The benches had blue upholstered cushions.

To her surprise, Paul led her to the very front row, right in front of the piano.

The first thing her eyes caught were the musical instruments hanging on hooks at the back of the podium, behind the pulpit.

After they were seated, Paul said, "I guess I should have warned you. A few of us take turns singing, and today is my turn."

"Do you play any of the instruments hanging up back there?" Callie asked.

"Yes, I play the guitar," Paul answered.

"What will you be singing?" asked Callie.

"It was supposed to be a surprise, but I'll be singing, 'Nearer my God to Thee,' and, 'I Saw the Light,'" Paul answered.

"Well, I have a surprise for you; I'll be accompanying you with the fiddle," Callie said.

"Me being surprised is an understatement. I didn't know you could play anything," Paul whispered.

"There's a lot you don't know about me. I just pray my fingers will hold up; they're mighty tender from washing so many dishes," Callie answered. She then added, "I've been dying to get my hands on a banjo or fiddle. I guess I'm just too frugal," Callie said.

"Oh, so you play the banjo too?" Paul asked.

"Oh, yeah," replied Callie.

Paul got up from the pew, stepped up on the podium, and returned with the two instruments, including the bow.

"We need to tune them," he said.

The young preacher soon arrived and stepped behind the pulpit, and opened the services with a prayer, then called out the names on the prayer list.

An elderly man sat behind the piano and he played for the two congregational hymns.

Callie had no idea what was coming up next; she thought you just went to church to hear a preacher, preach.

The baskets were passed around, and the tithes were put into the basket.

Callie noticed that Paul put ten dollars into the basket.

Next, Paul stepped up on the podium and without wasting time, he said, "My fellow parishioners, I'd like to introduce to you, Miss Betty Jean Dale."

Callie stepped up on the podium and stood beside Paul.

"On the count of three," Paul said.

They began with, 'I Saw the Light," and surprisingly, Callie didn't miss a beat, nor word, for she also sang along with Paul.

Everyone in the audience gave them thunderous applause. They then did, 'Nearer My God to Thee.' Once they had finished, the parishioners stood up, and were still applauding after Paul put away the instruments and they stepped off the podium.

When the smiling preacher stepped behind the pulpit, he said, "The only word that comes to my mind is, 'Wow!'"

"Just think I have to follow that," the grinning preacher said, as he picked up his Bible. "Okay, turn your Bibles to Matthew eleven, twenty-eight through thirty."

Callie didn't have a Bible, but on each pew there were two, so Paul got one, and went straight to the passages. They followed along with the preacher, and Callie absorbed every word.

Callie did have a Bible, and she read it at night sometimes. Not knowing she'd need it, she had left it at the diner.

When the services were over, Paul was asked to give the closing prayer, as the preacher made his way to the vestibule.

As everyone made their way to the front door, several ladies came up to Callie and introduced themselves, and welcomed her to the church. Every one of them said, "You must come back."

Several of them told her she was quite the performer.

Some of the men told her she made Paul sound good. To which Paul said, "Sure."

The preacher introduced himself as James Darby, as he shook Callie's hand. Near the front door was his wife, Linda, and she hugged Callie, then almost begged her to come back. "We need you," she whispered in Callie's ear.

Callie told Linda how pretty she was, and that she would be back.

Linda then said, "You two have so much in common."

Paul led the way to his car. He always opened the door for Callie, as she got in or out.

Callie never ate dinner; she ate breakfast, then supper, when she closed the diner.

"So, where would you like to eat dinner?" Paul asked.

"Baby, you know I never eat dinner," she replied.

"Well, do you want to go back to your place and make passionate love?" he asked.

"You talking like that, and we just got out of the church," Callie teased.

Paul laughed, then said, "Boy, we lit up that little church today, didn't we?"

"I haven't a clue; I've never been there before," Callie answered, as she gave Paul a smack on his cheek.

They wound up going back to Callie's room, and watching a football game until it began to get dark.

They did a little smooching, and Paul wanted more, but Callie pushed him away.

All she could think about was opening the diner on Sunday afternoons. Paul's advertisement had paid off and she was thinking about hiring another black lady. Her name was Judy, and she was Raymona's sister.

Callie knew she was taking a chance, but they wound up going to Morrison's cafeteria. She just prayed no one would be there that recognized her, for it was on the east side of town.

They got in line with everyone else. Paul was still talking about their performance at church. "We just have to go to Mom and Dad's church. It's the church I was brought up in. Boy, will they be surprised."

"You name the time," Callie answered.

She knew it was too good to be true, for about three couples ahead of them was Dan Booker and his wife. Dan had been a whiskey customer of hers.

*"He sure has aged,"* thought Callie, as she turned her face.

Morrison's cafeteria was a buffet place, so Dan was concentrating on the assortment of foods ahead of him, and never noticed her.

There were several different walls in the cafeteria; Callie guessed they were for privacy. She led the way with her tray of food, making sure Dan Booker wasn't in her section.

Callie dined on roast beef, creamed potatoes, butterbeans, a yeast roll, and lemon pie for dessert. She made it a point to linger just as long as she could to make sure that Dan and his wife had left.

While she was finishing her lemon pie, a man and woman sat near them. They'd undoubtably finished their meal, for they were smoking one cigarette behind the other.

"How sickening. I'm so glad you don't smoke," Callie said to Paul.

"I know, Baby. If you're through, I say we get outta here," Paul said, as he opened his billfold and laid a dollar tip on the table. He paid for their meal before they went out the door.

On the drive back to the diner, Callie told him her plans about hiring Raymona's sister and opening on Sundays after church.

"You'll pack the place; you're bound to be socking away the money as it is," Paul remarked.

"That's the idea. Before it's over, I plan on having a chain of 'Laken's,'" Callie said.

# Chapter 27

The morning after their Saturday show in Excel, the four of them really put on a show at the radio station. They played 'House of Gold' for the lady that had been at the Hi-Ho.

At the end of each program Laken said, "That's it for today; make sure you're on your way to the church of your choice."

The small room where they sang was separated by a soundproof room. When they opened the door to a small sitting room that led outside, it sounded as though the phone was going to ring off the hook in the manager's office.

Caleb, as usual, was waiting for the girls outside, but before they went out the front door, Miss Anne was tapping on the manager's door.

After church that day, Miss Anne stopped by the Beasleys' to tell the girls that she'd had a meeting with the manager at the radio station. "It's not much, but he's agreed to pay us fifty dollars each Sunday, providing we perform for an hour every week. The time will be from four to five o'clock," she said.

"That suits us; that way we won't have to rush back for church," Shelby said.

"That's right; you can just wear jeans if you want to, and with your money, I want you to save it. There'll be other engagements, and I want us looking like cowgirls or, in Buddy's case, a cowboy. There's a place in Atmore that sells nothing but Western clothes; they're expensive, though," Miss Anne said. She continued, "I've been thinking: we need a name. What about, 'The Bama Four?'"

156

"I like it!" Laken enthused, and Shelby agreed.

"I know that fifty dollars isn't much, but it's a start," Miss Anne said.

"Well, it's twenty-five dollars a week for each of them, and that sure beats what they were getting, which was nothing," Hiram said.

"Well, the manager is a swell guy, but let's face it, the only listeners he gets are just local people. Shoot, I have plans of getting us on the big WBAM in Montgomery before long, then on to Nashville," Miss Anne said excitedly.

"So, you think y'all are that good?" Hiram asked.

"Mr. Hiram, I've played with the best and you know it, and your daughters are right up there with the best of them. They need a little stage performance to put on a show. Buddy already has it. To put on a good show, you not only need talent in singing and picking, but you need to stand out. I intend on teaching your daughters that," Miss Anne concluded.

Thrilled, but coming down to earth, Hiram said, "Well, as long as it doesn't interfere with their school work."

"No, even I wouldn't allow that, but for them to be so young, they've got it," Miss Anne said.

Then, as if turning off a radio, Miss Anne suddenly said, "Well, girls, I've said what I've come here to say. I'll see y'all at the radio station next Sunday at four." She nodded her head at Hiram and Jimmie, then turned as if she was in a hurry and walked to her car.

After Miss Anne left, Hiram said, "Just think, all this started with a scared little five-year-old girl at Christmastime."

"Well, I was missing my mama and daddy, and I just didn't know what was ahead of me. The Lord had a plan, though; he gave me a family. Something that I had never had," Laken replied.

Laken's words were more than Jimmie's heart could stand. She rushed over to Laken and after she hugged her, she said, "Honey, there was never a doubt in our minds where you were going."

Caleb broke the nostalgic mood when he came into the house and told his mama that he had the hoes and yard rakes in the truck.

Jimmie had told them that after church, they were all going to the graveyard and clean around the graves.

"Oh my, girls, we've got to scoot," she said, as everyone went to their bedrooms to change clothes.

They'd already eaten dinner, so Jimmie made sure everything was covered and would be ready for supper.

Of course, they went straight to the Beasley plot, after they arrived at the cemetery, and began hoeing weeds. Hiram had brought a long sack to put the weeds and grass in.

There were three generations of Beasleys buried in the cemetery. Hiram made sure that each grave had a cement slab on it, so there wasn't much to be hoed. They looked a lot better, though, when they had finished.

Jimmie stood back from the graves, looking at them.

"Well, they look better, but the slabs sure need a coat of paint on them," she told Hiram.

"Oh, well, that sounds like a good job for Caleb. I'll send him over here tomorrow with a bucket of paint and a brush," Hiram said.

Laken saw a lone grave with its ornate tombstone and marble slab. It was sitting inside a wrought iron fence and gate.

"There's daddy," she said, as she walked toward the overgrown gravesite, and began to pull the weeds from around the marble slab. The others pitched in, and before long it was to her satisfaction.

Laken stood back and began reading aloud:
"Here lies James Robert Jordan
Born: October 26, 1924
Died: December 18, 1950
Beloved son of Willie and Victoria Jordan."

"Daddy would have turned twenty-one the year I was born," Laken said.

"Yeah, he was young," Hiram said, "But then, so was your mama," he added.

"Next time we come this way, I'm going to bring him a big bouquet of those camellias that are beginning to bloom in our front yard. I'll bet that fancy marble vase at the top of that slab has never had a flower in it," Laken told them.

"We'll make a point of doing that; just let them open on up," Jimmie told Laken.

Hiram made sure the squeaking iron gate was closed before they left to do their chores.

Laken was in a somber mood after leaving the cemetery, until Shelby suggested that they ought to try out for cheerleaders.

"That would be fun; heck, we'll be going to all the ball games anyway," Laken said.

The tryouts were for the next week, so the two girls practiced the yells all week.

Hiram and Jimmie thought seeing the girls hollering at the top of their voices was silly, but they didn't say anything.

The day of the tryouts arrived, and Jimmie broke down and allowed the girls to wear knee length shorts.

Jimmie drove them to the tryouts. She didn't tell Laken that she had picked a bouquet of the red camellias and put a pint of fresh water in the trunk of her car. She wanted Laken to be in top form during the tryouts.

When it came the girls' turn, they whooped and hollered with the best of them, but the cheerleader judges didn't pick them.

"Shoot, they picked the same ones that've been cheering," Shelby complained as they entered the car.

"Well, I guess playing a fiddle and banjo doesn't matter when it comes to cheerleading," Laken said.

Jimmie laughed, then stopped at the Big Store and bought them each a big cone of black walnut ice cream. Before they reached home, they put the bouquet of camellias on James' grave.

During their spare time, before school started, Shelby and Laken tried writing songs and picking out the tunes to them. They finally struck on one, titled 'Blue Alabama Girl.'

"You left me, saying you were going to see the world

Just an Alabama boy, saying you were gonna give things a twirl

But all you got were promises for jobs, and saw trashy girls

Remember, when all falls through, you can always come home to your blue Alabama girl."

Laken thought that Shelby really outdid herself on the banjo with that one.

School started for the year of 1959. The school didn't have air conditioning, and with all the body heat in the room, it was hot.

They didn't have air conditioning at home either, but at least they could go outside and find shade, or better yet, go to the creek.

The girls also discovered something new at school. Some of the boys began to flirt with them. The boys, like Caleb had been, were wearing Vitalis hair oil in their hair.

"Thank goodness, Caleb finally trained his hair, and we don't have to smell that Vitalis at home anymore," Laken laughed one day as they were coming home from school.

Their first performance at the radio station for the afternoon program was a success, and they'd put their money up, like Miss Anne asked.

They sang their version of, 'Blue Alabama Girl' to Miss Anne, and she loved it. Of course, they weren't allowed to sing it during their spiritual time on the air.

"You have something there; just keep writing songs. It's more than I can do. I'm strictly a mandolin picker," she had said.

At Caleb's ball games, they visited with their friends on the bleachers. Without realizing it, they mostly just sat with Hiram and Jimmie and cheered for Caleb from the bleachers.

Caleb was big for a quarterback. He was six feet, four inches tall, and weighed two hundred and ten pounds. If Caleb couldn't throw the ball, he ran it. Usually it would take two or three players from the opposite team to finally get him stopped. College scouts were looking at him. To Caleb, however, there was only one college he was interested in, and that was Alabama.

Coach Paul "Bear" Bryant had made a brief visit to one of Caleb's games, then talked to him and Hiram after the game. Coach Bryant explained the whole layout to them, and they were satisfied with it.

Hiram had a lot of respect for Coach Bryant. He had drafted a young fellow from Excel, and the young man was already doing miraculous things at the college.

Meanwhile, things carried on at the Beasley place as usual, until one early October morning.

Hiram was already outside feeding the calves, when Jimmie came out to milk the cow.

Belle had already made her way to the milking stable when she dropped dead.

Jimmie excitedly called for Hiram. Naturally, he dropped what he was doing and rushed to his wife.

He put his arm around Jimmie and said, "Go on back into the house; your milking days are over. It was fast, for she was mulling around in the pen when I came out. She was waiting for you to come out," Hiram told Jimmie, as he led her toward the back door.

"Reckon what killed her, Hiram?" the trembling Jimmie asked her husband.

"The same thing that's going to take us out, I pray: old age," Hiram told her.

"Well, I don't want to know what you're gonna do with her. We've had her since Shelby was a baby. She was different from those cows you sell; she was a member of the family," Jimmie said mournfully, as they wiped their feet and went into the house.

"I know, darling, but just think, your days of milking and churning are over. We can buy milk and butter now like everyone else," Hiram said, as they sat at the kitchen table and he poured them both a cup of coffee.

"Let's don't tell the children; let them find out for themselves," Jimmie said.

"Ok, darling, and I'll make you a promise, I'll give her a send-off like the queen she was," Hiram told her.

"I sure hope the chickens don't die. Do you know, that Caleb eats four fried eggs each morning, and four biscuits. It takes prodding to get the girls to eat just one," Jimmie said.

"He works it off," Hiram laughed.

After Jimmie had somewhat gotten over the shock about Belle, Hiram picked up a biscuit for Jim, then went back outside to his chores.

He thought he'd wait until the young folks were in school before he dealt with Belle's body. He'd finished with the hogs and was loading hay onto the back of the truck and wagon when he saw the three teenagers hurrying up the lane to catch the bus.

After Hiram had finished with the chores and making sure that Jimmie had turned the chickens out and fed them, he started with Belle.

The best way he could figure was to tie a rope around her head, and with the tractor, pull her to the deepest point on Persimmon Creek. It was on the corner of his land, as far away from the Pruitt place as possible. He then untied the dead cow and, with his tractor, pushed the body into the creek, with the help of a log.

"Well, so long, Belle; it's better than the buzzards getting you," he said, as the body of the old cow slowly and majestically made her way down the dark waters of the creek.

Of course, Jim followed Hiram and the tractor all the way to the creek, in an attempt to figure things out.

Another tragedy happened that weekend, one that would shake the very core of the family.

Both Excel and J.U. Blacksher high schools had won every game in the area. They were to tangle with each other that Saturday night to find out who the district champions would be. Both sides of the bleachers were filled to capacity, and Caleb was very anxious about the game.

It turned out to be a hard-fought game, with the scores going back and forth.

It was the last play of the game. Excel was behind by three points, and it was fourth down, but they had the ball in Blacksher's territory. The coach had decided against a field goal, as that would only tie the game.

The ball was hiked to Caleb. The linemen held them off for a few seconds. Caleb ran from side to side looking for someone in the infield to throw the ball to, but his men were covered.

There wasn't but one thing to do; he ran with the ball. He was tackled many times but eluded a takedown and continued on toward the goal line.

All of a sudden, someone tackled Caleb at his knees. He heard something crack, but the adrenalin kept him going until he reached the goal line, then he fell over.

The Blacksher players fell on top of him, in an attempt to take the ball away, but Caleb held tight.

He saw the referee raise his arms, signaling that Caleb had scored.

The other players slowly peeled off Caleb's back.

With all his strength, Caleb tried to stand up with the ball, but he couldn't manage to do it. All he could do was sit up.

Doctor Albert Boroughs was in the stands, and saw that something must be wrong, so he rushed down onto the field.

It took Dr. Boroughs only a glance, and he saw the trouble. Caleb's tibia bone was broken and was almost protruding through the skin.

"My God, son, you made that touchdown, running on a broken leg!" the doctor exclaimed.

An ambulance stayed on standby on all the games, so Dr. Boroughs motioned for it to come pick up Caleb.

By that time, Hiram had made his way to his son.

"Take him to Mobile Infirmary. We can't handle a break like that in Monroeville," Doctor Boroughs told the ambulance driver.

"Let me get your mama and the girls situated and I'll be on my way down there," Hiram told his son, doing his best to hide the tears that were trying to come to his eyes.

"This means I won't be going to Alabama," Caleb sighed to his daddy, then covered his eyes with his hands. He knew in his heart that his football career was over before it had really begun.

## Chapter 28

By the time 1962 rolled around, Callie had lived up to her promise to Paul. She now owned three 'Laken's:' the original one in Mobile, one on Dauphin Island, and one in Pascagoula, Mississippi. Her next goals were Biloxi, then New Orleans.

Paul was a big help to her with the legal work. He'd won a case concerning a shipping firm, so he now had money, and Callie was glad for him. The only change she saw in him, though, was that he bought a newer model car. He still wore the same two suits and ties.

They'd had their day of Callie playing the fiddle and Paul picking his guitar at Paul's home church, with both of them singing in harmony. They sang, 'I Saw the Light,' and 'House of Gold,' two Hank Williams songs.

They brought the whole congregation to its feet.

Charlotte and John weren't sitting at their usual spot in the church. They were sitting in the front pew, along with Paul and Callie. Callie could see the love and surprise in Charlotte's eyes as they did the "special."

At the end of the service, several people were led to the altar, including Charlotte.

Before they went out of the door, several people came up to them, telling them how much they enjoyed their performance. Both of them just responded with a thank you, not wanting them to think they were being proud.

They had a nice café in Pascagoula, and it was planned that they'd eat there instead of Charlotte having to cook. That's the day that Callie made up her mind for certain to open a 'Laken's,' in that city, for the restaurant was packed with people.

Over the years, Paul had noticed that Callie subscribed to the Monroe Journal, and at times some of the articles were cut out.

When asked about it, Callie told him that she had a friend from her school that worked there.

Telling Paul a lie tore at her heart, and she promised herself she'd never do it again.

*"Lord, what else could I have done?"* she asked herself that night when she was praying.

Not only had Callie's business grown, so had Paul's. He'd closed on quite a few big cases and was making a name for himself.

Now, several law firms were practically begging him to join them, but he continued on alone. He did hire a secretary, however; her name was Melissa. Melissa had studied to get her Juris Doctorate but had failed the bar exam twice. She was learning from Paul, though, and he told her when she passed the test to be a lawyer she could be his partner.

Callie liked Melissa. The woman was short, a little overweight, had two children and was married to a black man. Her husband was a foreman at the shipping docks in Mobile. His name was Sylvester Deas, and he was Paul's buddy. Callie thought their two children were the sweetest things. Their names were Sherry and Donald. Sherry was four and little Donald was two.

Callie and Paul found themselves visiting the couple at their home at least twice a week. They lived in a quaint little house. The house was on Heather Street, near Old Shell Road. Sylvester's mother lived with them and kept the children while they worked. Her name was Lilly. They went to a different church, though. It was a holiness church, while Callie and Paul continued going to the same Methodist church.

Of course, Callie saw to it that the whole family ate at 'Laken's' for free on Saturday nights.

Paul had been pressuring Callie to marry him for a year, but she kept putting him off, saying she was just too busy.

She did know something, though; she knew she had to make a move to the west. Luckily for her, the building she'd bought on Dauphin Island had a room in the rear that she could turn into a bedroom.

She hired a local woman, Sue Castillow, to cook and manage the 'Laken's' on Dauphin Island.

Cathy Jo, or C.J., decided to spread her wings and manage, plus cook at 'Laken's' in Pascagoula.

You'd think that good waitresses were a dime a dozen, but they weren't. Callie interviewed each and every employee. She understood that the waitresses were an important essential to her businesses. They were the ones that the customers saw.

Callie liked them with a high school education, slim, because they had to stay on their feet for several hours, and good to look at, with a sweet disposition. Above all, they had to have reliable transportation and a real desire to work.

Paul didn't like it, but he and Donald helped Callie make her move to Dauphin Island.

Since Callie's old room in Mobile was empty, Raymona's sister Judy chose to move into it. She said the rent would be cheaper than what she had been paying.

Callie didn't really want to move, but she knew in order to fulfill her quest she had to.

Paul found the shoebox of newspaper clippings, during the move. With Callie being at the new place on Dauphin Island, he took a short while to read the newspaper clippings. He found that almost all of them concerned a child by the name of Laken Jordan. He discovered that Callie had been following her for years.

"Aha!" he thought, "I'm going to check into this!"

In a way, he felt bad about it. *It's like I'm spying on her,"* he thought.

That night, Callie didn't know if it was the sound of the waves outside, or what it was, but after knowing Paul for five years, they made love in her new place on Dauphin Island.

All thoughts of Paul checking on Callie's past flew out of his mind.

Callie didn't know it, but it was Paul's first time.

Paul didn't know it, but it was the first time that Callie had enjoyed sex since James.

Afterwards, they sat on the side of the bed and caught their breath, then they did it again. That time took a little longer, but Paul had never felt so victorious, not even after passing the bar exam.

After a last passionate kiss, Paul asked again, "Now, when are you going to marry me?"

"Whenever you want, providing you don't interfere with my businesses; that's the main reason I've been holding off," Callie replied. They then kissed once more to seal the deal.

# Chapter 29

Also by 1962, Caleb's leg healed well, although he'd walk with a slight limp for the rest of his life.

He'd finished high school, and Shelby had been right about him from years back. Caleb decided he wouldn't go on to college; he decided instead to stay on the farm and help his daddy.

Hiram knew he needed to pay his son something, but he also knew he still had two girls to raise.

Willie Jordan continued to get money to Hiram some way. Willie had become frail and if he couldn't bring the money to Hiram, he'd see that someone would bring it over. Hiram never used the money to spend toward Laken's upbringing, though. Somehow, it just didn't feel right to him. Instead, he put the money inside a small metal toolbox and kept it locked with a small padlock. The money was hidden in the barn.

He thought about paying Caleb from the contents of the toolbox, but felt that wouldn't be right either, so he struck up a deal with his son. He allowed him to keep the books on the livestock from the farm. Caleb had to write down the expenditures of each animal on the place that they intended on selling. Upon the selling of the cattle or hogs, the expenditures were subtracted, and Caleb received a fourth of the profits. The cost of grain and peanuts, along with the cost of the propane gas that was used for drying, Caleb wasn't required to write down, as Hiram kept all the proceeds from the rents, grain, and nuts.

Caleb was satisfied with the deal, even though he worked even harder in the fields than he had during his school days.

Laken and Shelby were now seniors in high school, and were dating, but neither of them had found anyone special. In fact, when they'd get home after a date, they'd usually giggle and laugh at how silly the boys had acted.

Both of the girls could get in the kitchen and cook a meal, but their hearts weren't into it. Music was still their thing. Their hour on the radio station had continued. No one had to drive them anymore, as they had inherited Jimmie's '55 Ford.

Miss Anne had gotten them several paying jobs, most of which were local. Once, they had to go to Greenville, Alabama to perform for a new restaurant that was opening.

Miss Jimmie and Hiram were anxious about the girls driving such a distance. They assured them, however, that they'd be following Buddy and Angel on the way over there and back.

The girls, along with Miss Anne, now dressed as cowgirls. They didn't know how many outfits Miss Anne had, but the girls had three each, along with two pairs of cowgirl boots.

Buddy was a man of his own, and everyone knew it from his size and demeanor. He didn't care what Miss Anne said, he wore his usual, which was a pair of jeans, denim shirt, boots, and a wide brimmed hat.

Their route took them by the house that Hank Williams was raised in, and they were excited about seeing it.

They put on quite a show for the Greenville crowd that day, and Laken learned something.

She saw a few of the people clogging, or buck dancing, as they played. It looked simple enough, so she tried it while fiddling 'Cotton Eyed Joe,' and the crowd went wild. She never missed a beat, either. She learned that she could clog and fiddle at the same time, and she could turn in circles.

Both of the girls were blessed with beautiful hair and physical figures. When Laken turned her back to the crowd while dancing, people could see her long black shiny hair and also her shapely figure. When this happened, Shelby would put her banjo closer to the microphone, making it sound louder.

If there was a microphone involved, it usually stayed in front of them. The girls usually did most of the singing, with Buddy joining in on some of the tunes. With every performance, each instrument was given solo time with the microphone, even Buddy, who could pick the heart out of a bass fiddle.

As usual, they ended their performance with a spiritual song. This time they chose, 'Nearer My God to Thee.'

The manager of the newly opened restaurant, called 'Shoney's,' was elated at their show. He seemed happy to pay Miss Anne the hundred and twenty dollars, then invited them in for a free meal.

While they were eating, some young folks came by Laken and Shelby's table and made a lewd gesture at them. Buddy let it go the first time, but in a few minutes they returned and grabbed their crotches, then stopped in front of the girls' table.

Laken, Shelby and Anne soon found out what kind of a man Buddy was. He shot from his table, grabbed the two punks by the back of their necks, and dragged them to the front door. Pushing the double doors open with his foot, he flung them out onto the pavement.

From that day on, the three realized they didn't have anything to worry about, as long as Buddy was with them.

Buddy seemed to just have taken the incident in stride, for he calmly sat back down with his wife Angel and resumed his meal.

The manager of the place waited until he saw they were finished eating, then came over to Miss Anne's table.

"You know, after seeing the crowd's reaction, and your show, I've come to a conclusion. We're opening these things everywhere in the South. The next one will be in Montgomery, right off Highway 31 as you near the town."

He quickly drew a map of the location on a napkin. "I'd sure love it if y'all could come. I'll have y'all a covered stage and everything there," he said.

Miss Anne didn't waste any time.

"Boy, that's a long way from home, but we can do it for three hundred dollars, and eight free meals," She told him.

Without hesitating, he agreed to the deal, then when he walked by Buddy's table, he slipped a ten-dollar bill into his hand. "Good going," he simply said.

When they were outside, Miss Anne divided the money, then said, "I told you we'd get to Montgomery, and Montgomery we're going!"

"Woo-Hoo!" Buddy shouted.

"You heard what he said, they're building the things all over the south, shoot, no telling where all we'll go. I don't know about y'all, but I thought they served some good food," Anne remarked.

"They sure do," said Shelby.

Anne then told the girls the extra meals she'd bargained for were for their parents and brother, Caleb. She added, "The farther we travel, the more I'm going to bargain for."

"That's what I'm talking about," Buddy said, rubbing his hands together.

Anne looked at Shelby and said, "By the way, I've been meaning to ask you…what's your middle name?"

Shelby replied, "Rae."

"The reason I asked is, I have a daughter, and her name is Shelby Jean. She has the same appearance as Laken, though, with that mane of gorgeous black hair, and the dark eyes," Miss Anne said.

Her parting words were, "I loved the clogging you did, Laken, and the crowd did, too. Brush up on it, and let's have a safe trip home. Remember, next week, we'll need to leave Excel by eleven o'clock."

Miss Anne didn't waste time driving, so as before, Laken followed Buddy's truck home. The girls had made a deal: Shelby would drive on the way to their performances, and Laken would drive on the way back.

They did a lot of talking, as well as joking, on their way back home. They didn't hold back their feelings from each other. Shelby was turning out to be like her mama, mild mannered and understanding. Laken thought she herself must be more like her daddy, well mannered, yet when it came to decisions, she was the one who made them between her and Shelby.

They'd told each other things that, if Miss Jimmie knew about their thoughts, she'd have a hissy fit.

They were near Evergreen when Laken revealed a secret to Shelby.

"You know, with all the boys we've been exposed to, they all pale in comparison to Caleb. I mean, to me as of right now, he's the one. He's a hard worker, good-looking, caring, gentle, yet strong as an ox," Laken said.

"Yuck!" Shelby uttered. "All he wants to be is a farmer. You'll be slaving away like Mama all your life," she warned.

"You can take my word for it, there's worse," Laken replied. "There must be something lacking in me, though; I just don't know how to let him know my feelings."

"Dumb girl, that's because you have been raised like he's your brother," Shelby replied.

"Yeah, I reckon so. It's not like I'm going to go home and jump his bones or anything. Shoot, if he tried anything on me, I'd slap the fire out of him," Laken said, and they both laughed.

"Well, I've dated quite a few, but unlike you, that special one hasn't come along yet. All I've been concerned with is music, and getting away from here," Shelby said.

"Oh, me too, that goes without saying," Laken agreed. "I guess I was just looking too far into the future."

"Well, one thing's for sure, you need not worry about anyone else getting him, for he's not leaving Mama and Daddy," Shelby told her.

"Well, we have the radio station to do tomorrow. I'm sure glad we can just wear our pedal pushers and a blouse. This western outfit is H.O.T. hot. I know I'm changing the subject, but I'm going to see if I can persuade Caleb to take my boots to the boot place. Maybe he can get them to put taps on the souls. I might as well be making a sound when I'm clogging," Laken said.

"Where did you learn how to do that?" Shelby asked.

"It must have been from my mama; I can vaguely remember her doing it," Laken answered

They finally made it to their driveway, where they saw a hearse leaving from her Grandpa Jordan's place.

"Oh no! If I didn't have this cowgirl outfit on, I'd ride over there," Laken said.

"Hmph, and Miss Victoria would cuss you out, too," Shelby replied, so Laken made a left turn into the Beasley driveway.

The two girls were worn out from the performance, and the drive home.

Caleb and Miss Jimmie were on the front porch, so Caleb walked to their car, then after a brief hug, he got their instruments from the back seat. "Mama's got news for y'all," he said.

They made it to the porch, when Miss Jimmie told them that Miss Victoria had died. She then hugged Laken's neck and told her she was sorry.

"My goodness, what happened?" Laken asked, as she took a seat in the nearest rocking chair.

"We don't know yet, but Mr. Willie called over here and told me. I went out to the barn and got Hiram. He's over there with Mr. Willie now," Jimmie answered.

Jimmie got around to asking them how the singing went.

"Fine, we had a good time, too," Shelby said, as she pulled the money out of her cowgirl vest and flashed it at her mama.

"And guess what, Mama?" Shelby asked.

"What's that, child?" Jimmie asked.

"We have an engagement in Montgomery next Saturday at the same time. It's at a nice restaurant, Mama, and Miss Anne made a deal that you, daddy and Caleb get to eat free!"

"Oh my, y'all must've really put on a show over there," Miss Jimmie said.

"Not bragging, but we did. Laken even did a little dance on two of the songs."

"My goodness, Laken, you must've really gotten into it," Miss Jimmie laughed.

Caleb had overheard the conversation about Montgomery.

"So, we'll be going to Montgomery next Saturday?" he asked.

"If all goes as planned, we'll be making over three times the amount we made today," Laken said.

"I hope you haven't got a big supper cooking; we ate up there. We both had fried catfish and finished it off with sirloin steak. Of course, there were vegetables, and desserts," Shelby told her mama.

"Well, if y'all change your mind," Jimmie answered.

After about ten minutes, the girls got tired of waiting, so they went into their bedroom to change clothes.

Shelby and Laken had time to take a cool bath each and change into comfortable clothes, before they heard Hiram's voice in the kitchen.

"Well, let's go in there and get the news," Shelby said.

"Laken, I'm sorry. I shouldn't have said what I did about Miss Victoria. After all, she was your grandmother," Shelby told her.

"Ha, some grandmother. I'm seventeen years old, and she never even made one attempt to see me, so there's no hard feelings here," Laken said, then hugged Shelby's neck.

Everyone was at the kitchen table, eating. The table arrangement had always been that Shelby and Laken sat on one side with Caleb on the other, then Miss Jimmie and Mr. Hiram sat on each end.

Even though the girls weren't eating, they took their usual places at the table.

"So, I heard Grandma has gone to meet her reward," Laken said to Hiram.

"Yes, Darling, she's no longer in this world," Hiram answered.

"What in the world happened?" asked Laken.

"Mr. Willie said the servant had just brought her a cup of coffee, and she slumped over before she had time to take a sip. I'd say it must've been a heart attack," Hiram said.

"Is my grandpa there by himself?" Laken asked.

"Not a soul but him, the cook, and a servant," Hiram said, then added, "Mr. Willie must've loved that woman, for he's mighty torn up about it. Said they had been married for forty-four years."

"I must go to him," Laken said, as she pushed back her chair.

She asked Shelby if she wanted to go, but she answered, no.

"I'll go with you," Caleb said, as he swallowed the last drop of tea from his glass.

Laken didn't know who initiated it, but Caleb and she were holding hands when she rang the doorbell at the Jordan place.

Surprisingly, the lady that answered the door was a middle-aged white lady, wearing a light blue starched uniform.

They walked down a wide, cool hall, with portraits and paintings hanging on both walls.

"This is the sitting room; he's in there," the lady said, as she opened one of the double doors.

Laken found her grandpa sitting in an overstuffed cushioned velvet chair, and it looked like he had a big wad of tobacco in his mouth. Her eyes caught the cuspidor sitting on the floor in front of him.

"Grandpa!" Laken said and ran toward him, after Caleb turned her hand loose.

Laken ran to him and hugged his neck. She could feel the stubble of beard on his face and knew he hadn't shaved that morning.

"Thank you for the hug; it means so much to me. You and Caleb have a seat somewhere, Lord knows there's enough of them in here," he said.

"Grandpa, I'm sorry about Grandma, for your sake," was all that Laken could think to say.

"Well, she'll be missed—maybe not by too many folks around here, but *I'll* miss her. She kept my butt straight for forty-four years. We didn't have much when we married, but she had a knack about her; she knew how to make money. I can give her that. It all started during the Depression: when someone was losing their land, we'd buy it at half price. Somehow, she knew what to invest in and when. Shucks, I was just a poor farm boy when I married her.

"You know, when James died, she seemed to have lost her zest for acquiring things, so we've just been living on the interest of what we've invested," he said, as he seemed to have wound down.

"Is there anything I can do, Grandpa?" Laken asked.

The old man didn't answer her question, yet he started talking again.

"I'm sorry for the way she treated you over the years, my Lord, she would give me hell if she even found out I visited you. I never understood that. You're going to find that

179

things will be different around here. I want you to consider this place as yours, and you can visit any time you want."

"Thank you, I'd like that," Laken replied.

"As far as your question, yes, there is something you can do. Let's give her a real sendoff, by you singing at her funeral," he replied.

"I'd be honored," Laken told him.

"Thank you, and if you don't mind, ask Jimmie if she'll go to the funeral home with me tomorrow. Shoot, I don't know anything about such things," her grandpa said.

"I feel sure she'd be glad to," Laken replied.

"Yessir, things are going to change around here. She'd throw a fit if she knew I was sitting in her chair, and chewing my tobacco," he said, as he spat into the spittoon.

"Okay, I see that you have help, so I'm going home, but if you need anything, we're just a phone call away," Laken said.

She hugged him again, and they left the old fellow to his thoughts.

Laken grabbed Caleb's hand again as they made their way down the long brick steps outside.

*"It's a start,"* she thought, for they held hands until she opened the door to the car.

# Chapter 30

Callie and Paul married on New Year's Day, 1963, in Paul's family church in Pascagoula, Mississippi. She was thirty-six, and Paul was a year older; he was thirty-seven.

Callie never knew that life had so much happiness. It felt as though she was living in a fairytale, at times.

They continued to live at 'Laken's' on Dauphin Island.

Callie had never noticed it before their marriage, but Paul had quite the build on him. He reminded her so much of James! The black hair on his chest seemed to form the letter T as it ran from his chest to his navel. Like James, Paul was very bright, and not just in things concerning the law, but everyday things.

For the first time in her life, she didn't feel so alone. Callie loved the nights they'd just lie in bed, and with the radio turned down low, they'd just laugh and talk.

They continued their friendship with Sylvester and Melissa but didn't get to visit as often.

Paul's business continued to flourish, as did Callie's. They kept their two businesses separate, though. She didn't ask him to, but Paul paid for the utilities at Dauphin Island.

No matter how busy they were, they continued going to church on Sundays, and that was the day that bothered Callie's conscience most. Oh! How she wished she could just come clean and reveal her past to Paul, but she held off.

She grew to really respect and revere Paul's parents. She always tried to pop in for a visit when she was in Pascagoula. The best thing was that C.J. kept the restaurant running top notch. Callie absolutely loved Sue Castillow, and her daughter, Gena, who Callie soon nicknamed "Pretty Gena."

Sue and her daughter lived right down the street from the restaurant, so it wasn't a problem for Sue to get to work. As it turned out, she had worked in many restaurants, but never managed one. She appreciated Callie giving her the confidence and worked double hard to make 'Laken's' a success.

It so happened that most afternoons, Callie would have made her rounds to the other businesses and would get back to Dauphin Island about the time the school bus ran. That's how she became so close to Pretty Gena. As it turned out, the girl was a whiz in school. She'd finish her homework and over to 'Laken's' she'd come, for Krispy Kreme doughnuts.

After she'd eaten, Sue would put her to work cleaning tables or something.

Callie kept the two banks that she had always had, one for checking, to pay the bills, and the other for her savings account.

Sometime in April, she thought she had enough money in the savings account to open another restaurant. She was sticking to her original plan of expanding west to Biloxi, then on to New Orleans. She'd never been there but had heard many good things about the place.

She told Paul her plans about Biloxi, and she figured that he'd be upset about it, but he seemed all right with the idea. He even asked her if she'd mind if Sylvester and his family came along.

Callie was going to look for a place to start a place of business. She didn't understand why he wanted them to come, until his next statement.

"Biloxi is noted for its beautiful beaches. I just feel like it would give Melissa a break from work. We've really been at it here lately. I'd be willing to bet she's lost ten pounds, hurrying from my office to the courthouse. Another thing is, I've never seen you in a bathing suit. Get a red one and make it a two piece. I want you to show everyone how lucky I am. Heck, we'll make a night of it, and come back Sunday afternoon," he suggested.

"Well, I suppose I could look around for a suitable place on Sunday; there's bound to be "For Sale" signs in front of the buildings," Callie told him.

The next day was the day she would go to Pascagoula to collect the money. She collected on Monday, Wednesday, and Friday.

On her trip to Pascagoula the next day, she came to a decision. She'd decided to open a checking account at "First National Bank of Pascagoula." That way it wouldn't be necessary for her to come to the town three times a week.

Callie went by the old adage her Pap had told her, "When it comes to land or money, don't trust anybody." She trusted all her managers, yet she kept a tight ship. Callie wanted in print the expenditures of each place, the inventory, and the cash register tally for each day.

She kept her employees to a minimum.

More money was spent at the restaurant in Pascagoula, but it had a bigger business. There were three waitresses for the place, and two cooks, plus C.J. helping at places that were needed the most.

Callie just left signed blank checks at the place, and C.J. paid off the help on Fridays, as Callie did at the other places.

After arriving at 'Laken's' in Pascagoula, C.J. had all the records in order for her.

Callie asked C.J. if she had time to go to the bank with her. She then told her what she was planning to do. Callie continued, "Will you go with me somewhere to buy a bathing suit?"

"Well, if you hurry," C.J. answered.

First, Callie opened a checking account at the bank, introducing Cathy Jo to the manager, telling him that C.J. would be making the deposits from now on.

Next, they drove across the street to Gayfers, where C.J. picked out a pretty red two-piece bathing suit, a pair of sandals, a wide brimmed straw hat, and some sun shades. The last item C.J. got was some suntan lotion. "You be sure to rub this on your shoulders, face, and legs," she told Callie.

"My goodness, I'll be greasy as a hog," Callie protested.

"It's better than getting sun blisters all over you," C.J. said.

Callie wasn't too sure about the sizes, but she bought Pretty Gena a one-piece red bathing suit and a pair of sandals that looked similar to hers.

While she was in Pascagoula, Callie told C.J. that her real reason for going to Biloxi was to see about opening another 'Laken's.'

"Oh my goodness, just think, I knew you when! Please let me manage it for you, when and if it takes place," C.J. pleaded.

"Who's gonna run this one?" Callie asked.

"Loretta can. She's smart, quick on her feet and easy to learn. Last, but not least, she's honest as the day is long," C.J. said.

Callie told her what a wonderful job she was doing in Pascagoula. "Shoot, you make a lot more money than the other two," Callie told her.

"Do I?" C.J. acted surprised.

"You sure do," Callie answered.

"Well, I'd work my head off to see Biloxi does even better," C.J. pleaded again.

"Why are you so eager to go to Biloxi?" Callie asked.

"Several reasons. Pascagoula is centered around the shipyard. Biloxi is more of a tourist place, with its white beaches and tourist attractions. Too, my favorite boyfriend works there," C.J. answered.

"Favorite boyfriend?" Callie asked, surprised.

"Well, believe it or not, I'm not married to 'Laken's,' I do have a social life, you know," C.J. said.

"Lord, girl, when do you find the time?" Callie laughed as she hugged her friend.

At the end of their conversation, Callie agreed that she'd give C.J. a shot at it. She reminded her, however, that she expected Loretta to be fully trained when she'd take over the reins of the other location.

"I'll make sure of it," C.J. answered, excitedly.

Callie didn't take the time to go by Paul's parents; instead, she went straight back to Dauphin Island. She wanted to spend a little time with Pretty Gena.

Gena was right where Callie expected her, at the restaurant, eating doughnuts and sucking on a Coke. At seven years old, she was indeed a pretty little thing, with long blonde hair, and big brown eyes.

Callie hauled the things from her car, then went to her room with them.

It wasn't unusual to see people walking around on the island clad only in their bathing suits.

Callie walked to the door that led to the dining area and asked Pretty Gena if she come there for a second.

Of course, the girl hurried herself to Callie.

"Try these on for size," Callie said.

Gena looked into the bag, and said, "Boy, I sure hope everything fits," then she headed to the bathroom with the bag in her hands.

"If you need help, call me," Callie told her.

It didn't take but a jiffy before Gena came back into the room.

"Perfect fit," she said.

"Turn around, let me see," Callie instructed.

After Gena did so, Callie said, "Well, I'll be darned! I did a pretty good guess. "Now, go show your Mama."

Gena went running toward the kitchen, with her sandals clopping with every step.

Callie felt good, knowing that she had made a little girl happy.

*"It sure wasn't this way back home, we had the bare minimum,"* she thought, as she laid back in the bed for a few minutes, just to rest her back.

When she wasn't busy, her mind always wandered to Laken. She hadn't thought at the time she got married that she wouldn't be able to steal away and go for a visit back home, and maybe just get a glimpse of Laken.

She'd seen the occasional pictures of Laken in the newspaper and knew that she'd grown to be a beautiful young lady.

*"Oh, if only I could hug her and tell her how sorry I am!"* Callie thought. Callie also wondered if Laken ever thought about her.

Besides the occasional pictures, she saw that Laken remained on the honor roll every single year from first grade, and it was hard to believe that Laken would graduate that year.

*"Oh well, enough of this. I've got to tally these cash register tickets,"* Callie thought, as she sat up in the bed.

She had become a whiz with the adding machine that she kept on a little table in their bedroom. It didn't took her only about thirty minutes and she was through. As usual, everything checked out A-Ok.

She then gathered up Pretty Gena's clothes that she had been wearing and put them into the bag that Callie had brought the new ones in. She then went into the restaurant to see if Sue had things under control.

That night, after the restaurant was closed, Paul and Callie were alone in their bedroom, when Callie showed Paul her new bathing suit.

Paul gave her a wolf whistle and asked her to model it for him.

"You sex fiend, I'll model it for you tomorrow. You'll see plenty of it at the beach," Callie said.

"Chicken, squawk, squawk, squawk," Paul said, making fun of her.

"Squawk, squawk, yourself," Callie said, as she began to remove her clothes.

Paul lay in bed laughing at her, as she kept attempting to poke her boobs into the top part of the bikini.

"That C.J.! She did this on purpose," Callie complained.

"Well, the bottom fits good, so face it, you have big boobs," Paul laughed.

"Laugh if you want to, but I have an idea," Callie said, as she plundered through the closet until she found what she was looking for. She sat down on the edge of the bed, topless, with scissors, needle and thread, with the piece of white lacy material.

Seeing his wife exposing herself, clad in only the bottom part of the bikini, was too much for Paul. He raked everything off the bed, then grabbed Callie by the shoulders and pulled her toward him.

After making passionate love for thirty minutes, Paul went to the bathroom, while Callie complained about having to change the sheets on the bed.

Paul decided to take a shower and shave while he was in the bathroom. When he came out, he saw that Callie was sewing the piece of material between the cups of the bikini top.

Paul slipped on a pair of clean boxers and eased into the bed, not wanting Callie to stick herself with the needle.

In a short while, Callie strapped the top on again.

"There," she said, "You can't see anything but just the crease at the top," she then modeled it again for Paul.

"Hmm, you'll still knock 'em dead," Paul said.

While Paul lay in bed, looking through the paper, Callie went into the bathroom for a quick shower.

The next day was heavenly. Sylvester and Melissa had left the children at home with Lily. They had driven to Dauphin Island from Mobile. They decided to go in two vehicles, as Melissa said their car was loaded with beach paraphernalia.

"All you need to bring is your beach towels," she told Callie.

Both Callie and Melissa were dressed about the same. They were both wearing different colored pedal pushers, and loose blouses. Paul and Sylvester were dressed in Bermuda shorts and T-shirts. Unlike the girls, they wore loafers instead of sandals.

They weren't aware of it, but Paul had been loading the trunk of Callie's car all morning. "Jesus, you'd think we were going to the moon," he said, as he put the last suitcase into the trunk.

"Well, we're doing other things besides just going to the beach," Callie told him.

Paul had checked the weather forecast in the paper the night before and saw that the weather was going to be beautiful.

Callie almost sat under Paul on the trip to Biloxi, she was snuggled up so close to him. They were both wearing their shades and listened to "Rock and Roll" music the entire trip. The Beatles had invaded American music, so they listened to several of their songs, and The Beach Boys.

Callie had never been further than Pascagoula, so from there on was an adventure. The towns followed Highway 90, which was along the coast. She paid close attention, in case she'd be making the trip alone in the future.

There were several bridges, for there was a lot of marsh land. As they were going over a long bridge, Paul said, "Look, Baby, at the fishing boats; that's the Gulf of Mexico you're looking at."

"Shoot, we have the Gulf of Mexico back on the island," Callie said.

Every now and then she would look behind them and saw that Sylvester and Melissa were still hanging in.

After going over a long, curved bridge, Callie saw a sign that read, "Welcome to Biloxi."

Just the sight of the place was breathtaking. On the left of the road were occasional eating places for quick foods, and the most beautiful beaches Callie had ever seen. To the right were hotels, occasional old homes, and more eating places. She noticed that most of the places were geared toward young people.

"A 'Laken's' would go good here," Callie said, as she pointed to a long brick and lumber building on the right. "It has a for sale sign out front, too," Callie said.

"It has a number on the sign. You can call them tomorrow; today and tonight is all about having a good time," Paul said, as he hugged Callie closer to him.

The first place to find was a hotel, so they pulled into the parking lot of a beautiful building that had an ornate water fountain on the outside.

Sylvester and Melissa pulled in beside them.

"You guys probably haven't thought of this, but due to Sylvester's color, we're not welcome in many of these places," Melissa said.

"You're kidding!" Callie responded.

"No, Sylvester checked, and the hotel that we can stay in is up the road a bit, so y'all follow us," Melissa said.

They passed Jefferson Davis' house, and Paul pointed it out to Callie.

"Well, it seems that ol' Jeff's rules are still hanging tight," she said.

They finally pulled into 'The Blue Knight' parking lot. There was a sign outside that read, "We welcome all people."

"Not bad," Paul said, as he looked across the road. "They still have a beach here," he added.

First, they checked into the three-story hotel, then went back to their vehicles for their clothes. Their rooms adjoined each other, so they agreed to meet in the lobby in half an hour.

By eleven o'clock they'd all eaten a good breakfast and were lying on the beach.

Melissa had brought a homemade quilt which Lily had made, that she and Sylvester sat on. The two of them seemed to be having a good time, sitting under a huge, red, white and blue umbrella. They brought a transistor radio and were listening to the music and just relaxing, while watching people play in the salt water.

It had been a long time since Callie had been swimming, so both she and Paul were enjoying the salt water, and the waves.

Paul had no idea that Callie was such a good swimmer. There were some rocks about a hundred yards from the beach. At one point, Paul saw his wife swimming toward the rocks, and worried that she wouldn't be able to make it to the rocks and swim back. He knew that oysters attached themselves to the rocks and the outside of their shells were very sharp if you touched them with your bare skin.

She must have found that out on her own, since before he could make it to her, she was on her way back toward the beach. Right before she reached Paul, she dove under the water and pulled his trunks down to his knees.

He exposed his buttocks briefly as he attempted to swim with one hand and pull his trunks back up with the other. He looked around and saw that Callie had swum close enough to the beach to stand up.

"Do you need any help?" she cupped her hands and shouted.

Paul didn't say anything, but just kept swimming toward the beach.

Callie knew him and guessed that he was up to some trickery, so she half swam, and half ran, back toward the beach.

"Boy, what a lily white behind!" Melissa exclaimed, as Callie reached her and Paul's beach towels and umbrella that were beside Sylvester and Melissa's.

"Hey, say something to him when he gets here," Callie whispered, as she sat down on her beach towel and reached for the sunscreen.

"Darn, girl, I had no idea you were such a mermaid," Paul said, as he reached them. Of course, Callie had never told him that she'd learned to swim in Persimmon creek, as a toddler.

"Good gracious, Boss, I've never seen a pair of hams so lily white," Melissa said.

Paul wasn't going to allow her to get the best of him, so he pulled his trunks down far enough to just reveal the crack of his behind.

They all laughed at that, including Paul.

There was a pier near them and at the end was a very high diving board.

"Come on, Paul and let's show these girls what kind of men they married," Sylvester said, as he got up from the quilt.

Paul had no idea what he was planning, until they stepped onto the pier.

*"Oh Lord,"* Paul thought to himself, but realized it was too late to back out now.

Callie guessed what they were up to, so she ran to the pier. *"Shoot, I've dived out of trees that were higher than that,"* she thought.

Melissa watched with her hands over her eyes, as Sylvester, Paul, then Callie climbed the long ladder that led to the diving board. Both men were unaware that Callie was following them until they reached the diving board.

"Why, you little stinker, you never cease to amaze me. I don't know about you, but I'm scared to death," Paul said.

"Are you, baby? Well, don't do it," Callie told him.

"I can't let him show me up," Paul said, as Sylvester sprang up and down at the end of the diving board and dove toward the water.

"Just do a cannonball. You won't go as deep, and you'll be swimming toward the beach in just a jiffy. Besides, I'll be right behind you," Callie said.

When Sylvester was clear of the area below, Paul sprang off the diving board in a cannonball, and made a big splash.

Both Paul and Sylvester were swimming on their backs so they could see Callie making a spectacle of herself.

After seeing that Paul was all right, she walked to the end of the diving board, and after springing up and down, she jumped, making a perfect swan dive.

Paul waited anxiously until he saw his wife clear the water, and wave at them.

"My Lord, I've married another Johnny Weissmuller," Paul said.

"You can say that again. Hell, Melissa won't get in the water past her knees," Sylvester said, as he waved back at Callie.

After the exhilaration of the diving, they all persuaded Melissa to get into the water and they tossed a volleyball around to each other.

By three o'clock, they all decided it was time to go back inside and just relax before supper.

The first thing that Callie and Paul did was take a shower together. They must have stayed under the cool water for thirty minutes. They might have been a little sunburned, but it didn't stop them from making love. Afterwards, they showed each other their suntans.

Dining out that night was just as marvelous as the day at the beach.

They all rode in Sylvester's car. They went to another place that had a sign outside that read, "We serve everyone."

They ate while they listened to a string orchestra. Callie wasn't sure of some of the things she ate, but it was all good. Paul insisted on paying the tab, and Callie was astounded at the price.

That was one thing they didn't do. Callie never asked Paul about his finances, and he didn't ask about hers.

After eating, they moved into the dance room, paying five dollars a couple. The orchestra played mostly old swing hits. They even had a gorgeous blonde that stood in front of the orchestra and sang.

Of course, she had to be paid, too. There was a dainty little basket with ribbons that read, "Tip the singer here."

The two couples danced until ten o'clock.

"Boy, have I had a great time today," Callie said, as they drove back to the hotel. She then asked Paul if he had a license to practice in Mississippi.

"Sure, I do, but most of my clients live in the Mobile area," he answered.

Both Sylvester and Melissa laughed at Callie's words, knowing she was already thinking about business again.

The next day, on the way out of town, Callie wrote down the realtor's number that had the building for sale. The sooner she called the number, the closer her latest 'Laken's' would be to becoming a reality.

# Chapter 31

Only a handful of people had shown up for Miss Victoria's funeral, and they were from the church that she and Willie attended.

Laken played the violin and sang 'Precious Memories,' and 'I'll Fly Away.'

It was a graveside funeral, and Mr. Willie was the only one there that seemed to have expressed a feeling, one way or the other.

On the way back home, Miss Jimmie told Hiram that she knew Mr. Willie had a cook, but she was still going to cook at least a pound cake and take it over to him.

Laken and Shelby continued going to grand openings and such, and they were building their money to quite a sum. They had plenty of costumes to wear on such occasions, so the money continued to build. Miss Anne went over and above to see that they had an engagement nearly every weekend.

Mr. Hiram told the girls he knew that Miss Anne didn't need the money. "I believe that she does it to just have something to do," he said.

The last few engagements, Miss Anne's son Brad had accompanied them.

Brad was a couple of years older than Laken and Shelby. He still lived at home and had his own mechanic shop in Miss Anne's backyard. He also did a little gardening with a small tractor.

Shelby thought he was a dreamboat. He was tall, muscular, and spoke only when he was spoken to.

Brad mostly went with them when they had to drive quite a distance. He led the way by driving Miss Anne's car, and doing odd jobs, once they arrived at the sites.

It was April, and they'd be graduating the next month. The Prom was that month as well, and the girls had plenty of boys ask them to the Prom, but they kept turning them down.

Shelby finally told Miss Anne's son, Brad, that she'd be pleased if he'd go with her to the Prom. When he responded that he'd be pleased, too, Shelby was excited and the word, elated, wasn't big enough.

Laken held off, though, waiting for that certain one to ask her. She couldn't quite understand her feelings toward Caleb. One moment he felt like her brother, but the next she saw him as her beau.

Caleb certainly didn't help her feelings, either, for he continued treating her as his sister.

She had dared Shelby to say a word to him about the strange feelings she had for him, because, really, she didn't know herself. She knew that on the few dates she'd had, all of them failed in comparison to Caleb.

Laken believed that Miss Jimmie had something to do with Caleb telling her, "The boys around here must be crazy. Would you allow me to take you to the Prom?"

Laken squeezed his work-roughened hands, and where she got the nerve, she never knew, but she said, "I thought you'd never ask me."

"Why, you little rascal," he responded. He then said, "For that, you get this for punishment." He then leaned over and gave her a passionate kiss, while embracing her tightly.

It was better than she had ever imagined, but she couldn't dare let him know her feelings, so she slapped him on his back and pushed away from him.

"I said you could escort me to the Prom, and that's all," she told him.

They were alone in the den when the event took place.

"Shhh, Mama will hear you," Caleb whispered, with his hot breath in her ear. Again, Laken could almost feel her knees buckle, and she felt ashamed of herself, and sat down on the couch, quickly.

The first thing that ran through her mind was, *"I wonder if Mama felt like this?"*

She snapped back to the present when she heard Caleb go out of the front door.

Quickly, regaining her strength, she ran to the door and asked him, "Well, are you still going to take me?"

Caleb never turned around, he just kept walking toward the barn, but he did say, "Yeah, yeah, I'll take you."

Trying her best to not act excited, Laken casually walked into the kitchen and told Miss Jimmie and Shelby that Caleb would be taking her to the Prom.

"Oh, I'm so glad, dear," Miss Jimmie said.

Shelby just looked at her and smiled.

You could rent all manner of things from Katz Department Store in Monroeville. Taking it for granted they'd be going to the Prom, the girls already had their dresses hanging in the closet. They had rented them for a week, making sure they could get the dress they wanted.

Both dresses looked similar, only Shelby's was red, while Laken's was pale blue.

Both girls' gowns required strapless bras. They also were lucky enough to be blessed with bigger than the average breasts, and the gowns really accented that part of their body. They both knew they'd have to really keep the tops of their gowns pulled up until they got away from the watchful eyes of Miss Jimmie. Too, each gown came with a lacy shawl, so they'd wrap it around their shoulders until they reached the Prom.

"We'd better be careful when we bend over, or do that 'Jerk' dance," Shelby laughed after trying on the dresses for the first time.

As they waited for the Prom that was still two days away, Hiram decided to put a new tin top on the old log cabin.

As usual, Jimmie didn't ask where the money was coming from. In reality, Hiram knew he had more than enough money to do the job. Both he and Caleb had finished laying the crops by, so they had the time.

After finding out about the new top going onto the house, Laken asked if she could go inside.

"Sure you can, I'll pull the nails out of the front door tomorrow," Hiram said.

The girls waited until dinner the next day, while Caleb and Mr. Hiram were eating dinner. They finished first, so over to the log cabin they went. Of course, Jim followed them, but he was getting old and didn't run ahead of them as he had in the past.

Luckily, Mr. Hiram had pulled the lock and nails out of the door, so the girls just walked inside.

"It's just as I remembered things," Laken said, as she looked around in the dusty room.

She made a beeline to the hearth of the fireplace. She picked up the loose rock and looked underneath.

"It's just as I expected, it's empty, which means she's out there somewhere," Laken whispered to Shelby.

"Wonder why she never bothered to come after you?" Shelby asked.

"Hmph, she was more concerned about herself. Too, she had to be the one that whacked Calvin on the head with the sling blade. Thank God, I'd left by then. She couldn't go over to y'all's house to get me, for it would be known that she was alive, so she left with what money she had," Laken said.

"I can tell you one thing, I was a pleased little girl to have a sister, and it's stayed that way," Shelby told Laken.

"The feeling is mutual. I thank God every night that she didn't come after me. I believe I would have run out the back door if she had. I was tired of her kind of life," Laken said.

The girls continued to look around.

"You know, if we'd clean this place up it would make a good little getaway," Shelby said.

"Yeah, if you like living without electricity and running water. I do have to admit that, for a while, I missed the sound of Persimmon Creek when I'd go to bed at night. That was what lulled me to sleep," Laken admitted.

"Who are the people in the pictures?" Shelby asked, as she pointed to three pictures that rested on a shelf.

"That's Mama on the left, then her mama and daddy to the right," Laken answered. She gently brushed the dust away from her mama's picture with a shirt she'd picked up from the floor.

"Boy, she was a looker," Shelby said, as Laken placed the picture of her mama back on the shelf.

"Yeah, she was," Laken said, never bothering to tell Shelby about the crooked nose that her mama had, because Calvin had broken it.

"The infamous chifforobe, I want to see it," Shelby requested.

Laken opened the door to her old bedroom, and they walked in.

"There it is," Laken pointed to the tall piece of furniture, and they both walked over to it. The key was still sticking out of the mirrored door, so Laken turned the key, and they looked in.

"Wow, look at all the old clothes!" Shelby exclaimed.

"Yeah, that's what I'd hide behind," replied Laken. "That hatbox—I always wanted to see what was in there, but I was too short to reach it."

She used the same small key to unlock the hatbox. Inside, they found some old purses and an 8x10 framed picture of Callie and James.

"Wow, I've never seen this," Laken said. "Now, this one, I'm taking with me."

"Why not the others?" asked Shelby.

"They remind me of a terrible time in my life; I'd see them every day. But this one, I've never seen before," Laken replied.

"Just looking at the backdrop, I'd say the picture was taken at a carnival," Shelby said. "What about the chifforobe—are you still going to destroy it?"

"No, at least not today. Mr. Hiram and Caleb will probably be back shortly," Laken answered. She then walked over to an old oak dresser, that had wheels on all four legs. "Come help me," she said as she began tugging on the heavy dresser.

"Caleb will absolutely love to have these if the sheriff didn't find them," she said, as the two of them pulled the squeaking dresser away from the wall.

Sure enough, just as her grandfather had left them, were an old cavalry sword, and a muzzle loader.

"Look! Each corner of the woolen blanket is stamped CSA," Shelby remarked. She then continued, "You're right about that, ol' Caleb will love to get his hands on these."

On the sword was stamped, "3rd Alabama Cavalry."

They rewrapped the gun and sword in the same blanket, then headed back toward the house, making sure the cabin was secure.

Luckily for them, Caleb and Mr. Hiram were just gearing up to return to the log cabin by the time Laken and Shelby returned to the house. No one noticed them as they sneaked into the house with their treasures.

All Miss Jimmie saw was the old, rolled-up blanket. The girls went directly to Caleb's room and laid the objects across the foot of his bed.

When they came back into the den, where Miss Jimmie was, Laken showed her the picture.

"Is that your mama and daddy?" Miss Jimmie asked, then exclaimed, "Lord, Laken, you are your daddy's child, the spitting image!"

"I know. Shelby and I are going to run across the road and show it to Grandpa," Laken told her.

"I'm sure he'll be thrilled. I remember seeing your mama at the Big Store in Excel; she was beautiful," Miss Jimmie said.

Laken hugged her, and confessed, "The biggest favor she ever did for me was allowing me to come over here. Daddy was the one who talked her into it."

"You two go on out to Mr. Willie's before you have me crying," Miss Jimmie said. She then added, "Just look what you've done for this family. You're the one that got our

Shelby to picking that banjo. Shoot, Shelby loves you like a sister, and we love you like you're our own. We did from day one."

"Me, have *you* crying?" Laken asked, as she hugged Miss Jimmie again, then she and Shelby went out of the door, carrying the picture.

They found Laken's grandpa sitting on the back porch, chewing his tobacco.

There was a row of rose bushes planted around the porch. They saw that when a fly would land on the roses, Mr. Willie would spit a wad of tobacco juice on them.

"Look what I found," Laken said, as she brought the picture from behind her back.

"Well, sir, would you just look at that," the old fellow said, as he reached for it, with trembling hands.

"Boy, she was a pretty little thing. It's a shame that Victoria had to show her butt so. James and your mama could've had a happy life. No telling how many grandchildren we'd have had," he smiled ruefully as he handed the picture back to Laken.

"I've been seeing you girls going in and out in Jimmie's old car. I want you to go to the Ford place in Monroeville tomorrow and pick y'all out a brand-new car. Don't get a secondhand one, either. It's my gift for y'all graduating. Don't argue with me, now. I've already made the arrangements, and they're waiting on you," he said.

The girls knew it wouldn't do any good arguing, so they both hugged his neck and thanked him profusely. They were both so excited that it seemed like their old car floated back home.

"Oh my Lord!" Miss Jimmie said, just as excited as the girls were when they told them about the new car.

"Yeah, he told us to not bother with the cheap ones, to get us the one that we wanted. He said it was a graduation present!" Shelby exclaimed.

"Well, it was mighty good of Mr. Willie to include you, honey," Miss Jimmie told Shelby.

"He has the money, and I agree with Jimmie," Hiram said.

They were all sitting at the kitchen table when the girls made the announcement. Caleb was nursing a sore thumb, caused by whacking his thumb instead of a roofing tack, making it difficult for him to hold his fork as he ate.

All he said about the affair was, "You lucky things."

The girls didn't eat much. They were too excited, not only about the car, but also, wondering what Caleb would say when he found the old musket and saber.

It was just their luck that Caleb and Hiram did as usual. After supper, they went directly outside to feed the livestock. The days were getting longer, so the girls and Miss Jimmie had plenty of time to clean the kitchen before they fed the chickens and gathered the eggs.

Miss Jimmie was still selling her eggs at the Big Store, and at church. It was hard for the girls to believe, but Miss Jimmie still said now and then that she sure missed Belle.

All three of the womenfolk were in the den, watching the Lawrence Welk show, when Hiram and Caleb returned. They could hear the men scraping their feet on the thick mats on the doorsteps and porch.

Caleb headed straight to the back of the house, presumably to the bathroom or to his bedroom.

*"Where in the world?"* They heard Caleb's voice, as he came clanging into the den. He spread the musty-smelling

blanket onto the den floor, then laid the old musket, saber, and sheath on the blanket.

"They belonged to my great-grandpa, and I'm giving them to you," Laken said.

"Let me see the saber, son," Hiram requested.

Carefully, Caleb handed it to him, as the sword was razor sharp.

Hiram looked at the saber and saw that it was stamped 3rd Alabama Cavalry.

"Wow, it's authentic! My grandpa and Mr. Pruitt fought together in the battle of Atlanta, nigh on a hundred years ago," Hiram told them. He continued, "Pruitt lived in that very log cabin that we're putting a new top on."

"Gracious, I knew the place was old," Laken said.

"I'm gonna oil these things up, get me some black powder and I'm gonna be shooting this baby," Caleb said.

Laken was so glad that Caleb loved her gift to him.

"Whoa there, buddy, you need a bullet of some type," his daddy said.

"There's one of those thingamajigs over there that you make the bullets with; it's out in the barn. Heck, I've seen Pap make them," Laken said.

"Good, I love anything that's pertaining to the Civil War. we'll go get it tomorrow," Caleb said eagerly.

"No, tomorrow we're getting the car, then we're coming back home and getting ready for the Prom," Laken reminded him.

"Shoot, tomorrow we'll be through with the house," Caleb said.

"Yeah, and you're not going to be plundering around in that shop or cabin until Laken is with you," Hiram told his son.

"Caleb, aren't you even going to thank Laken for her gift?" Miss Jimmie asked.

"Oh, yeah, thank you Laken," Caleb said.

Both Laken and Shelby smiled, and Laken said, "You are most welcome." She then went into the bedroom and brought back the picture and showed it to Mr. Hiram.

After giving the picture a good going over, Hiram remarked, "You know, some folks around here owe your mama a big apology. She was judged by a lot of people around here. I'm so glad we weren't one of them. The Bible plainly warns us, 'Judge not, lest ye be judged.' I think she was judged because she was so pretty," Hiram said.

"Thank you, but she was a mess," Laken countered.

Caleb looked at the picture and said, "Boy, you look just like Mister James."

After listening to the Lennon sisters sing on the Lawrence Welk program, the girls went to their room, hoping that if they went to bed early, it would make the morning come sooner.

Laken placed the picture on the little table next to the head of her bed. After saying her prayers, she smiled and murmured, "Thank you, Lord, for Mama still being alive."

The two girls were at Ford Motor Company when they opened their doors.

All the new cars were parked across the street from the office building.

The girls had already picked out the car they wanted. It was a Ford Fairlane, white in color, with red interior. It was loaded with chrome, too. It was a four door. The two-door looked better, but they thought about needing room for their instruments. The best thing was that it had air conditioning. They wanted to get inside, to try out the seats, but all four doors were locked.

A smiling, casually dressed man, who seemed to be in his late forties, came outside, and crossed the street to talk with them.

"Can I help you?" he asked.

Even though the man never revealed his name, the girls told him their names and why they were there.

"Oh, yes, Mr. Willie's granddaughter and her sister," the smiling man said.

He finally introduced himself as being Luther Lee.

"So, did you see anything you like?" he asked.

"Yes, could we test drive the white Fairlane?" Laken asked.

"Sure, let me run inside for the keys," he said.

In less than five minutes, Laken was driving the dream car down North Mount Pleasant street.

While Laken was driving, Shelby was turning and punching different buttons to make sure everything worked.

Before they got out of the residential area, Laken turned the car around and let the eager Shelby drive it back to the Ford Place.

Mr. Lee was still outside the building, chatting with someone.

"Well, what do you girls think?" he asked.

"This is the one we want," Shelby said.

"Good. Follow me inside, and we'll call Mr. Willie," he said.

Mr. Lee then told the man he had been talking to, to "Just look around."

When the salesman placed the call, Laken could hear her grandfather's voice over the phone.

"Well, if that's what they want, and it's a good vehicle, let 'em have it.

Lee told Laken's grandfather the total price.

"Well, I'm going to add another hundred to that, so they can get a license plate and fill it up with gas. You let 'em have a hundred out of your pocket. I'll call the bank, and your money will be waiting for you," her grandfather said.

"Yes, sir, Mr. Willie, I'll take care of everything," Mr. Lee said.

After the salesman hung up the phone, he opened his wallet and took out five twenties.

Smiling, he told Laken to sign the long paper in three or four places, then gave her the hundred dollars.

"I'm sure you overheard Mr. Willie. Now, y'all will need your driver's licenses to get your tags. Good luck, and if you have any trouble with it, feel free to bring it back and we'll straighten it out," Mr. Lee said.

As Laken pulled the new car out of the parking lot, Mr. Lee was already talking to the customer he was speaking with earlier.

After leaving the courthouse with the tags, they stopped at Pete Black's filling station and filled the car with gasoline. Shelby said they'd get Caleb to put the tags on when they got home.

Of course, their next stop was at Mr. Willie's, to show off their new purchase and thank him once more for the generous gift.

# Chapter 32

The time had come for the biggest event of high school besides graduation itself: the Prom. The event wasn't being held at Excel High School; instead it would take place at the Community House, in Monroeville.

Brad wasn't wasting any time. The Prom didn't begin until seven o'clock, but he pulled into the driveway at six p.m. sharp. His tall self was all decked out in a white tuxedo, with a red vest and red bow tie to match.

Caleb and Hiram didn't get through topping the house until five o'clock. When he got home, Caleb went straight to the bathroom, and he stepped into the den at six fifteen. Unlike Brad, Caleb was dressed in his blue suit, and was wearing a red necktie.

Laken thought he looked mighty handsome, with his blond hair combed back on the top and sides.

She noticed that he had his dancing shoes on, or at least, that's what he called them. She was glad, because she was planning on doing plenty of that. Both she and Shelby were wearing low heeled flats.

Making sure the bodices of their dresses were pulled to the very highest, and with their white laced shawls firmly in place, they walked out with their dates for the evening. They left the house at six-thirty.

Miss Jimmie was dabbing at her eyes when they went out the door.

Caleb was driving Miss Jimmie's car, and they didn't know where Brad had come up with the big, long car he was driving.

A local band was playing. Laken knew one of the guitar players; his name was Tommy Chandler. She figured he must like bluegrass, because he'd shown up for several of their performances.

The big dancing area was really decorated, too, with twisted crepe paper ribbons and colorful balloons hanging everywhere from the ceiling.

There was a row of tables and chairs on the sides of the dance floor, with two tubs of iced down sodas.

After the principal gave a short speech, congratulating everyone for graduating, the band immediately began playing.

Most of the songs were popular songs from the current era, and Laken thought they were very good. They even had a young lady to sing some of the songs, and she was amazing. She would later find out the girl's name was Della Anne Downing.

Laken was really surprised at how well Caleb could dance. They must've danced for a solid hour before the band took a break. As they were walking hand in hand toward the tables for a cold drink and to sit down, Caleb pulled her near him.

"Yes?" Laken asked.

"You might want to pull your dress up or something; your boobs are about to pop out of there!" he warned her.

Not wanting Caleb to get the best of her, Laken responded, "You don't like to see my boobs?"

"Yes, I'd like to see even more, but they're meant for me to see, not everybody else. Besides, I'd imagine you're making some of these girls jealous," Caleb said.

Knowing he was right, Laken said, "Hmph!" and pulled her bodice up.

Of course, Shelby and Brad joined them at the table, and when Shelby bent over to get a coke, Laken noticed that she could almost see everything, so she whispered in her ear.

"Oh, I know it. You know, we really shouldn't have gotten these dresses; I've been pulling the darn thing up all night."

The dance was over at ten o'clock. Some said they were going to stay out all night, but Laken and Shelby knew they'd be headed straight home. At least that's what Laken thought, because it was Shelby's and her turn to sing in church the next day.

Caleb and Laken held hands until they went through Excel, then Caleb laid their linked hands on top of her upper thigh.

Laken didn't say anything, for she knew they'd soon be home. She had a strange feeling with Caleb. She felt safe. She knew if he did anything inappropriate, all she'd have to tell him was to stop, and she felt like he'd do it.

Her heart sped up, though, when Caleb pulled the car down the old trail that led to her old cabin. She didn't say anything but knew she should.

Caleb switched the car off, but left the radio on, turned down low. Brenda Lee was singing, 'All Alone Am I.'

Before Laken knew what was going on they were kissing. Not the "peck on the cheek" kind, but the hot, passionate kind, with their tongues touching. Yet, she was still embracing him tightly, and he was holding her just as close.

He tried to run his hand between her legs, but she grabbed his hand and pushed it back. Next, before she realized it, he had his rough left hand in her bodice and was fumbling her at breast.

*"He must think I'm like Callie,"* she thought, as she reared back and slapped his face.

"What do you think I am, a cheap whore?" she demanded, as she attempted to get out of the car.

"Ok, I'll be good, just stay in the car. It sure wouldn't go good on me if you walked home," Caleb said, as he expelled the air from his lungs.

"You asked for it, though," he said, "Look at the bosom of your dress."

Glancing down, she saw that nearly all her breasts were clearly visible, even in the moonlight.

"This darn dress!" she exclaimed, as she exhaled, shifting her breasts so they fell back into her dress.

"Okay, I'll admit it, I'm sorry for slapping you in the face. Just don't do anything like that again. That is, unless I allow it," Laken said.

"And when will that be?" Caleb asked.

"You'll know," Laken said, as she pecked Caleb on his cheek.

They embraced and kissed each other once more, but not the passionate kind as before.

"Well, at least I can say I was the first to feel them," Caleb said.

"I'll let you in on a secret, you'll be the only one. Just give me some time. There's so much at stake. Miss Anne and Shelby have their hearts set on going to Nashville after we graduate. Let me see what develops from that, but no matter what, you're the one. I've loved you since I turned twelve years old," Laken admitted.

This time, their kiss seemed to really mean something, for Caleb told her that he loved her, too.

"It's going to be hard, though, with us living in the same house," Caleb said.

"Nah, we'll behave," Laken said.

"Are you still gonna let me go through the cabin and the shop tomorrow?" Caleb asked.

"Just as soon as church is over, and we take the new car for a spin," Laken promised.

That night the girls liked to have never gone to sleep, from talking about the night's events. As it turned out, Brad had tried about the same maneuvers on Shelby as Caleb had tried on her.

"I like him, though; in fact, I like him a lot," Shelby told Laken.

"Well, I love Caleb. I just hope he'll wait on me until we find something out about this music," Laken said.

"Caleb? He's so slow to make up his mind about something, you needn't worry, he'll be right here," Shelby said.

"I don't know, he's mighty handsome, and he wasn't so slow tonight," Laken told her. She then said that she and Caleb wanted to drive their new car around the next day. "After he goes through the old cabin and shop," Laken said.

"Boy, do our minds work on the same track! I told Brad that if it was alright with you, we'd take the car for a spin tomorrow. He's even coming to our church," Shelby told Laken.

"I'll tell you what, since the car belongs to both of us, you can have it until three o'clock, then we'll have it until five," Laken answered.

"Fair enough," Shelby agreed.

"We'll have to take those gowns back to Katz's Monday after school. I guess they did what they were cut out to do," Laken said. They both had to put their pillows over their mouths to stifle their laughter.

Since both Mr. Hiram and Miss Jimmie had gone to bed before they came in the night before, first thing in the morning Miss Jimmie wanted to know how things went.

"Well, we danced, drank sodas, then came home. All in all, we had a good time. Laken said Caleb was a perfect gentleman, and so was Brad," Shelby answered.

They were all sitting around the breakfast table, and Caleb seemed to have strangled on a swallow of milk, but after coughing a few times he got straightened out. Hiram and Jimmie exchanged a long, knowing look, but neither of them said anything.

The girls drove their new car to church that morning, with their instruments on the back seat.

The girls sang, 'Oh, Come Angel Band,' and 'Farther Along.' Thinking it might be the last time they'd sing in the church for a while, the girls really accented their selections.

After church, the temperature had risen a good bit, so Laken decided that she'd take a dip in Persimmon Creek, after they had eaten.

Caleb was anxious to get to the shop and cabin. Hiram told his son to take the hammer and nails with him. "Be sure to nail the door back, before you leave," he said.

Brad showed up, and both he and Shelby left.

Not wanting to tempt Caleb again so soon, Laken decided to just wear some cutoff jeans, and a blouse that she tied in a knot.

The two of them were soon crossing the pasture in Hiram's old truck.

Not only had Caleb brought along a hammer and nails, but he'd also brought a shovel to probe around in the dirt.

Laken showed him where she remembered seeing the bullet mold. Of course, once they were in the darkened old log barn, Caleb slid his arms around her. He squeezed her so hard, while kissing her at the same time, until he lifted her off the ground.

Caleb was well over six feet tall, while Laken was barely over five feet.

Her heart was racing, realizing that although it was a little rough, she was enjoying the passionate kissing and caressing. She could feel her breasts against his chest.

Suddenly she realized she had a choice to make: give in to the young man she loved so deeply, or protect her career.

Her mind whirling, she thought about what Shelby had said, "Caleb would never leave his folks," so she did the only thing she could think to do. She kicked him on his legs.

He almost dropped her to the ground, but she landed on her feet. Crying, she said, "Caleb, I love you with all my heart, but I'm not that kind of girl."

He used his shirt tail to wipe the tears from her face.

"I'm sorry, Laken, but you're just so irresistible that I was carried away," Caleb said.,

Laken briefly kissed Caleb on the lips again, but not like the long, passionate kiss earlier.

"Give me some time, at least until next summer. I can tell you this, though, we're not going all the way until we're married. I'm not that kind of girl. I'd be letting down Shelby, Buddy, and Miss Anne. Can't you understand, I have a dream? You're in it, but a little further down the road, I'd be honored to be Mrs. Caleb Beasley," Laken said.

"So, you will marry me?" Caleb asked.

"Caleb, you've been my hero since I was a little girl; again, give it a little time," Laken said.

With her senses coming back to her, she said, "Wow, I see that Mama's old still is hacked to pieces." She then turned around and ran out the barn swiftly, and around the house, then dove into the cold water of Persimmon Creek.

Caleb followed behind her until he reached the bank of the creek.

"You need to be in here; it'll cool you off," Laken teased, as she wiped her wet black hair away from her face.

"Maybe later. Right now, I'm going to be looking for old stuff," he said.

"Well, you'd better not plunder too long. We get the Fairlane at three o'clock, and I'll be expecting a chocolate sundae from you," Laken told him.

Laken must have stayed in the water for about thirty minutes, before she swam to the shallow part, and enjoyed sitting on the creek bank in the warm sun.

About two o'clock, she heard Caleb as he nailed the door back, then shortly he made his way to her, carrying a cardboard box.

"I figured I'd find you here. Boy, did I find some treasures!" he said, as he emptied the contents of the box on dry ground.

"Just look at all this Confederate money, and a Confederate belt buckle, not counting the two bullet molds," he said.

"Just look how dirty you've gotten," Laken countered.

"I know; I crawled up into the loft. That's where I found the Confederate money. When I have time, I'm going to dig around the old house and barn. No telling what I'll find," Caleb said.

"You'd better not dig up Mama's daffodils; they're in full bloom," Laken said.

"Just think, in little over a month the house and land will be yours," Caleb reminded her.

"Yeah boy, I'll be a woman of worth then," Laken laughed.

She then told Caleb that if he looked on the porch, he'd find a bar of soap. "Shelby and I use it. Go back up there, pull off your clothes and take a bath. No way am I going anywhere with you like that, much less in our new car!"

"I will if you go with me," Caleb said.

"Ha ha," she replied, then added, "Thanks, but no thanks. You can put on clean clothes when we get to the house."

"Well, okay, but you'd better not bring your behind up there, thinking you might see something," Caleb told her.

"Again, ha ha," Laken said, as Caleb made his way back toward the house.

When he came back in about twenty minutes, she could tell that he'd taken a bath. All men in the south always carried a sharp knife in their pocket, so he'd cut her a big bouquet of the daffodils.

"Oh, you are so sweet. You still owe me that chocolate sundae, though," she teased, as she kissed him on his clean-smelling cheek.

Laken knew she didn't have to worry about repercussions, for he had both hands on the cardboard box that held all his treasures.

The girls were so busy the next month with graduation, that they hardly had time to think. Both of the girls came close to being valedictorian, but a girl in their class, Bobbie Wright, was chosen.

They got their diplomas, and rings, however, and that was what mattered in their book.

That very night, they began to pack things in the Fairlane for their trip to Nashville.

Of course, both Hiram and Jimmie had all kinds of things to tell them, including offering them money. Both girls assured the adults that they believed they had enough saved back to last them for a while.

Laken and Shelby made it a point to avoid Caleb and Brad as much as possible.

Before they left the next day, Miss Anne assured them that they'd be safe. "Buddy and I will see to that," she said.

Over the last couple of years, Laken and Shelby had written several bluegrass songs. Miss Anne told Hiram and Jimmie that she was going to try to get them recorded.

At ten o'clock the troupe pulled out for Nashville, with Jimmie crying, and Hiram and Caleb waving goodbye.

# Chapter 33

*"There's no doubt about it; prayers work,"* Callie thought when she closed on the building in Biloxi.

Of course, some remodeling had to be done, and that's when C.J. came in handy, as her latest boyfriend was a general contractor. His name was Bryson. He and his crew could do anything when it came to remodeling.

When Callie gave the nod to open the place for business, there was new flooring, electrical system, sparkling new stainless-steel appliances, and freshly painted ceilings. The building had a stage, and a nice dance floor, which was separated from the dining area with thick red curtains that were trimmed in gold. Like her other establishments, Callie had the traditional neon sign outside, that flashed in red letters, 'Laken's.'

Callie kept her word; she moved C.J. to Biloxi, and allowed her to pick her own help, as C.J. never ceased to amaze Callie. Miraculously, C.J. had never married.

Callie thought C.J. was a beautiful young woman. She was of average height, with straight, natural blonde hair. She had a perfect build and posture. Even at her most tired, C.J. could bounce around like a young girl of sixteen. She was now, and had always been, Callie's "go to" girl when she needed to know something.

By the time 'Laken's' opened in Biloxi on Friday, August 9th, C.J. just knew the place was going to rocket, so she hired an assistant manager, whose name was Krista. She was not only C.J.'s friend and confidante, but she could juggle numbers in her head faster than a computer. Like C.J., Krista did a little of it all. Where they were needed the most, that's where they'd be.

There were three cooks, three waitresses, and a bouncer for the weekends. Even though there was no alcohol served, some customers would come in inebriated, or would have it hidden in a purse, or a flask that was tucked away somewhere on their body. Most of the time, though, all the bouncer did was flirt with the customers, or with C.J. and Krista.

His name was Leon, and just from the looks of him, you could tell that it wouldn't pay to fool with him. Leon was handsome enough; he stood about six feet four inches tall and weighed about two hundred and fifty pounds. Cassie wondered how C.J. found him, but was afraid to ask questions, for you could see when he flexed his muscles that he was ready for almost anything.

Callie put C.J. in Biloxi, Sue in the Dauphin Island location, and Loretta in Pascagoula in charge of the entertainment, and the three also had her permission to write checks for all expenditures. The restaurant in Mobile, Callie oversaw. Of course, as always, she personally kept up with every dime.

Paul's parents visited infrequently, but not knowing when they'd catch him and Callie together made it hard for them.

With each passing day, Pretty Gena became closer to Callie's heart. She made a special effort to attend all of Gena's school functions, her little plays, sports events, and such.

Callie was very frugal with her money, except when it came to Pretty Gena. She just loved the child's southern drawl, and her brainy talents. Both Paul and her were grooming Pretty Gena beyond her knowledge to become a lawyer, for she was slick, and very advanced for her age.

Callie made sure the girl had plenty of pretty clothes, so she could attend church with them, for Sue liked to rest as much as possible on Sundays.

There was a nice home for sale on Dauphin Island. Callie could tell that Pretty Gena wanted her and Paul to buy it, so she would have a bedroom to spend the night with them. As bad as Callie wanted the house, she stuck to her original plan, and that was to save up to have a 'Laken's' in New Orleans.

*"After all,"* she reasoned, *"Houses are a dime a dozen, and they cost so much, especially on the island, while restaurants make money."*

Callie thought she'd get a nice house on the island one day, when she was finished with the restaurants. Until then, they'd live frugally. As always, she never asked Paul for a dime. She didn't know a thing about his bank account, and he didn't know the details of hers.

They ate at the 'Laken's' restaurants a good bit of the time. Occasionally they'd go to another restaurant or go out for a movie. Both of them liked bluegrass and country music, so if a singer or group came to town, they'd go see the performances.

Callie wasn't a sports enthusiast, but Paul was a big fan of Alabama football, and so was Sylvester. Since they didn't have a living room, both he and Sylvester would get together at Sylvester and Melissa's house.

They also were avid golf players and went golfing a lot. Callie didn't say anything, but she thought the clothes they wore while golfing were comical.

Somehow, in spite of their differences, their love for each other continued to grow. After their lovemaking at night, Callie and Paul would talk about their events of the day, and many nights Callie would wake up with her head on

Paul's chest. They both liked to sleep with the radio turned down low.

Callie just loved the little Baptist church they had always attended. Just about everyone in the church was on a first name basis with her by now. Of course, they all knew her as Betty Jean. Occasionally, she and Paul would sing together in front of the congregation, and everyone always told them how much they enjoyed it.

It was strange to Callie that even though her businesses were making money, especially in Pascagoula and Biloxi, there still seemed to be something lacking.

She talked to Paul about her feelings one night, and he told her he'd watched her with Pretty Gena. "Maybe if we had a baby before we're too old, it would help your feelings," he said.

Callie didn't dare reveal her suspicions that she could no longer bear children, for to do that, she'd have to reveal her sordid past to Paul. She didn't know if she'd ever be ready to trust him with her secrets, but every day that went by, it was harder to stay silent.

# Chapter 34

It was the biggest crowd their band had ever performed for, so they went over and above. They were at Lakewood Amphitheater in Atlanta, Georgia. Miss Anne had told them the place would hold over 18,000 people, and Laken didn't see an empty seat. The tickets ranged from ten to twenty dollars for each individual. Laken attempted to tally the money in her head but found it to be impossible. They'd really made a name for themselves in just five months. Meanwhile, she and Shelby continued to write new songs.

So far they'd recorded one album, and two of their songs on the album had become hits.

When they first arrived in Nashville, they performed for many producers and were turned down. After being in Nashville for a month and paying for food, plus hotel rooms, the girls' money was getting low. Miss Anne kept encouraging them, though, saying, "Just hang on; there's too much talent here for someone not to take notice."

Another one that kept them going was Buddy, with his funny antics.

Both girls spent their eighteenth birthdays away from home.

They ate mostly at McDonalds or other fast-food places. Miss Anne even paid for all of them to go to the Grand Ole Opry once. The main attraction that night was Roy Acuff. Of course, they had other singers too, but no one beat Mr. Acuff singing 'The Great Speckled Bird.'

The second week in July, on a hot summer's day, they auditioned for "Ten Records," and the owner of the company liked them. They sang two songs that Laken had written, 'Wildflowers for my Mama,' and 'Jumping Jehosaphat.'

The owner, Sam Randall, called another fellow in from across town. His name was Lee Peacock, and Sam convinced him to come and listened to the group sing and pick. They wound up going into the recording studio and recording the two songs.

Mr. Peacock would be their booking agent and promoter. He started out saying he usually got fifty per cent of all revenues. The girls and Buddy were willing to settle for almost anything, but Miss Anne haggled him down to twenty-five per cent of all ticket sales. T-shirts, records and other paraphernalia the group might sell at events would be strictly "The 'Bama Four's," Miss Anne said.

Mr. Peacock rubbed his chin, and said, "That doesn't give me much leeway."

"Baloney! The only expense I see, are telephone calls," Miss Anne responded tartly.

Mr. Peacock, realizing he was haggling with a professional, took the deal.

"My going rate for an unknown artist is five percent per record, and I don't haggle," Mr. Randall said.

They each signed contracts after Miss Anne marked through a few words, and they were on their way.

Mr. Peacock got the phone number of Miss Anne's hotel room. They waited for a week before Mr. Peacock called. Miraculously, he had lined up ten engagements for them. They were at different towns in Georgia. The last one was at Lakewood amphitheater, in Atlanta.

Miss Anne waited until the group had a little money and she designed, then ordered five hundred T-shirts in various sizes. She then had the group dress in their finest and took them to a photographer. After looking over the finished photographs, she ordered a thousand of them, in color.

Spending her own money, Miss Anne found and purchased an old touring bus that had belonged to Johnny Cash. The bus was in miraculous condition. It was equipped with everything that a hotel room had: air conditioning, heat, a small shower, and even a small gas stove. The electricity was from a small generator that ran off diesel. The only drawback to the electricity was that there were only three plug-ins, one in each sleeping area.

The bus was also equipped with three tiny bedrooms, cordoned off from each other with fold-in doors. Buddy was the driver. When they reached each location, all they had to do was step off the bus, after they'd readied themselves inside the bus.

Laken had to admit to herself that after their Fairlane was sent back home, she sort of felt unattached to the only life she'd ever known, and to the small town of Excel.

One day, during a layover in Rome, Georgia, Miss Anne had a painter write, "The Bama Four" in red lettering on each side of the gray and white bus.

Of course, the girls wrote home regularly, and called at least once a week. Laken also wrote to Caleb, and Shelby corresponded with Brad. Brad proved to be a better letter writer than Caleb. When Caleb did write, he wrote about duties on the farm. At the end of each letter, though, he always wrote, "I love you."

One letter he sent had a black and white picture of him standing in front of the old log cabin. After looking closely, Laken saw that he was wearing the oval shaped C.S. belt buckle.

What she wondered was, who took the picture? So, she called home that night. First, she talked to Hiram, since he answered the phone, then to Miss Jimmie, and last but not least, to Caleb. She didn't ask him right off the bat, but eased into it, and he replied that his daddy had taken the photo.

"We were mending the fence behind the place, so after dinner I took the camera back with me."

He told her that they'd put the Fairlane in the barn. This phone call was like all the others. He never failed to ask, "When are you coming home?"

She always gave him the same answer: "When our contract is fulfilled."

"I love you, darling, and thanks for the record. Monroeville is proud of y'all too, for they get plenty of requests for it," Caleb said.

"Yes, baby, I'll have to admit, it felt strange hearing our voices over the radio there for a while," Laken replied.

After blowing each other long distance kisses and saying "I love you" to each other, they hung up the phone.

The front of the bus had four seats, sort of like a school bus on each side. While Miss Anne stayed busy typing on the typewriter, tallying every dime from concerts and the sales of the merchandise, Laken and Shelby were busy thinking up songs. Angel somehow became the cook, and she was a good one, too, even with the small stove and oven. She could cook the best casseroles, and it sure beat stopping at a burger place.

Not that they didn't trust Miss Anne's book keeping, but she said the IRS didn't, so she always gave them a copy of the money made and the expenses. Anne said she wasn't going to take any of their money she'd spent on the bus, but they all had to pay for the diesel, oil, and tires.

"I know it might seem foolish, but Mr. Peacock is getting one fourth of the tickets sold at concerts. Just the one in Atlanta brought him in over fifty thousand dollars, more than we make as individuals. I'll admit that at Lakewood Amphitheater, we made our biggest amount. Mr. Peacock is already pressuring me to sign another year's contract. I'm holding off, though. Shoot, he's not having to buy diesel and spend time away from home. When that time comes, if we decide to go another year, I'm going to work up another contract with him myself," she said.

Miss Anne gave each of them two hundred dollars a week, excluding Angel, who she gave fifty dollars weekly for keeping Buddy straight and for cooking.

With the rest of their money, she invested in stocks, telling them they would thank her later.

From the sales of their album, Mr. Randall sent them a check once a month. It, too, was divided four ways. They were making more money than they'd ever dreamed. Laken and Shelby, not being accustomed to so much money, simply stashed it in their little compartment and just lived off their share of the concert money.

The girls surprised Miss Jimmie by calling McPhaul's Hardware in Excel and had them deliver and install an automatic washer and dryer for her.

Never forgetting their roots, they mailed Miss Jenny, the mayor of Excel, one of their albums, and yes, 'Pretty Polly' was the first song on the record.

They had all planned on making occasional visits to home, but Mr. Peacock kept them on the road.

To begin with, Laken and Shelby admitted to each other that they got the jitters, but after performing in so many places, they soon felt comfortable on stage.

Their concerts after the Christmas holidays for the month of January were in North Carolina and West Virginia. Some of the towns were so small that they performed in school gymnasiums. It didn't matter how big or how small the crowd, the "Bama Four" always put on just as good as a show.

After each performance, they spent an hour or more signing albums, T-shirts, photographs, dollar bills, you name it.

Miss Anne soon tired of all four scribbling their names on various items, and just said they'd take turns. This made it possible for the others to go back to the bus, so they could relax.

It was nigh impossible for Angel to cook a good meal while Buddy was driving, so at the end of a concert, they knew they could look forward to Angel having them something good to eat.

While looking out of the window one day as Buddy passed a mountain that had snow on top, Laken wondered how her family managed to settle in Excel all those years ago.

She said something to Shelby about it, and she replied. "Simple enough, you can't farm the top of a mountain to any extent, but Excel is flat, making it possible to farm nearly every inch. Our ancestors came to Excel looking for land to farm, and they found it.

"That may be true, but it's sure some pretty country up here," Laken replied back.

The first week in March, they performed at Manchester Music Hall in Lexington, Kentucky. It had a seating capacity of eleven thousand people, and like in Atlanta, there was standing room only.

After sneaking a peek from behind the curtain, Shelby told Laken, "Lord, folks must have come from miles around!"

"Your nerves aren't getting the best of you, are they?" Laken teased.

"No, but what would people think of us in tiny little ol' Excel, if they were standing where I am now?" Shelby asked.

"They'd say, 'Bring the house down, girls," Laken replied.

Usually, their performances would last a little over an hour. It was according to how many jokes Buddy told.

Laken didn't do her jigging at every performance, but in Lexington she jigged around in circles with her boots tapping on three separate occasions. She never missed a beat with the fiddle, either.

They all put on a good show in Lexington. Their next stop was three days later in Louisville. Miss Anne said they ran out of both albums and T-shirts in Lexington and she had ordered a thousand each, the week before. "Maybe they'll catch up to us in Louisville," she said. They'd stopped autographing their pictures, as they had a tendency to stick together. Miss Anne had no intention of throwing away money by wasting precious merchandise.

Most of the places they performed had hawkers that sold their albums and T-shirts. They wouldn't be leaving the places, either, until Miss Anne counted the inventory and the money.

Miss Anne had the albums and T-shirts sent to the post office in Louisville.

The day after they arrived there, the items came in. Anne had made arrangements for payment when she ordered them. She'd chosen a bank in Nashville when they first started out. She always saw to it that the balance would have a few hundred dollars more than the next order, after making sure of that the money was split as usual.

The place they'd be playing in Louisville was the Robert Whitney Hall, with a seating capacity of two thousand four hundred seats.

The only places they didn't care to perform was the outdoor stadiums at night. Bugs and mosquitoes swarmed the places, and Buddy even swore a big bug flew down his throat one night. With their closeness of performing and living on the bus, they formed a fondness for each other that would last a lifetime.

Even though they didn't realize it at the time, they would always look to Miss Anne for advice, as she seemed to know something about most anything. Angel had a habit of working crossword puzzles. She soon learn that she'd better not leave it so that Miss Anne could find her puzzle books, for she'd work the whole book in just a short while. Money seemed to be her specialty, though. She knew the right people to call that could turn a nickel into a dollar. Miss Anne also knew the Bible. She could quote verses without opening the book. She saw to it that they all attended church too, usually one of a Baptist or Methodist faith.

Oh, how Laken loved going to the little churches in the Appalachian-mountain areas! They seemed so sincere, and she believed they cooked each Sunday. The food would be delicious homegrown foods, too, things that Miss Jimmie cooked. They all made sure that they always left their tithe.

Buddy showed his worth several times. Once, while he was filling the bus with diesel, he saw two men run inside and heard the girls scream. Buddy cut the diesel off and ran to the door. The two men were exiting about that time, each with a cloth sack in their hands. Buddy didn't recognize the sacks, so he knew the robbery was planned.

The girls were still screaming, so one at a time, Buddy closed his huge fist and popped each of them square on the nose, knocking them under the bus. Buddy retrieved the sacks they dropped, stepped up into the bus and said, "Make sure everything is in there before I let them go."

The girls made a quick assessment, then said, "Our class rings are missing; they jerked them off our fingers and stuck them in their pockets."

The two men were moaning and groaning, attempting to crawl out the other side of the bus.

Buddy caught them just in time. Using his strength, he grabbed each of them by their heels. Having no mercy on them, he dragged them across the hot asphalt, leaving a bloody trail behind them. The girls, Angel, and Miss Anne were staring out of the windows of the bus and saw what transpired.

"Alright, empty your pockets," Buddy told them, as he helped them to their feet. The two young men did as they were told, and Buddy heard the girls' rings as they made a tinkling noise when they hit the sidewalk.

"Now, get your little change," Buddy said.

Still reeling from the hard lick on their nose, when they bent over to retrieve their few coins, Buddy snatched their sagging pants down to their ankles. He then gave them a swift kick to their behinds, knocking them down again.

"Now, let this be a lesson to you: don't *ever* fool with a man that just got out of church," Buddy said.

"Yes, sir," one of them said, as the other rapidly nodded his head, and they hobbled painfully away.

Buddy quietly went back to the diesel pump and continued to fill the bus. He never said another word about the incident

"Bless his heart, he laid his life on the line for us! They could have been armed. Thank goodness for Buddy," Miss Anne exclaimed.

"Oh, that's the way he is. I don't have to worry about things when my Buddy is around," Angel said.

The event happened in Paducah, Kentucky, and they were scheduled to perform at the Market House Theater that night. It was a small building; the theater only had a two hundred seat capacity, but someone seemed to be in every seat.

If Buddy's hand was injured in any way, they couldn't tell it, and he carried on with his usual shenanigans. Ticket sales might have been small, but Angel sold several T-shirts and albums. Miss Anne didn't use "hawkers."

Laken thought that Paducah was really a pretty town, with the Ohio River running beside it. Not having to perform the next night, and since they had plenty of fuel, they spent the night on the banks of the Ohio. Angel decided to take the night off, so they all had cold cuts for supper, which was fine with everyone.

Buddy and Angel chose to walk down by the river's edge, to watch the big boats as they went by. The girls wanted to go, too, but Miss Anne grabbed them by their collars and

232

shook her head. After making sure the door was secure, Miss Anne told the girls that Buddy and Angel were married and needed a little time alone.

"Oh!" the girls said, as they laughed.

Their next concert was at Ward Oates Amphitheater. It, too had a small seating capacity. It was located in Frankfort, Kentucky, and Buddy liked to have never found it. They put on a good show though, and Angel sold ninety-nine T-shirts, and a hundred and twenty albums.

When Miss Anne was paying everyone for their share of the merchandise sold, she said, "I have something to say. I'll admit at the beginning, I figured we'd make a little money, have some adventures, then go back home, but people, we've made a name for ourselves. I don't mind admitting, I'm a little scared. I don't know what I'm going to do. I called Mr. Peacock today and he's pressuring us to go to England. Brad is pressuring me to come home, and my daughter, Shelby Jean, is, too.

"What did you tell Mr. Peacock?" Buddy asked, as he gave Angel his share of the money.

"The same as always; I told him we'd give him an answer when our contract was up," Miss Anne said. She then added the frosting to the cake. "We're booked to sing at the Grand Ole Opry, in June.

"I'm not telling anyone to give me an answer now; we have two and a half months to make up our minds," she said.

Everyone screamed, "The Grand Ole Opry!"

"Yes but hold on to your panties. The way I have it figured is, we'll only be making about ninety dollars each, for they pay by the union scales," Miss Anne said.

"Who cares? People everywhere can hear us, even Mr. Hiram, Miss Jimmie, Caleb, and all the folks in Excel," Laken said.

"You forget Brad," Shelby said.

"Well, everyone in Monroe County, and the surrounding counties," Laken added.

Everyone had grown accustomed to performing, so Buddy put in his two cents worth. "Just wait until I'm on that stage. They'll never forget The Bama Four!

"Just remember, they can't see your antics over the radio," Miss Anne said.

Buddy already had a good idea rolling in his head, when he said, "No, but the folks in the audience can."

# Chapter 35

It was July of 1964, and things were happening to Callie, things that she didn't understand. After tallying up the expenses and revenue from different restaurants, she found that the Biloxi store was nearly doubling the amount of revenue as the Dauphin Island location. She knew, though, that the business at the restaurant in Pascagoula would pick up after the summer vacationers left.

Callie had begun to read the Bible. Since reading the holy book, she felt better about herself, and she'd learned so much. Words that she didn't understand, she'd ask Paul when he came in. She began to feel comfortable in church, taking every word to heart.

There were several performers in the church, some good, and some not. It didn't matter; they each got a good applause. As the verse Psalm 98-4-9 reminded them, "Make a joyful noise unto the Lord. All the earth: Make a loud noise and rejoice. Sing and praise."

Like all her other employees, Laken attempted to hire religious people. They might have to come to work after church, but they were there to feed the church people anyhow.

The longer she was around that crazy C.J. and Krista, the more she loved them. They ran a ship-shape operation, and customers kept coming back. The only reason a bouncer was hired at Biloxi was because teenagers frequented the place, but the bouncer, Leon, soon took care of the problem.

Secretly, Krista sneaked and told Callie that C.J. had a thing going on with Leon.

Callie just laughed and said, "That C.J., maybe she'll find the right one, one day."

Pretty Gena was coming right along with school and cheerleading at Dauphin Island Elementary school. She was always on the honor roll. Callie was so proud of her, and as a reward, they'd always go out to the movies. Gena liked any movie concerning animals, especially dogs. Callie talked Sue into letting her take Gena to the nearest animal shelter and getting the girl a dog.

"Lord, you already have her spoiled rotten!" Sue said. She then took a deep breath and said, "Just so it's not a puppy, and get her a small one."

Callie smiled, and hugged Sue's neck.

Callie tried her best to keep up with Laken; she was so proud of her! Callie had bought the Bama Four's album at the nearest record shop and played it over and over. She had thought about booking the group to play in Biloxi but knew her place wasn't big enough. Chills ran over her body when she heard Laken's voice, and when the fiddle came in.

The very next Saturday, Callie took Gena to the nearest animal shelter and the girl picked out a cute little, tan-colored Chihuahua. Their next stop was to pull into a pet store and buy a food and water dishes and a sack of dog food.

The dog took an immediate liking to Pretty Gena's hugging and loving.

"So, what are you going to name him?" Callie asked the exuberant child.

"I'm going to name him Pepi," she answered.

"You know you can't bring Pepi into the front of the restaurant, and especially the kitchen?" Callie asked.

"Oh, yes Ma'am, it's the back door as usual," Gena agreed obediently.

It was the following Sunday when all of Callie's bewilderment and strange feelings came to a head. Brother Darby had preached out of the book of Revelation. At the end of the sermon was the altar call. It hit Callie like a bolt of lightning. She shouted from the pew, "Oh God, deliver me of my sins, help me dear Jesus," and almost ran to the altar.

Paul followed her up there.

Callie got down on her knees and voices came from her throat that were alien to her. Her actions brought several other people to the altar.

Paul was so proud of her, for he knew she'd been holding back something since their marriage.

It was seldom heard from anyone to speak in unknown tongues in a Baptist church, but still everyone was proud of her, including Brother Darby.

Callie couldn't wait until they got home to begin telling Paul the truth about her past. She started talking as soon as they got in the car to leave the church.

"You just don't know how it hurt me all these years, running off and leaving my baby girl, but I had to. I would have gone to jail for murder. I went back a couple of times to get her after I sort of got established, but saw she was being raised by the neighbors. They are real good Christian people. The neighbor's daughter, Shelby, Laken must have taught her how to play my banjo. I disguised myself one night and saw them play at the theater in Monroeville. I saw that Laken was well dressed and looked happy, so after their performance I left. I drove half the way home squalling like a baby.

"I've thought about it for years, and now I realize that I put money over everything, even Laken, and that's the bad part. You see, due to my last name, folks in the area looked down on me, and I knew once Laken started school, they would look down on her too. I saved every dime, so that we could get away from there. Maybe things would have been different if I just had someone to keep Laken when she was a baby. She was born right there in that old log cabin, and I nearly died having her. I thought that I couldn't get out and get a job, or someone had to keep Laken, so I did what I knew best. I made and sold whiskey," Callie confessed.

"Well, who is Laken's daddy?" Paul asked.

"James Jordan, the man that Neeley killed. He came from the richest family in the area. We couldn't be together, though, because of his Mama; she hated me. James knew that Laken belonged to him, so he helped me financially with her. Being money crazy, I saved most of it. Both Laken and I survived on bare necessities," Callie told him. Then she went silent, scared to learn what he would say.

"Hard to believe, but Lord, you've got to be incredibly strong to hold all this in, and prosper," Paul said.

Callie let out a deep breath she hadn't realized she was holding. "You just don't know. I stayed scared to death someone would recognize me," she answered.

"So that's why your places are called 'Laken's,' Paul said.

"Yep, and I'm not starting up one in New Orleans, as I had planned. Money is not everything. Shoot, with just the money that Biloxi is making, we can live comfortably. Folks have got to eat. I'll probably sell the old store in Mobile and the one in Pascagoula," she told him. I already have enough money to build us a house on stilts, right here on Dauphin Island."

"So, you're not selling the 'Laken's' on Dauphin Island, because of Sue and Pretty Gena, I'll bet," Paul said.

"You know me so well, and I'm holding onto the money maker, Biloxi, because of C.J. and Krista," Callie said.

"So, what do I call you, Callie or Betty Jean?" Paul asked.

"Well, I like it when you call me "Love," Callie said, smiling.

"Well then, Love, when are we going to see Laken?" Paul asked.

"Well, she's the fiddle player for the Bama Four, so I guess, when they get back in this area. Right now, they're somewhere in Tennessee, or that's where they were the last I heard," Callie said. She then continued, "Shoot, they even played on the Opry, and of all things we missed it. We were over at Sylvester and Melissa's house."

"The Bama Four. Wow!" Paul exclaimed.

"They're a big thing right now, and just think, I taught her how to play on our beat-up old front porch," Callie told Paul.

There was something else that Callie wasn't telling Paul. She thought she'd wait until she went to the doctor to be sure, but she knew in her heart that she was pregnant.

How she managed to conceive with Paul after she had failed to get pregnant with her erratic past was beyond her. *"It must have just been God's will,"* she thought.

# Chapter 36

The Bama Four's next concert was in Bristol, Tennessee. It was being held at the Viking Hall, with a seating capacity of six thousand, one hundred people.

Miss Anne was excited that they'd be playing closer to home. She'd also realized that the closer to their contract date, the closer to Nashville they came.

She hadn't heard from the others, but her mind was made up; come July 15th, she was bringing her tired body home. The ends of her fingers on her left hand were as tough as whet leather, from chording the mandolin. She thought that she'd have someone build her a frame with a glass front and hang the mandolin on the wall.

Both Laken and Shelby had talked about it privately, and they too, were coming home, to get married and live like normal people. They were so tired of all the traveling! They were pleased that they'd made their hometown proud of them, not to mention Hiram and Miss Jimmie.

It was hard to tell about Buddy, though; he acted as though everything was all right with him 24/7. Angel was more down to earth. They all had a sneaky feeling that Angel was ready to come home. She and Buddy lived between Excel and Monroeville. The girls saw their house every time they went to Monroeville. It was a beautiful home, and they'd hired a caretaker to keep up the grounds while they were gone.

The Viking Hall was a beautiful place. They discovered that there were two Bristol's, with one in Tennessee, and then across the state line the town continued into Virginia.

As usual, they played to a full house, and everyone played and sang beautifully. The bravado in the girls and Buddy's voices were remarkable, Miss Anne thought.

After signing autographs, for it was Laken's turn, she walked back to the bus with Buddy, for Buddy always hung around when it was the girls' time to sign autographs.

When they returned to the bus, Miss Anne had already counted the money. They'd brought in twelve thousand, four hundred dollars. Mr. Peacock's share was three thousand, one hundred dollars, leaving them a balance of nine thousand three hundred dollars. She quickly counted the money that the merchandise had brought in, which was two thousand, three hundred dollars, giving each of them five hundred and seventy-five dollars.

As usual, Buddy handed his share over to Angel, while the girls hid theirs in their usual places, which were battered make-up cases.

Miss Anne always gave each of them a carbon copy of all the paperwork and receipts. "Now, this is not counting the money that's going into stock. As it is, just leave it in there and you won't have to pay taxes on it," she told them.

"Angel said, with some of our money she was going to get her a new Harley," Buddy said.

Angel slapped him on his shoulder and said, "Buddy Cater, can't you just see the folks in Excel goggle when I go by?"

They all laughed, for they could just see Angel tooling down the streets of Excel astraddle a motorcycle.

Their next performance was in Knoxville, Tennessee, which gave them two weeks off. It was a good thing, too, for the next morning when Shelby called home, Miss Jimmie was all up in the air.

"Honey, Mr. Willie Jordan was found dead this morning, Laken needs to know. Baby, I'm so proud of you girls. Every time I wash a load of clothes, I cry, just thinking about y'all. Of course, Caleb would die before he'd tell us, but I think he dearly loves Laken. He's been working in his spare time fixing up Laken's old place into a picnic area. I shouldn't be prattling on so, knowing Mr. Willie is lying dead just across the road."

"You mean they haven't picked his body up yet?" Shelby asked.

"Must not, because your daddy hasn't come back from over there yet," her mama answered.

"Mama, I'll tell Miss Anne, after I tell Laken. We have a two-week layover, and I'm sure Buddy will put the bus in high gear coming home," Shelby promised.

"Oh, praise be to the Lord!" her mama exclaimed.

Miss Jimmie never could keep one thought in her head, before she'd switch to another.

"You girls doing alright, with all that cold weather up there?" she asked.

"It was pretty cold weather in the mountains, but it's started to warm up some. Mama, I could talk to you all day, but let me get off his phone so I can tell Laken about her granddaddy," Shelby said.

"One other thing, let me know when y'all are coming in, so I will have plenty cooked," her mama said.

"Mama, don't worry about it. I'm sure there will be plenty of food at Mr. Willie's; we can eat there or go out. Bye, Mama, I love you; tell everyone else I'm sending my love," Shelby said. Shelby practically had to hang up the phone, while her mama was still talking.

When Shelby left the phone booth at the service station, Buddy was just finishing pumping the diesel.

Miss Anne was inside buying cold drinks and snacks, so Shelby went inside to tell her the news.

"That does it. We're heading home. I'll go to the phone and call Mister Peacock but assure him we'll be back in time for the Knoxville show," Miss Anne said.

Laken was sad when she heard the news about her grandpa, but it wasn't a devastation to her, not like it would have been if it had Miss Jimmie, or Mr. Hiram.

*"He was a good old fellow; he just married the wrong one,"* Laken thought to herself. She was certain in her heart that she and Caleb would be a better match than her grandparents had been.

Buddy was burning up the road, and they all screamed with delight when they read the big green sign that read, "Welcome to Alabama, the Heart of Dixie."

Miss Anne knew for certain, then, that come July 15th, they would be through with the road.

They left Bristol on a Sunday Morning at ten a.m. and rolled into Miss Anne's yard at two a.m. on Monday Morning. Buddy set down on the air horns. Brad was soon outside. Before hugging his Mama's neck, he kissed Shelby. It was a long, passionate kiss, too. Shelby knew everyone was wanting to get home, so she told him she'd see him that afternoon, and they held hands until Shelby stepped back into the bus.

The girls thought it would take forever for Miss Anne to get her things from the back of the bus, even with everyone helping.

Buddy would have to drive the bus to his house.

When they reached the Beasley place, Buddy didn't want to show disrespect, being so close to the Jordan house. He didn't pull down on the air horns as he had at Miss Anne's. Instead, he and Angel helped the girls get their things out of the bus. They then waited patiently until Caleb came out and swept Laken up in his arms.

"Aw, to be young and in love; I can remember," Buddy said.

"Shut up, Buddy Cater, before I slap you upside the head. Let's go home," Angel said, then pecked him on the lips. "Boy, it'll be good sleeping in our bed tonight," she said, as he hit the blacktop road and turned the bus toward home.

"Yeah, sleeping is right, I'm tired, it's been a long drive," Buddy said.

"I know it has been, baby, but who else could have done the things you have? My Lord, you were the bodyguard, driver, and performer, and you know what?" Angel asked.

"What?" Buddy asked.

"I love you, and wouldn't have you any other way," Angel answered.

"I love you too, baby," Buddy said, as he pulled the bus into their yard. "Welcome home."

## Chapter 37

Not a single person at the Beasley place went back to bed. Instead, they ate an early breakfast, and the girls answered at least a million questions.

It was a crucial time of the year for a farmer, though, so at eight o'clock, Mr. Hiram and Caleb crawled up on the tractors.

About nine o'clock, Shelby rode with Laken in the white Fairlane over to Mr. Willie's house.

After talking to Mrs. Tammy Ikner, one of the caretakers, she showed Laken the life insurance policies.

"Wow!" was all that Laken could say, for she was the beneficiary of Willie Jordan's life insurance for fifty thousand dollars.

"I have several things to tell you. Of course, the main one is that Beverly Mohn at Monroe Chapel funeral home is waiting on you to come by and make the arrangements. Next, as ordered by Mr. Willie, his will is to be read directly after the funeral, so you need to be there. Attorney Robert Barry will be reading the will in the church study.

"Lastly, my husband has opened a business on Highway 84. I'm going to stay here two days after the funeral, then I'll be helping my husband with his business," Mrs. Ikner said.

"Thank you, I understand, so I guess I need to be on my way to talk to Mrs. Mohn," Laken said.

"One other thing, not pertaining to Mr. Willie's funeral," Mrs. Ikner said, then added, "You just don't know how proud folks are around here with your success. Y'all have put this little town on the map," Tammy concluded.

"Thank you so much," Laken and Shelby said, and had turned to leave, when Tammy said, "Oh, scatterbrained me, I almost forgot. Here's a list of pallbearers Mr. Willie has written down. Most of them work here, except for Caleb Beasley," she said.

The girls thought about taking Miss Jimmie with them to the funeral home, but they figured she'd just be useless, for she cried at the drop of a pin. When they hit the highway, Laken turned left, which headed toward Monroe Chapel, which was about four miles away.

The funeral home was a beautiful building, with a cemetery in back that was barely visible. Mrs. Mohn must have been waiting on them, for she met them at the main entrance.

"Oh, I'm so sorry for your loss," she said, as she hugged both of them.

"Thank you," Laken said. All the while, Mrs. Mohn was leading the girls toward her office.

Once they were seated in the cramped little room, Mrs. Mohn said, "Well, I guess the first thing I have to say is, I have your album. It's unreal that y'all wrote a lot of those songs."

"Thank you. We can let you in on a little secret: when we get back to Nashville, we're planning on cutting a new one," Laken told her.

"That's wonderful. Before we get down to business, would you mind signing my album, please?" she asked, as she pushed the familiar album cover their way.

Both Shelby and Laken politely signed the album.

"Oh, thank you. Now, I'll treasure it that much more," Mrs. Mohn said.

"Well, I guess we should get down to the arrangements. First, does he have a life or burial insurance?" Mrs. Mohn asked.

Laken pulled the life insurance policy from the small leather bag that she used for a purse and handed it to Mrs. Mohn.

"My gosh! Excuse me while I make a call," Mrs. Mohn said.

After calling the telephone number on the policy, then giving them the policy number, she thanked them, after telling them she'd be sending them a death certificate.

"I know this may not be the right place to say this, but congratulations. Your granddaddy has left you a lot of money. The most expensive funeral we offer is roughly three thousand dollars. The money will come here, I'll notify you, and you can stop by after it. Of course, my fee will be deducted first," Mrs. Mohn said.

"There's a slight problem; we'll probably be back on the road when the check comes in. Can Mr. Hiram Beasley pick it up for me?" Laken asked.

"Sure, I'll put it in a sealed envelope. Now, would you care to take a look at some of our caskets?" Mrs. Mohn asked.

"No, Lord, just give him the best you have," Laken answered.

"Okay, that'll range around three thousand dollars, as I said, and please, call me as Beverly. We're all grown," Mrs. Mohn said.

"Now, I have a few more questions. His parents name, his birthday, including the year. All living relatives, both deceased and living."

"I'm the only living relative. My daddy was James Robert Jordan, his son. His wife's name was Victoria, and my full name is Laken Chandler Jordan. I'll ask Mr. Hiram if he knows who my granddaddy's parents were," Laken said. She then handed Beverly the list of pallbearers.

"One other thing: I'll need a suit of clothes to bury him in," Beverly said. "Also, it's such a short obituary…was he a member of a church, or any other organization?" Beverly asked.

"They were of Baptist faith, but whether they were members, I don't know. I'll have his clothes here, and hopefully the other information you need this afternoon," Laken told her.

"Another thing, due to your notoriety, this place will probably be packed," Beverly warned. "Would you prefer the family room? It's more private, and you'll still see and hear the funeral, just no one can see you until after the services. And are there any special songs you'd like sung at his funeral?"

Knowing her mama would cry through the whole ordeal, Shelby answered for Laken. "We'll take the private room."

Laken knew what Shelby was thinking, and said, "I'll ask Mrs. Ikner if she knows about the songs; I'll tell you when I bring his clothes back."

Beverly followed them to the door and opened it as if they were special.

"She is one more beautiful lady," Shelby said, as they pulled out of the driveway.

"She sure is, but I had no idea a funeral was so hard to plan. I guess I should have gotten to know daddy's people better, but with Victoria being as she was, it was impossible." Laken said.

248

"She was something else, that's for sure," Shelby said.

"You know, I've thought about it for a long time; we owe my mama a lot. She may have abandoned me, but all this bluegrass singing we do, came from her. She's the one who kicked it off. Her folks must have come from Ireland," Laken said.

"I don't know, it just came natural to me," Shelby said, then laughed.

Lakin laughed along with her.

Shelby then asked, "Laken, what are you going to do with all that money?"

"I don't know. Shoot, the last time we counted, we had fifteen thousand dollars each in our make-up cases. I think from all the ticket sales we have another thirty-five thousand each in stocks," Laken answered.

"You know we couldn't have done it without Miss Anne, and Buddy," Shelby said.

"No, and it all started by Miss Anne hearing us on the radio," Laken reminded her.

"You know, before I started eating at your house, we usually just had one thing to eat at meals. It was usually grits, or just scrambled eggs. Wherever Callie is, I pray that she's eating properly and behaving herself," Laken said.

"So, you think your mama is alive?" Shelby asked.

"Oh yeah, she's out there somewhere," Laken answered.

Laken knew that she was feeling nostalgic, both due to her granddaddy dying and the realization that their time on the road had come to an end. But for some reason, she was missing her mama more at that moment than she ever had before. Somehow, she was no longer angry with her mama, either. *"I guess maybe I'm just growing up,"* she thought.

# Chapter 38

They had a special baptism for Callie the next Sunday at the baptismal pool in back of the church.

It was an experience like none Callie had never had.

Pretty Gena even came along with them. She wanted to bring Pepi, but Callie told her that puppies didn't get baptized, so the child left Pepi in his pen at home. He had all his toys in the pen that she and Callie had bought him, to gnaw on.

"Oh, I feel so good!" Callie told her husband. "Before I was saved and baptized, it was as though my heart opened up. I had a hard, bitter life in the past, but since I've truly accepted God's love, it's as though my heart is open to accept happiness. I can't quite explain it."

"I know the feeling. Now, don't think all your troubles will go away. You'll still have them, but now, you have someone to turn them over to; let the Almighty fight for you," Paul said.

"That's right; no man's law is greater than his," Callie told Paul.

"I'm working on something. It might take a little time, but I'll explain it to you when we get home," Paul said.

"Yeah, and I have something to tell you," Callie told him.

She had bought Pretty Gena several crossword puzzle and coloring books and kept them on the back seat. She could see that Gena was busy figuring out a crossword puzzle and wasn't paying them a bit of attention.

Naturally, the child wanted to go home to play with Pepi. She said that she'd just walk home from the restaurant.

After he and Callie were in the privacy of their room, Paul said, "Now, I think I've found you a buyer for the

'Laken's' in Mobile. She's one of my clients, and I just settled her case for a huge sum of money. I might add that I'll be getting quite a chunk, too," Paul added.

"That's great, but why would she be wanting to buy my restaurant, if she has a large sum of money?" Laken asked.

"Simple, the same reason you've been getting by so lightly on your income tax, you've been re-investing," Paul answered. "Another good thing, she's willing to keep Raymona and Judy," Paul added.

"Well, that's good; that place has become home to them. As you know, they're living in my old room in the back. So, how much did she offer?" Callie asked.

"Hold on to the bed post. She offered one hundred and twenty-five thousand dollars," Paul answered proudly.

"Does she have experience working in a restaurant?" Callie asked.

"As a matter of fact, she does. She's worked as a cook in three or four places," Paul reassured her.

"I'll tell you what, see if you can get one hundred and thirty-five out of her. That way, I can give the church ten thousand, and we should have enough left over to buy that lot next to Sue and Pretty Gena. I want a nice house built on stilts, for when the hurricanes come. We've been lucky so far," Laken said.

"I'll contact her tomorrow. Now, what is it that you want to tell me? Paul asked.

"Now, it's your turn to grab a bedpost. I went to the doctor Wednesday, he called me back Friday and said we were going to have a baby," Laken told him.

She looked over at Paul, and he was crying.

Finally, he said, "My Lord, at our age! I can say one thing, we've certainly been working on it."

251

Callie laughed, and said, "I'm already taking the vitamins. The baby should make its arrival about the middle of March."

"Just wait until mama and daddy find out about this," Paul said.

"I'll be going to Pascagoula tomorrow; I'll stop by and tell them," Callie said.

"No, with news like this, we should be together," Paul answered.

Paul hugged and kissed her. "I'll tell you what, we'll go ahead and buy that piece of land. From now on, your money and my money are going to be our money. Whether the deal goes through or not, I have enough to build our house."

It took two weeks, but the deal for the sale of 'Laken's' in Mobile, went through. The buyer's name was Amanda Ward, and Callie really liked her.

Paul knew a contractor, Carlton Sturdivant, and he started building the house right away. Needless to say, Pretty Gena was thrilled, to say the least. It was looking like their growing family would finally have a place to call home.

# Chapter 39

While they were at the Jordan house to pick up Willie's burial clothes, Laken learned from Tammy Ikner that her great-grandparents were Samuel and Bessie Jordan. They were from Butler County, Alabama. "Mr. Willie had migrated to Excel following a sawmill and got to know Miss Victoria, whose folks lived near Excel," Tammy told her.

Laken then went into Willie's bedroom and brought back a pretty blue suit, socks, underwear, and his best pair of black shoes. The suit smelled of mothballs and was hanging on a wooden hanger. The other, she'd put in a double bag.

She thanked Tammy for her help, then Shelby and Laken rushed back to the funeral home. They both were still worn out from the trip, plus they were hungry for some of Miss Jimmie's food.

They were back at the funeral home in a jiffy with the clothes, and the meager amount of information concerning her grandfather's lineage.

Laken decided to just let the intercom at the funeral home play, 'In the Sweet By and By,' and 'Farther Along' at the funeral.

Beverly thanked them for the clothes and information, then asked Laken if Thursday at 2:00pm suited her.

"Yes, that'll be fine with me, and it'll give us another day to rest some," Laken answered.

On the way back home, Laken commented, "You know, it's not really fair to Mr. Willie; he was my granddaddy and lived right across the road from us, yet I hardly knew him."

"Well, how could you get to know him? You were grown before you had a chance to know you ought to," Shelby answered.

"You know, choosing the wrong partner in marriage is such a big deal. It can affect you your entire life," Laken told Shelby.

"You're not having second thoughts about knucklehead, are you?" Shelby asked.

"Heck no, Caleb Beasley is the only one for me," Laken answered.

"For the life of me, I don't see what you see in him. All he studies is keeping his behind on a tractor, and going hunting and fishing—that is, when he finds the time," Shelby said.

"Well, that's because you look at him differently; he's your blood brother. I see a tall muscular blond, that's certainly not lazy. He's very caring, a Christian, and having those sexy blue eyes doesn't hurt the matter, either. I'll bet he could father some pretty children, and I want a half dozen of them," Laken confessed.

"Yuck, stop, you're making me sick," Shelby told her.

"I love you, Shelby Beasley," Laken laughed.

"I love you, too. We've been through life together; let's keep it that way," Shelby answered.

"Well then, is Brad willing to move over this way, or are y'all going to move in with your mama and daddy, or have y'all gotten that far?" Laken asked.

"Shoot, that boy would starve to death if we lived on our own; you know I can't cook. I'm staying with mama and daddy. I have enough money in that cosmetic box to build a wing onto the house," Shelby answered. She then added,

Brad wants to get married as soon as possible. I think those dresses we wore to the Prom put the icing on the cake."

They both laughed so hard that Laken had to tell her to shut up. "I have to keep this car on the road!"

After they stopped laughing, Laken said, "I just hope that Brad and Caleb get along."

"Brad's what's known as a "good ol' boy;" they'll get along. Besides, he's already worked on some of daddy's farm stuff. What we're gonna need is more land for them to work if you're planning to have all those young'uns," Shelby laughed.

"Aw, I was just talking. Caleb is enough for the moment." Laken said.

They were about to pass the cemetery, when Laken said, "I know we're starving, but I want to stop by and see Daddy's grave."

"You're the driver," Shelby said.

There was a road that went all the way around the cemetery. The Jordan plot was in a row at about the middle of the cemetery and on the very end, so you could drive right up to it.

What they saw sort of scared them. James' tombstone looked as usual, but someone, or some people, had blown the name off Miss Victoria's tombstone. You could plainly see that it had been shot several times with a shotgun.

"Oh my! I guess her reputation lives on," Laken said.

"Are you going to replace it?" Shelby asked.

"No, Mr. Willie's name wasn't touched. All it needs is the death date, and Beverly will see to that," Laken said. She then added, "You know, I feel sorry for my grandma; what a miserable life she must have had! A fine example that money can't buy you love."

255

Laken then patted her daddy's tombstone, remembering the night that she had jumped into his arms, and him hugging her and telling her to run to the Beasley's.

She said aloud, "I'm gonna have you some fresh flowers on your grave tomorrow, Daddy."

It was good timing, Miss Jimmie was putting dinner on the table when they walked into the kitchen.

"Is that your famous chicken and dumplings we smell?" asked Shelby.

"It sure is," Miss Jimmie said, then hugged both of the girls, making sure she didn't get flour on them. "You also smell fresh creamed corn, turnip greens, and butter beans, sliced tomatoes, and fried squash, all fresh out of the garden."

"And bread pudding, for dessert," Laken added.

By now, it was a known fact that Caleb and Laken were planning on getting married. Caleb had shown his parents the engagement and wedding rings that he'd bought at Johnson's Jewelers. He was planning on putting the engagement ring on Laken's finger that very night, so they weren't surprised when Mr. Hiram and Caleb came in for dinner, and Caleb kissed Laken.

"That's not fair; I have the whole side of the table by myself," Shelby said.

Both her daddy and Caleb had silly looks on their faces.

"I heard that, and no, you're not eating alone," Brad said, as he entered the room.

Shelby jumped up from the table, and they too hugged and kissed, although briefly.

"Ol' Brad has been working on one of the corn pullers," Hiram said.

Brad pulled up a chair beside Shelby, and Caleb blessed the food.

Both the girls and Brad complimented on the food throughout the entire meal. Shelby and Laken ate like two starved hounds, but they didn't care who noticed it.

"Boy, if mama could cook like this. She's more of a one dish meal kind of gal," Brad said, after he'd cleared his throat with a big gulp of iced tea. "Oh, she can cook, but she mainly stays at her desk tallying up things. I can say one thing, though, she won't allow anyone to walk around in the house with their shoes on, not even the preacher. The house is spotless 24/7," he continued. "Mama loves to work in her flowers, though; she has them everywhere. And "I know one thing, she has nothing but admiration for both of 'her girls,' as she calls you," Brad finished.

"Oh, we just love Miss Anne," Shelby said, and Laken chimed in. "We couldn't have gone anywhere without her, She's kept the group running like a well oil machine."

"Yep, you'd be surprised at the people on the higher level that would have taken advantage of our inexperience, but she kept them in line," Shelby agreed.

"We just love her, and that's all there is to it, period," Laken said.

"Why, thank you, and I feel the same way," Brad told her.

After bragging on the meal again, and giving their respective women a peck, including Miss Jimmie, the menfolks went back to work outside. The girls dove in and helped cleaned the kitchen, against Miss Jimmie's protest.

"I'll be so glad when my fingertips get normal again," Shelby said, as she rinsed the dishes, while Laken dried them and put them away.

"What's wrong with your fingers?" Miss Jimmie asked.

"It's from chording our instruments, mama," Shelby answered. "They're as tough as old shoe leather."

"Oh, I see. I'll be glad when you girls are through with that traveling around and come on back home. We'll manage; we always have," Miss Jimmie said.

The girls nodded their head at each other, agreeing that it would be alright to tell the precious woman.

"Mama, our contract runs out on July 15th, and we're planning on coming back home. Laken and Caleb will be marrying, and I guess it isn't a secret: Brad and I will also be getting married."

"Well, it's no surprise to me about the marrying part, but Lord, I've prayed and prayed for my girls to come on back home," Miss Jimmie said. She then sat down at the kitchen table and wiped her eyes. "Just think, Laken, honey, you can then call me Mama," she said.

"Miss Jimmie, I've thought about it for years, and love you with all my heart, but I have only one Mama. She was a lazy, slovenly creature and had no scruples at all. I would consider it an honor if you'd allow me to call you Mother, instead," Laken told her. They both wound up in each other's arms, crying, but they were happy tears.

Finally, Miss Jimmie said, "Now, why didn't I think about that?" All three girls had to grab napkins to blow their nose and wipe their eyes.

"I'm so proud for both of you girls. It's going to be cramped here, but Hiram said he'd build on," Miss Jimmie remarked.

"No, don't do that, we both have our own money for that," Shelby said.

They wound up talking about Mr. Willie's funeral.

Later, the girls made excuses for themselves, then went into their room for a nap.

After they both tossed and turned for a while, Shelby said, "You know, it feels strange in here with all this room. I miss the security of the bus, and the protection of Buddy, knowing he was almost within arm's reach."

"So, that's it, I knew it was something. We're too late for him, though, Angel has him," Laken laughed. "Besides, they were meant for each other," she added.

The girls soon settled down and went to sleep, each one dreaming of a happy married life once they were off the road for good.

# Chapter 40

Laken knew that she should be ashamed of herself, but she felt very little grief at her granddaddy's funeral. She laid the blame on Caleb, for she was sporting a beautiful engagement ring. So was Shelby, but it wasn't her granddaddy they were burying.

Beverly was right; the little Woodlawn Church was filled to capacity, and droves of people were outside. They waited to not only see the corpse of Mr. Willie, but The Bama Four, and Beverley made sure that Miss Anne, Buddy and Angel had reserved seats with the family. The house servants also had front row seating, including Tammy Ikner and her husband, Daryl.

Laken thought that Beverly had done a fine job, and her granddaddy looked good with the wad of tobacco out of his mouth.

Brother Kenneth Johnson preached the funeral. He spoke some quotes from the Bible, and talked about the good that Mr. Willie had done for the community by hiring local people. The two hymns were sung that Mrs. Ikner had suggested.

Somehow, Mr. Hiram had kept Miss Jimmie quiet until they reached the cemetery, and he told her to just sit in the car.

After another passage from the Bible was said at the cemetery, the funeral was over.

Attorney Barry was there, and he told the ones that were mentioned in the will to meet him back at the church.

Caleb was driving the Fairlane, and Laken was the passenger. Shelby had ridden with Brad and Miss Anne.

After they returned to the church, Laken saw only two people there, besides attorney Barry. The two were Ms. Jenny Countryman, and Tammy Ikner.

Mr. Barry called them into the back of the church, where there were tables and chairs; it was actually the fellowship hall where the church held potlucks and special events.

First, he said they were there for the reading of the will. He sat at one of the tables and called Ms. Countryman's name. Jenny walked to the table.

"I, Willie Jordan, give and bequeath the town of Excel fifty thousand dollars, to be used as Ms. Jenny Countryman sees fit."

Jenny signed a paper, and Mr. Barry told her the money was in the Monroe County bank. He then told her she could leave.

Tammy Ikner was called next.

Mr. Barry rattled off, "I give and bequeath Mrs. Tammy Ikner twenty thousand dollars, for her devotion, and seeing that the household, as well as myself, were seen to."

Tammy signed the paper, and he told her that the money was in Monroe County bank. He then told her she could leave.

Tammy hugged Laken as she walked by her.

"Now, young lady, I've called you last for a reason," attorney Barry said, and then he began.

"I, Willie Jordan do give and bequeath my one and only granddaughter, Laken Chandler Jordan, all my property, businesses, and money. The property is roughly four hundred acres that adjoins the house, which you now own and everything in it. There's also two whole tracts of land, each containing six hundred and fifty acres, more or less. Mr. Barry will give you descriptions of the land. Both tracts are on Butler street, below Excel. The sawmill, which employs about twenty people. All my vehicles, including tractors, trucks, cars; in short, everything I own.

"I have money in two banks, seven hundred and eighty thousand dollars in a savings account in Monroe County Bank, and roughly three hundred thousand dollars in the People's Bank in Frisco City. That account is used for business purposes only. Of course, you can use it at your own discretion.

With love and devotion:

Willie James Jordan."

"Bless his old heart, I loved you, granddaddy," Laken said, as she cried on Caleb's shoulder.

"You're a mighty lucky girl. Your only requirement is to go by each bank and give them your signature; I'll tend to the transfer of the lands and property.

"Mr. Willie would like for you to keep the sawmill in operation. He knows your circumstances and said to turn the sawmill over to Joshua Sheffield; he's the general manager. He's a good honest man, and he'll see to its management. Until you can take care of things, just sign a book of checks from the People's Bank and leave them with me. I've already been paid to handle everything. I'll write every cent down in a ledger," Mr. Barry said.

"Mr. Barry, I've been knowing you all my life and know that you're a good and honest man," Laken said. "I trust you completely."

"Okay then, just bring the signed checks by my office tomorrow, as the men will be getting paid then as usual," Mr. Barry said.

"Yes, sir, I'll go by the bank in the morning," Laken said.

"Mr. Willie has a stack of checks at his…excuse me, *your* house. I'm sure Mrs. Ikner will direct you to them," the attorney told her.

"I'll visit both banks tomorrow morning, and I'll get in contact with Mrs. Ikner," Laken said.

Mr. Barry held out his hand to each of them. After shaking hands, he said, "Nice having you as a client."

Laken's legs were wobbling so, that she could hardly make it back to the car. After they were both seated, she exhaled, and said, "Just think, we're millionaires!"

"I know, and with all that land," Caleb said.

"I might have known you'd be thinking about the land," Laken laughed. "I've been saving my money that I made selling the albums and T-shirts. I'm going to deposit it with all the other, then go to the Ford place and buy us one of those new Mustangs they've just started making. Heck, I'll just sign the title of the Fairlane over to Shelby.

"We need to go to the sawmill after we find the checks. It'll be so much more convenient if Mr. Sheffield has the signed checks. I don't see the need of Mr. Barry having to leave his office in Monroeville every Friday."

"That's what I was thinking, too. I know Josh, and he's a good man," Caleb said.

There was no need for them to knock on the door this time, so Laken and Caleb just walked into the giant foyer of the Jordan house.

"All of this mess has got to go," Laken told Caleb as she pointed to the marble statues and other stuffy things that were just for show.

"So, this is where we're going to live?" Caleb asked.

"Sure. Brad and Shelby will be moving in with Mother and Father, so we can't move in there," Laken answered.

"Wow!" Caleb responded.

"I'll put a sticker on everything I want moved out of this house. I want it gone when I come home in July. You'll need to hire someone to help you. I'll leave money so you can pay them," Laken said.

"What's all this about "Mother and Father?" Caleb asked.

"From the moment you put this beautiful ring on my finger, they became Mother and Father to me," Laken said.

"I'm glad," Caleb responded.

They opened the door that led to the sitting room, where Mr. Willie had stayed all the time. They called for Mrs. Ikner, and she soon entered from another room.

Laken told her why they were there, and she led them to Mr. Willie's bedroom.

There was a huge roll-top desk with pigeon holes in the back.

"He kept the checks in the desk," Mrs. Ikner said. "The reason I'm not asking questions is because I know Mr. Willie left you everything. I was the one that drove him to Mr. Barry's office to do his will. I didn't know he was leaving me anything, though. Lord knows we need it, with Daryl opening the new business."

"Well, I'm glad he left you something," Laken said.

"I called Daryl and told him the good news, and he's thrilled to death," Tammy said. She then added, "He wanted me to go to the bank today, but I thought I'd wait until tomorrow. That way, Mr. Barry will have had time to go by the bank."

"Me too. It's all still so unbelievable," Laken replied.

She rolled the top back on the desk, and sure enough, she found three books of unsigned checks. Each book contained five hundred checks.

"This should do it until I make it back," Laken said, as they thanked Tammy, and turned to leave.

"Here, I need to give you the keys to the house. The other keys on this ring are for various barns and sheds. They're all labeled. The keys to every vehicle are hanging on nails at the back door. I really don't see the need for me coming back, so I'll lock the front door before I pull it to," Tammy said.

"Do I owe you anything?" Laken asked.

"No, you don't owe anybody anything. The cook and housekeeper were paid the day he died, so I just told them they could go home," Tammy said.

Laken laid down the heavy book of checks, hugged Tammy and thanked her for everything she had done.

"Think nothing of it. You know where our business is, it's across the road from Pensacola Salvage on 84. If I can be of further assistance, I'll be there," Tammy said.

Caleb drove, while Laken started signing checks. She tore out the first three and gave them to Caleb.

"What are these for?" he asked, as she continued signing checks.

"The electric bill has to be paid while I'm gone," Laken told him.

"Oh!" Caleb said, as he rolled them up and stuck them in his coat pocket.

"Now, don't lose them," she said.

"Boy, you sure have become bossy since you've come into money," Caleb teased.

"I'm sorry, darling, but I need to get this done. Shoot, I wish we could go home and change clothes, not to mention telling everyone what's transpired," she told him.

Jordan's Sawmill was about a mile from the house, down Butler Street. Laken sat in the parking lot until she'd signed all the checks.

Caleb had already gone into the little office and told Josh why they were there.

When Laken handed him the book of checks, she told him to give everyone there a ten cent on the hour wage. "Also, give yourself a ten dollar a week raise," she said.

"Boy, having all these signed checks could be risky. I have a safe here, though, and I'll make sure they'll be protected. Also, I always kept a ledger of everything that I spend. I'll make sure it'll be up to date. I turn every penny over to People's Bank in Frisco City, three times a week. This place clears an average of about twelve hundred a week, if we have no major breakdowns," he said.

"Well, maybe Caleb will take interest in the place, for I don't know a thing about a sawmill, so it's all on you, Mr. Sheffield, to keep this place running," Laken said.

"Well, the men will appreciate the raises, and so do I," Josh said.

"I'm so pleased," Laken said. She then told Mr. Sheffield that he'd have to get with Caleb after she'd gone back on the road.

"I understand, and everyone around here are so proud of y'all," he said.

"Well, I'll be at Mr. Beasley's or the Jordan place for ten more days. I don't know what else I can do, so until then, goodbye and I pray everything works out," Laken said.

"It's my pleasure," Josh told her.

After they finally reached home, Laken told Mr. and Mrs. Beasley about the inheritance.

"Oh, my word!" Miss Jimmie exclaimed.

"Congratulations, honey, but money comes with problems, so be careful. Always remember to put God first, and that money can be a blessing to you," Mr. Hiram said. Don't get me wrong, though, I'm very pleased for you," he added. Laken hugged both Hiram and Jimmie, then asked where Shelby was.

"Honey, they came by just long enough for Shelby to change. They said they were going to Miss Anne's, but there's no telling where they are," Miss Jimmie said.

"I don't see how she does it, her being as old as she is, but as for me, I'm taking a shower, then just relax," Laken said.

Both Jimmie and Hiram laughed at the beginning of Laken's sentence.

"Yeah, I guess five days does make a difference," Miss Jimmie said.

After Hiram figured Laken was out of hearing distance, he said, "Bless her heart, I know today has been trying for her. Now that I know they're safe, I'd better tend to the chores. Tell Caleb, when he gets through changing clothes, I'll be at the silos."

"I'll tell him," she said.

Laken heard what Hiram had said, and thought, *"How blessed can a girl get? With me and Shelby riding on that bus to all those places, how worried they must have been."*

# Chapter 41

Laken bought the Mustang car the next day, although Shelby called her a "show-off."

They both had already gone to the bank and arranged to have checking accounts and deposited all but a thousand dollars each of the money they had earned from performing.

Just for kicks, Laken asked for the balance on her savings account, and it was exactly what Mr. Barry had said, seven hundred and eighty thousand dollars.

Laken still couldn't believe her good fortune, although she was paying for the Mustang with the money she had earned.

She followed Shelby back to the Beasley place, for she wanted to ride in the new car to the bank in Frisco City. The mustang was similar in color to the Fairlane; both were white with red interior, only the Mustang was a two-door coupe.

Shelby didn't give her mama time to come out and look at the new car; she just yanked open the passenger door and sailed inside, and they left. She didn't tell Laken, but she wanted to go by and see Brad while they were in town.

Laken thought about her Grandpa Pruitt being killed at the railroad tracks, when they crossed them.

The ladies at the bank were so friendly, and Laken was even introduced to the president of the bank.

She signed the necessary papers, including telling them from now on to make the checks out to Caleb and/or Laken Beasley.

Shelby talked Laken into going by Miss Anne's, since they were so close by. They didn't see Brad's work truck, but they stopped anyway.

Laken could see why Miss Anne insisted on a clean house, for not only was the house gorgeous, but also the yards. They saw flowers, shrubbery, and trees blooming everywhere.

"I'm going to see if I can get her over to my new place," Laken said.

There was a swing on each end of the porch, and they saw Miss Anne swinging away on the one that was shaded by a giant live oak tree.

Lying like a dog, Shelby said, "We were in the neighborhood, and thought we'd stop by."

"Uh-huh. Brad's not here, but you girls come sit on the porch with me, it's such a lovely day," Miss Anne said.

"Oh! Miss Anne, I'm going to have to get you over to my place and see what you can do with it. Your yards are beautiful," Laken said, as they climbed up the doorsteps.

"Thanks, but Brad mowed down a bunch of my babies with the mower while we were gone," she said. "I heard about your good fortune, Laken, and I'm so glad for you, but getting back to your statement, I'd be glad to come over there and help with the grounds. That is, when we get through with our contract," she answered.

"We just thought we'd stop by here and tell you that we're not going back on the road after July 15th," Laken told her.

"I hope it's not because of me," Miss Anne said.

"No, the main thing is, as you know, we're both getting married. I just can't see Caleb, or Brad living on that bus," Laken said.

"Well, I guess Shelby has told you that I've already congratulated them, and I'd like say the same to you and Caleb," Miss Anne said. "I think you both have made good choices," she added.

The girls had taken a seat in the same swing that Miss Anne was sitting it, due to the hot sun.

They laughed and talked of some of their experiences on the road for about fifteen minutes, and then Laken said they had to go. "I've got so much to do!" she exclaimed.

"I can imagine, but you two need to rest some, for we're pulling out on the 12th. Buddy already has the word, and I'll tell Brad that y'all came by. By the way, that sure is a snazzy little car y'all are driving," Miss Anne said.

"It's Laken's," Shelby said, as they stood up and hugged Miss Anne's neck.

"Just think, I'll soon have two daughters with the same name, Shelby Jean, and Shelby Ray. What a coincidence," she laughed.

The girls were laughing, too, as they left Miss Anne's place.

"I barely know Shelby Jean, but she's a pretty girl," Laken said, as they drove away.

"You'll love her; she's the sweetest thing. She and her husband live in Monroeville, and they have the cutest little boy," Shelby told her.

The girls almost felt like they were using Miss Jimmie, for they stopped by the house just long enough to eat and change clothes before going over to the Jordan house. They found one of Mr. Willie's trucks that cranked and backed it to the back door, then went to work.

They started in the foyer. Some of the items were so heavy that they had to roll them or use a dolly to get them to the truck. They'd have to wait until Caleb came in from the fields to load some of the things. The marble statue was the heaviest, but they managed to roll the thing to the back of the truck. Tall vases, about four feet in height, were in each corner of the foyer, and they were filled with cat tails, and plastic flowers. These, they also rolled to the truck.

Laken thought some of the oil paintings must be some of her ancestors. She didn't know them, so they went into the back of the truck, along with some other useless items that were just for show.

"We're just common people, and that's the image I want to project. I can hardly wait until I get into Victoria's room," Laken said.

After loading the heaviest items into the back of the truck and surveying the remainder of the house, Caleb told Laken there was no way they could finish up by themselves. He said he had a friend named Victor that could help them. "He's a good fellow, and strong as an ox. All you need to do is pile what you want to discard, and he'll take care of it," Caleb said.

"Whew! What a relief. Some of it can be taken to the Goodwill store, some can be burned, some can be put in the attic, and some can be stored away in one of these barns. Speaking of the barns, I haven't even had time to look into any of them," Laken said.

"Just leave it to Victor in the morning, he'll take care of it," Caleb said.

"You see, my goal…and this is just the beginning…my goal is to clear out as much as possible, at least downstairs, and have it all painted by the time we get back from Nashville," Laken said.

"It's not fair," Caleb said." We only have a few days together, and you're too exhausted for us to do anything for ourselves," Caleb said.

"Honey, this *is* for us. Can you just imagine us moving into this monstrosity the way it was?" Laken asked.

"Well, to be frank, no," Caleb said, as he put his arms around Laken and kissed her.

Shelby said, "Yuck," and went outside.

In just a few minutes, though, Caleb and Laken walked out hand in hand.

"We've locked up the house, and you can drive the Mustang home. Thank you for your help, Shelby; we'll get back on it tomorrow. All we'll need to do tomorrow is tell Victor and his crew what we want done," Laken said.

"His crew?" Shelby asked.

"Yes, Caleb said Victor had some men that could help him," Laken said.

Shelby laughed to herself, and said, "Okay, I'll see you guys when we get back home.

Very little intimate time was spent for either Laken or Shelby, for they stayed busy with the Jordan place until it was time to go back on the road. Both girls promised their fiancés that things would be different after they were married.

Between the girls and Victor, they got the house the way Laken wanted it. To top things off, Victor said his crew would have the house painted, both floors, by the time Laken returned.

Both Laken and Shelby discussed how Brad and Caleb must have felt. It was as though they were avoiding them the whole time they were home. What Caleb and Brad didn't know was that it was hard on the girls to keep saying, no.

Caleb was a little more understanding, however, when Laken wrote him out a check for fifty thousand dollars for cows. He'd mended fences on the Jordan land and intended on putting the beeves there.

The remainder of their time in Tennessee seemed to fly by. Laken grew to really love the state and its people. They met all their tour dates, and Buddy wasn't lying when he said he was going to put on a show the Grand Ole Opry wouldn't forget. Near the end of their act, he had his pants rigged somehow, and they fell to his ankles, only to reveal that he was wearing white underwear with big red roses that covered his legs all the way to his ankles.

The crowd at the Opry went wild, and so did Buddy. Each time he'd pull his drawers up, they'd fall back down, until the end of their performance.

After they performed on the Opry, they still had almost a month left to go, so Mr. Randall had them cut another album while they were in Nashville. It took them a week to get the album to suit him.

They were in Chattanooga performing when their contract expired. That very day, Miss Anne called both Mr. Peacock and Mr. Randall to tell them they were through.

Mr. Peacock threw all kinds of threats at Miss Anne, but she knew there was nothing he could do.

Mr. Randall simply told Miss Anne that he'd forward the sales from their newest album to her address, and she could disperse it accordingly.

# Chapter 42

Not wanting to spoil each other's wedding, so that each could attend the other's, the two couples chose different dates. Laken and Caleb were married at five pm on Saturday, July 25th. Brad and Shelby were married the next evening. Both ceremonies took place at Woodlawn Methodist Church.

The two couples went to the beach in Gulf Shores, Alabama for three days and nights for their honeymoon.

On the day they were to come back home, the girls went into the bathroom together in Mobile.

They hugged each another and said, "Finally!" They asked each other how things were going, and both agreed that they had gotten their partner for life.

"Good," Laken said, "Now, let's go home and be old married women and start living life; our childhood is over."

"And the best is yet to come," Shelby added.

# Epilogue

Paul had won a legal case, concerning a big industry. They settled out of court for a million dollars. Paul's fee was two hundred and fifty thousand dollars.

To celebrate, the very pregnant Callie went out that night with Paul for a good meal. Of all the people that were there, was the owner of the industry that had settled out of court that very morning. It suddenly became clear how unhappy he was with the verdict the judge had imposed.

When the fellow saw Paul, he came at him with an open knife, swinging the blade back and forth. Paul backed up as far as he could go. People in the restaurant were screaming.

Callie had a sudden flashback, so she picked up her wooden chair and slammed it over the man's head, knocking him down. The manager called the law, while Callie stood there with the remnants of the chair, still threatening her husband's attacker with the raised object.

A photographer from the Mobile Press was there and snapped a picture of Callie holding the broken chair over the man. Paul was pleading with her to put the chair down. She kept the man on the floor, though, until the police arrived.

The next day on the front page of the paper, there was a long article about it. Above the picture of Callie, the caption read, "No need for a bodyguard for attorney Paul Lindsey, he already has one: his wife, Betty Jean."

Laken had been married for two months when she read the article, and she immediately called information and got the number for attorney Lindsey.

Melissa answered the phone, then buzzed Paul's phone.

Laken didn't beat around the bush; she told Paul who she was, then said, "I believe you're married to my Mama. Can I have her number?"

Paul didn't hesitate; he'd been looking for things to come to a head one way or the other, so he gave Laken Callie's number.

Laken called it without hanging up the phone; she just jiggled the lever on the handset and dialed.

When Callie answered, Laken said, "Mama?"

"Who is this?" Callie asked.

"It's Laken, your daughter."

Callie's knees went so weak she collapsed onto the side of the bed, and cried, "Oh, my baby, my baby, my baby!"

www.ingramcontent.com/pod-product-compliance
Lightning Source LLC
Chambersburg PA
CBHW070748280626
47162CB00018B/2771